Death by Fame

Also by

_____ *Andrew Sinclair* _____

Prohibition: The Era of Excess (1962)

The Better Half: The Emancipation of the American Woman (1965)

The Last of the Best: The Aristocracy of Europe in the Twentieth Century (1969)

Dylan Thomas: Poet of His People (1975)

Jack: A Biography of Jack London (1977)

John Ford: A Biography (1979)

Corsair: The Life of J. Pierpont Morgan (1981)

The Other Victoria (1985)

War Like a Wasp: The Last Decade of the Forties (1989)

Francis Bacon: His Life and Violent Times (1993)

Arts and Cultures: The History of the Fifty Years of the
Arts Council of Great Britain (1996)

Death by Fame

——A Life of Elisabeth, Empress of Austria——

Andrew Sinclair

St. Martin's Press　New York

Library of Congress Cataloging-in-Publication Data

Sinclair, Andrew.
    Death by fame : a life of Elisabeth, Empress of Austria / Andrew Sinclair.
        p. cm.
    Includes bibliographical references and index.
    ISBN 0-312-19852-3
    1. Elisabeth, Empress, consort of Franz Joseph I, Emperor of Austria,
    1837-1898. 2. Empresses—Austria—Biography.   I. Title.
    DB88.S55   1999
    943.6'044'092—dc21
    [B]
                                                          98-50901
                                                             CIP

First published in Great Britain by Constable and Company Limited

First U.S. Edition: April 1999

10 9 8 7 6 5 4 3 2 1

To Sonia

Contents

Illustrations

between pages 178 and 179

A HABSBURG GENEALOGY

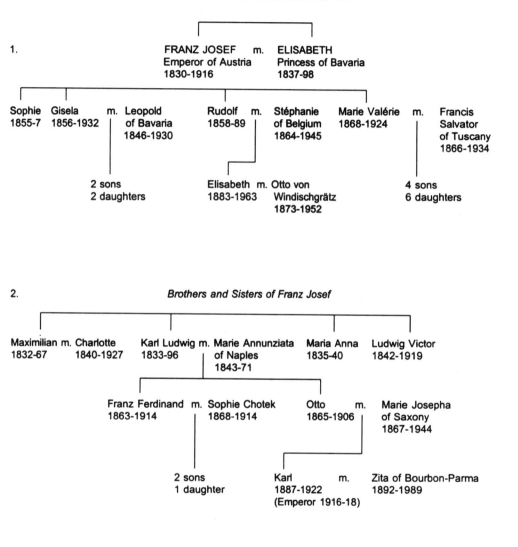

1.

FRANZ JOSEF m. ELISABETH
Emperor of Austria Princess of Bavaria
1830-1916 1837-98

Sophie   Gisela   m. Leopold   Rudolf m. Stéphanie   Marie Valérie m.   Francis
1855-7   1856-1932   of Bavaria   1858-89   of Belgium   1868-1924   Salvator
                        1846-1930   1864-1945   of Tuscany
                                                                                        1866-1934

            2 sons   Elisabeth m. Otto von   4 sons
            2 daughters   1883-1963   Windischgrätz   6 daughters
                                                     1873-1952

2.   *Brothers and Sisters of Franz Josef*

Maximilian m. Charlotte   Karl Ludwig m. Marie Annunziata   Maria Anna   Ludwig Victor
1832-67   1840-1927   1833-96   of Naples   1835-40   1842-1919
                                         1843-71

            Franz Ferdinand m. Sophie Chotek   Otto   m.   Marie Josepha
            1863-1914   1868-1914   1865-1906   of Saxony
                                                                        1867-1944

                        2 sons   Karl   m.   Zita of Bourbon-Parma
                        1 daughter   1887-1922   1892-1989
                                                    (Emperor 1916-18)

Death by Fame

CHAPTER ONE

Young and Free

❖

Royal marriages rather than wars made the shape of kingdoms of the West until the age of nationalism. The map of Europe did not have to be rolled up; it was blessed and inherited. The Victorian age was the last century when the sovereigns of German stock still had enough family influence to stop conflicts as well as start them. Cousins communicated with other cousins from their courts, ignoring their generals and prime ministers. They married each other, risking the mental instability and haemophilia of the inbred. They hardly trusted anyone outside the hereditary circle of a few hundred of their blood. They feared assassination by anarchists and republicans, the enemy and the insane. They did not take kindly to their proscription by history. They still tried to rule and live by form and wed their daughters well.

The relationships between the Austrian Habsburgs and the Wittelsbachs, who had been supreme in Bavaria in southern Germany for more than seven hundred years, had more to do with alliances and diplomacy than love and kisses. The Habsburg Empire in Central Europe was the heir of the Holy Roman Empire, which had included most of the German kingdoms and principalities and duchies. Yet the rise of Prussia in the eighteenth century had given an alternative leader to the gaggle of German-speaking states, as well as reviving memories of a Thirty Years Civil War between the

Protestant north and the Catholic south. Who was to head a united Germany? Which would be the capital, Vienna or Berlin?

The wounds which gaped between the ambitions of the expanding powers of Prussia and Austro-Hungary, of Russia and of Britain, were bandaged by the royal sympathies and ties between the four countries. After its Revolution, France had fallen out of the game of marrying between the crowns, while Spain faded into irrelevance and Italy struggled towards unity. Born as the contemporaries of the new technology which would destroy their traditions, four connected children would play out their roles of privilege and decline. These were Victoria, the eldest daughter of the Queen of the British Empire; Ludwig the Second, the King of Bavaria; Franz Josef the Second, the Austrian Emperor; and his wife Elisabeth, whose life was both a tragedy and a prophecy.

The marriage web between the crowns of Bavaria and Austria and Prussia was woven into a net of fragility. Curiously, the conquering Napoleon had converted Bavaria into a kingdom in 1805 to create a French buffer state between the rival Germanic powers. By the astute marriages of his daughters into France and Austria, the Wittelsbach King had maintained his rank after Waterloo and the Congress of Vienna. For Max Josef the First had married twice and had twelve children. His first wife was a princess from Hesse-Darmstadt, connected to the British royal family. His successor was King Ludwig the First, an eccentric and artistic monarch, whose cousin was Duke Max in Bayern. His heir, who would become Ludwig the Second, was born just before his grandfather was forced into abdication and exile by a scandalous affair with the dancer Lola Montes and the revolutions of 1848, which shook so many dynasties. The capital Munich, however, had been rebuilt by him in the classical and Mediterranean mode, another Athens and Venice of the North on the Isar River.

Duke Max of Bayern had interbred into the eligible Wittelsbach royal women. His wife Ludovika had made a bad match by taking her cousin. Her sister Elisabeth was the Queen of Prussia, while Sophie was married to the Archduke Franz Charles, the heir to the Austrian Empire. Ludovika lived in minor style, very much the poor relation. Her winter home was a palace in the new Ludwigstrasse beside the attractive English Garden. Its large rooms were decorated with frescos by Kaulbach, but its size was petty compared with the vast residences of her sisters. Duke Max, however, bought a summer castle on Lake Starnberg only eighteen miles from Munich, over-looking the Wetterstein mountains. But Possenhofen was ugly and rural, the four squat towers round its keep flanked by stables and out-buildings. Only its magnificent park and rides made it a very heaven for children, who could run down its wooded slopes and banks towards the water.

The first child born to Ludovika in 1831 was called Ludwig and the second Hélène – her husband so admired Greek names. Six years later, Elisabeth was born in the Munich palace on a Sunday on the eve of Christmas, which would become her favourite festival. Her godmother was her aunt, the Queen of Prussia, but her father soon deserted her to visit his nephew Otto, who had reached the throne of the new kingdom of Greece, before he continued on to Turkey and Arabia and Egypt, where he bought four Sudanese slave boys in the market to bring home. Although a cavalry general in the Bavarian army, he preferred to ride with the circus performers or the gypsies, also playing his zither and singing and drinking with them. His familiarity with the peasant who taught him to twang strings had no sexual overtones: the Duke loved women far too much and too often. He set a pattern of rebellion to his children by preferring to wear Loden and Lederhosen, while spending his time in taverns rather than Court occasions. He loved hunting in the mountains and the forests; but in the city, he sought the company of dramatists and poets. He wrote under the pen-name of 'Phantasus', and his works were as fantastical on the whole as his life, most charming with little meaning, and seductive without commitment. He even set up a drinking club of fourteen Knights of the Round Table, at which, as King Arthur, he drank them under it.

Duke Max officially sired five girls and four boys, one of whom died as an infant. He had dozens of other children among the actresses of Munich and the peasant girls near Possenhofen. When his infidelities became too public, his wife would not speak to him and brought up the children in a separate part of the Munich palace.

They only knew that he was home by his faraway whistling. The periods of distance, however, were always ended by another pregnancy and birth, for Ludovika could not finally resist her handsome and engaging husband, who did at least teach deportment to all of his daughters. As if they were ponies in dressage, they learned to trot elegantly. Their father told them to be angels with wings on their ankles.

Among the brood, her second brother Karl Theodor became the favourite of Elisabeth. He was known as 'Gackel' or 'Cock', she was called 'Sisi'. The older Hélène was more beautiful than the young Sisi, who was round-faced with almond eyes, although she grew a magnificent crop of auburn hair; but their governess, the Baroness Luise Wülffen, kept them apart, because of Sisi's bad influence on her elder sister. She was a day-dreamer, lost in her imagination of the ancient Germanic myths and legends, the tales of chivalry and giants. Restless and energetic, she had literally to be tied to her chair, for she was too active to do her lessons. Only sketching the landscape and the horses made her sit quiet.

Sisi always adored her wandering father and tried to join him in his sports and games. She became a fearless rider, loving the park of Possenhofen and her ponies. Occasionally, Duke Max took her out on his expeditions into the country to meet the people and join in their pursuits. 'If you and I, Sisi,' he told her, 'had not been princely born, we could have performed in a circus.' His frequent absences from home only made Sisi admire him and seek his affection even more. When she later became an empress, she said that the only honest money she had ever earned was the copper coins tossed to her father and her, when they performed outside beer gardens for a song and dance act, dressed as strolling players on their long rides.

She was eleven years old in 1848, the year of the revolutions. Her future husband Franz Josef of Austria was eighteen, slender and strong and hardly ever out of uniform and braid. Even as a youth, he learned to be a stickler for duty under the fierce guardianship of his Wittelsbach mother Sophie. Her cousin and later her close friend, the young Ludwig of Bavaria, was only three, but he would turn out to be even more artistic and otherworldly than her father or his own grandfather, who had made a Mediterranean city out of Munich. Both Franz Josef and Ludwig found their lives forever changed by the forced abdication of the ruling sovereigns of their states in the aftermath of the repression of the flames of the revolts in Vienna and Munich. Franz Josef himself would become the Austrian Emperor, and the infant Ludwig's father, the Crown Prince, would become King Maximilian the Second, while his heir was already building dream castles with toy bricks. At the age of eleven, Sisi would meet Franz Josef for the first time at Innsbruck, where his family were compelled to flee in the year of revolutions before he assumed power; but he ignored his childish cousin, leaving his intense younger brother Karl Ludwig to court her hopelessly with flowers and sweets and a watch on a chain.

England was singular in being spared the turmoils of that turbulent year. It was already a democracy, in which the popular Queen Victoria and her Consort Prince Albert ruled through their ministers, who advised them. Their eldest daughter Victoria or 'Vicky' was eight years old and would marry the heir to the throne of Prussia and become the mother of the Kaiser Wilhelm the Second, while her sisters would be the wives of the Grand Duke of Hesse-Darmstadt and the Prince of Schleswig-Holstein, claimed by Prussia as well as Denmark, whose royal daughter Alexandra would be united with the Prince of Wales. The Queen's grandchildren also would wed well and occupy the thrones of Russia and Norway, Spain and Rumania and Greece. Through her progeny, the sovereign of the British Empire would create the most extraordinary and personal intelligence system in Europe of the nineteenth century. And the purpose of all her incessant diplomacy would never alter. She wanted peace between the nations, so that none of her widespread relatives went to war against each other. How could her children or their offspring try to kill their nephews or cousins because of a strip of land?

Of the young people brought up strictly within royal conventions, Elisabeth was almost the only one who ran wild in her summer and salad days. With her boyish father as her model, she became a fine horsewoman and a trick rider and something of an athlete, impossible to achieve for the other princesses of Europe, who were cooped inside their corsets and their crinolines from an early age. Vicky had some exercise as a child, because of her mother's belief in sea bathing. If Elisabeth was to be the first empress dedicated to fitness and travel, Queen Victoria had already set the fashion for holidays by the beach. Until the reign of her predecessor, King George the Fourth, the seaside had seemed to promise an early death from exposure. Sun was to be avoided, certainly on ladies' complexions. But the British Queen entered the waves discreetly from her bathing machine, still preserved at Osborne House in the Isle of Wight. And where she dipped, her children and the nation followed.

Hunting and riding had long been the recreation of kings, and some rulers followed Duke Max in preferring the company of foresters to courtiers. Duke Max himself always went out with Johann Petzmacher, the son of a tavern-keeper from Vienna and an expert on the zither: when his daughter Elisabeth rode with them, she was introduced into blood sports without a tremor. The aristocrats had always hunted, and they always would. However romantic and sensitive she and her father were, the killing and eating of animals in the chase seemed natural to Elisabeth. Also from her father, Elisabeth took her love of poetry, while his tales of his travels incited a wanderlust in her. Both of them were under the spell of Heine's lyrics, yearning and melancholy and witty. She hid copies of his *Nocturnes* and *Intermezzo* in a little case at the bottom of her wardrobe, her most intimate possession. In one epigram the poet pretended to be King Ludwig the First writing to the King of Prussia:

> You Hohenzollerns of my blood,
> Don't make a fuss of the Wittelsbach mode.
> Don't go at me over Lola Montes,
> I knew her more, you knew her less.

As a poet, Elisabeth imitated her father in his facility and his output. Hundreds of her early poems are still preserved in the Swiss Federal Archives. They show a love of nature and a shy and adolescent heart, which she lost to a young man with brown eyes, who was sent away, and then to a count with blue eyes, to whom she sent 'the moon as a whisperer'. She did not take too well to formal education, unlike her elder sister Hélène, who was being groomed in conscientiousness and duty to serve Franz Josef as his wife, if he should ask her to become the Empress of Austria, as her match-making mother dearly desired. Determined to marry off her five daughters well after the disappointments of her own marriage, Ludovika would scheme more assiduously than a general in her strategies for success.

Bavaria was still the piglet in the middle between Austria and Prussia. Two years after the fires of the revolutions were put out, Prussia proposed the creation of a North German Federation, which would include Hanover and Saxony, and so end the Federation of all Germany, led by Austria, which itself proposed a separate southern group. Aided by Bavaria, Austria put four army corps in the field against weak Prussian forces in Silesia. The King of Prussia hesitated before deciding to fight and wrote to the young Franz Josef: the Queen of Prussia wrote to her sister Sophie, the Emperor's mother. Royal intercession prevented an armed confrontation. Yet this diplomatic triumph for Austria had a black lining. 'War would perhaps have been better,' the Austrian statesman Prince Schwarzenberg said, 'and would have brought a peace lasting fifty years.'

Royal marriage was still diplomacy by other means. And so Franz Josef paid a visit to Berlin in the winter of 1852. His eye fell on one of the King's nieces, Princess Anna, who was intelligent and hand-some and slender. Unfortunately, she was already committed to another princely alliance with the Hesse-Kassel family, and she was a Protestant, although she could convert her faith and break her engagement. The objections were far from insuperable. The Austrian Emperor's mother Sophie thought that Anna would be manageable, and so she implored her sister Elisabeth, the Queen of Prussia, to help her pull off the match. But nothing that the two Wittelsbach women might do would persuade the King to agree to an alliance by blood with the power which had just humiliated him. Franz Josef would have to seek a wife within his mother's family in Bavaria.

First, he would have to survive the nightmare of the royal families of Europe, the attack of an assassin. He had supported the brutal repression of Hungary in its fight for independence led by Kossuth. Strolling round the walls of the Hofburg in Vienna, he was assaulted by a tailor's apprentice, who stuck the point of a long knife into the back of his neck through the gold braid on the collar of his uniform. Cut and bleeding, he fell to the ground. His military aide, Count O'Donnell, caught the culprit and delivered him to the police. No reprieve was granted, and the Hungarian Libenyi was duly hanged. For a month, the Emperor had to convalesce from his wound and loss of blood. But when he took up public life again, he did not forget or forgive the country of the would-be murderer, and it was more important than ever that he should produce an heir before another assassin cut him down.

Therefore, in the summer, his mother Sophie invited her other sister Ludovika with her two elder daughters, Hélène and Elisabeth, to stay with her family at the retreat of Ischl among the mountain lakes of Salzkammergut. Hélène was intended to be the right wife for the young Emperor. Nobody considered that Elisabeth would attract him, although she had grown into a beauty with an oval face set on a long neck under coils of auburn hair that reached undone to her knees. Later in her life, she would remark, 'Marriage is an absurd arrangement. One is sold as a child at fifteen.' But as a Catholic and a virgin and a princess, she could not avoid the matrimonial market, in which the Wittelsbachs had traded their girls for so long and with such profit.

The Emperor tumbled at first sight of Elisabeth with her slender and elegant bearing. Invited to tea with his Bavarian relations, the moment that he saw her in a simple black mourning dress, 'he was then convinced that his choice would fall upon her. He shone,' his mother wrote to the Queen of Saxony, 'and you know how his face shines when he is happy. The dear little one did not doubt the deep impression which she had made.' She was embarrassed by all the people around them and did not dare to eat, although she was always gracious in spite of her timidity.

At a following ball, Elisabeth wore a modest gown of rose and white. Weckbecker, the adjutant to the Emperor, found her 'of enchanting grace although completely incapable of controlling her embarrassment'. Deeply blushing, she told him 'that she did not know how she would be able to get through it all without the assistance of her dancing master.' The adjutant further heard from her mother that she was not sure of her daughter's ability ever to fulfil her future duties, if she were elevated to the throne while she was still so near to the nursery.

Yet Franz Josef had made up his mind. He would insist on what he wanted. When he was on the parade ground, he used to shout at any error in the manoeuvres, 'I command to be obeyed!' Already sexually experienced as a military officer, he was not at his best in the ballroom. Yet he was a dashing and correct dancer; and he took Elisabeth over at the cotillion. To his mother, she was like 'a rosebud, which opened under the rays of the morning sun'. He gave her the dance bouquet as well as all the flowers that should have been presented to the other ladies. Such a breach of etiquette was almost an official proposal, and Elisabeth was deeply embarrassed.

The following morning, the Duchess Ludovika told her child Elisabeth of the Emperor's intentions, and then told her sister Sophie of her daughter's answer. 'She burst into tears and assured her mother that she would do all she could to make the Emperor happy,' Sophie wrote, 'and to be for me the most tender of children.' What Ludovika did not pass on were the feelings of the spurned Hélène, who would now have to be found a less exalted husband.

Two days later after hearing the ceremony of the Mass, Franz Josef asked the priest to bless him and his future bride. Then an official reception took place, at which Princess Elisabeth was congratulated by the Austrian courtiers on her betrothal. These were led by the Emperor's Adjutant-General, Count Karl Grünne, a worldly and reactionary disciplinarian who also acted in the interests of his master's mother. 'The entire Suite was presented to the future Empress,' Weckbecker observed. 'Grünne spoke eloquently. The Princess could hardly speak a word.' After the banquet, the Duchess Ludovika also confided her worry over the merciless judgement of the women of the Viennese aristocracy in the future, once they had to deal with an innocent and defenceless child Empress.

Elisabeth had her own doubts about the sudden engagement. When her mother asked her whether she could love the Emperor, she wept and said she did. Yet what did he think of somebody as young and unimportant as her? She would do all she could to make him happy, but would it be a success? Yes, she was 'already fond of the Emperor, if only he were not an emperor'. But as her mother knew, if he had not been an emperor, she would not have been put in his way.

In spite of his state duties, the wooing of Elisabeth by her Emperor took her to the age of sixteen. He found it sad and depressing, as he told his mother, to leap from the earthly paradise of Ischl back to his writing table and masses of papers. He commissioned a portrait of his betrothed and sent her a miniature of himself on a bracelet studded with diamonds, also an imperial brooch of gems in a spray of flowers. He visited her at Possenhofen, even joining in the fun and games there and admiring her balance in the saddle, before taking her to the opera in Munich to see Rossini's *Wilhelm Tell*. The Bavarian Court exploited the occasion to throw numerous parties, which annoyed the Prussian ambassador, who saw the enthusiasm of the kingdom for an alliance with Austria. He reported back to Berlin that 'the little Princess seems to take the parting from her family and her homeland very hard. My impression is that a faint shadow has fallen over the grace and beauty of her bright young face.' She was, indeed, far too young to leave her family and take up the life of an empress.

Elisabeth was assigned tutors in the history of the empire which she was to rule; one of them was a Hungarian, Count Majláth, who began the fire in her for Hungarian independence. Although business in Vienna summoned Franz Josef away, he returned to Munich for Christmas Eve, before another recall to his imperial duties. The details of the marriage had to be arranged, even a dispensation from the Pope because of a breach of canon law. The Habsburgs and the Wittelsbachs had already intermarried so much that Elisabeth was Franz Josef's second cousin on his mother's side and fourth cousin on his father's side. Rome was willing, a trousseau as large as the whole collection of a couturier was ordered and fitted, while a

selection of the imperial jewels was brought to Bavaria. On 20th
April 1854, Elisabeth left among cheering crowds in a procession of
carriages along the Ludwigstrasse for the Habsburg yacht, waiting to
take her down the Danube to Vienna and her fate. One of her girlish
poems showed her apprehension:

> Your swift wings let me borrow,
> Guide me where you fly far,
> How glad to be free, Swallow.
> Break out from prison bar.
>
> With you in flight to the blue
> And the infinite sky,
> I would sing with all I knew
> Of divine Liberty.
>
> My sorrows would be over,
> Gone new love and old.
> Tomorrow, to fear no other,
> No tears and nothing cold.

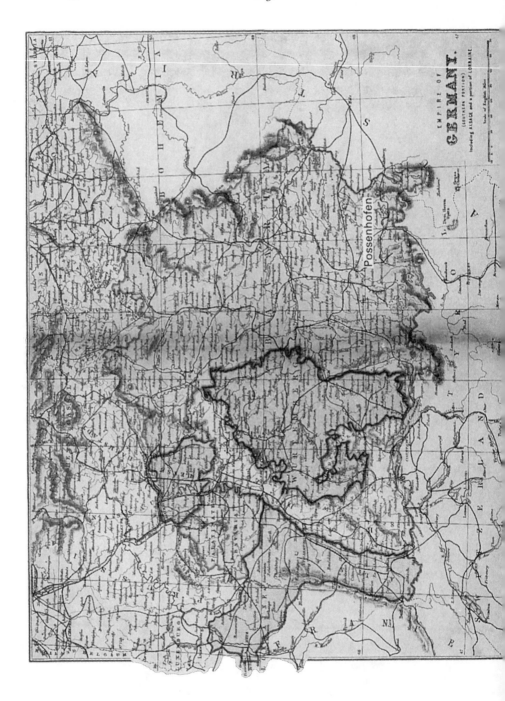

CHAPTER TWO

A Wedding and Confinement

❖

As a floating Ophelia in a boat surrounded with flowers, Elisabeth arrived in Vienna. Franz Josef boarded the state steam yacht and kissed her. The next day, she was taken in a closed glass coach with panels painted by Rubens and drawn by eight Lippizzaner greys for a state procession through the capital. She wore pink and silver; her long hair was coiled beneath a crown of diamonds. Her reaction from the cheering crowds came out in a remark to her mother, 'I am on show like a freak in a circus.' Her new celebrity would become the running sore of her life.

Received by the Emperor at the Hofburg, she was given two 'Most Humble Reminders', interminable briefings about the procedure at the wedding and the greeting for each distinguished guest at the following reception. The next day, the ceremony took place at the parish church of St Augustine. Elisabeth wore white and silver and carried myrtle blossom; her crown was studded with opals as well as diamonds. The resplendent congregation was treated to a long ceremony and a sermon without end from the Cardinal Prince-Archbishop of Vienna. That was succeeded by the embarrassment demanded of Elisabeth by protocol, the kissing of the hand of the new Empress by all the nobility, including her mother-in-law Sophie. When she objected to the bowing and scraping of distinguished ladies old enough to be her grandmother, her husband told her that she would have to grin and bear all the curtsies of the future. She was trapped in homage. Even ancient duchesses would have to bend the knee to her in public, whatever they said behind her back.

The marriage also had to be consummated. Franz Josef was no virgin as she was. Like her father, he had been provided with dancers and singers from the opera ballet in Vienna and young peasant women in Bohemia. The news of his success with his wife was announced by the Emperor two days later at his daily breakfast with his mother at eight o'clock – he usually rose at five to begin his duties. The Archduchess Sophie had already taken steps to keep the ungrown Empress tied to her whip hand. Rather as the young Marie Antoinette had been put under the guidance of the Comtesse de Noailles, Elisabeth found her household run by the Countess Sophie Esterházy-Liechtenstein, a severe and uncompromising woman old enough to be her grandmother and a confidante of the Archduchess. Elisabeth had been allowed to bring nobody from Bavaria; all her ladies-in-waiting were strangers and examiners of their childish mistress, who had to be taught her imperial manners. No matter if the lessons went against her grain, now she was constrained by the most formal Court in all Europe.

Most of her time was spent dressing and undressing in order to receive the state delegations in the correct costume. While she had often worn the fashions from the Tyrol in Bohemia, she enchanted the Hungarians by wearing the embroidered skirt and velvet top of an aristocrat of their country. More depressing were the Court balls, in which her gowns were so elaborate and form-fitting that she had to be stitched into them. One of the festivals delighted her. A circus rider named Renz performed a quadrille with his mounted company in medieval costume, followed by a personal demonstration of *haute école*. Already the Empress was known sometimes to prefer horses to people.

When she became pregnant, Elisabeth was sent to the rural palace of Laxenburg, about fifteen miles from Vienna. This Gothic building with its battlements was no Possenhofen. It had public gardens instead of a wild park. Voyeurs looked out for a sight of her condition; in fact, she was told by the Archduchess Sophie to show herself off, dressed in the height of splendour. She was also prevented from escaping with her saddle and bridle by her mother-in-law, in case the heir to the throne were to be harmed. She found Laxenburg a sad spot and wanted to follow her husband on his daily duties at the Hofburg. She was reproved again for running after the Commander-in-Chief like any young subaltern. She had her place in things, and she had to stay there.

The intrusion of the domineering Archduchess turned Elisabeth against her. Through the recollections of her later confidante, the Countess Festetics, she revealed her obsessive hatred of her mother-in-law, who could herself not stand being superseded in importance by this chit of a princess from Bavaria. So Elisabeth found herself being reminded time and again that people did not know how to behave as they should in southern Germany, while manners were perfect in Austria. Elisabeth was beginning to prove with her determined chin that she had a strong will of her own, not just the whim of youth. Although her husband was in awe of his mother, he was in love with her. She could begin to recruit her own supporters in this alien and difficult world.

Her husband was being drawn into the tangles of the Eastern Question, which would lead to the Crimean War. He now turned against the Tsar Nicholas the First, who had helped him to crush the rebellion in Hungary. The Romanov ruler was claiming that his attack on Turkey was a last crusade for Christendom, while France and England should not back Islam against a holy cause. Both Austria and Prussia, however, refused to support the aggrandisement of the huge Russian Empire, which always threatened their eastern frontiers. Franz Josef even refused to allow the Russians to cross the Danube and advance on Constantinople. That was the price of his neutrality, or else there would be war. He sought to preserve the Austrian Empire with its multi-lingual subjects. He would rather maintain than aggress. He followed the advice of the great statesman Metternich, the architect of Europe after the fall of Napoleon, that Austria should never be the vanguard of the East against the West or the West against the East.

Another Napoleon, however, ruled in Paris following a new revolution and a *coup d'état* there. Prince Louis seemed as dedicated to the overthrow of the dynasties of Europe as his predecessor. Certainly, he supported Italian nationalism and the cession of Lombardy and Venetia, which were still held by Austrian troops. He was only waiting his time to invade the Po valley with the support of Victor Emmanuel the Second, the King of Sardinia and Piedmont. He was further antagonised when Austria refused to send troops to aid his forces and the British in the Crimea, where they were fighting the Russians. Both powers were even more shocked when Austria moved its army corps into the Danubian principalities of Moldavia and Wallachia, forcing the withdrawal of the Russian invaders, but staking a claim to those provinces, if the Ottoman Empire were to be dismembered. Franz Josef saw a future empire in the East by pushing back the power of Tsar Nicholas, who now died, giving away to Alexander the Second. A strategy of security demanded further protection, and Vienna now signed a treaty of alliance with Britain and France to the anger of Prussia, which felt isolated. Even if nearly half a million Austrian troops had been mobilised, they never went to war in the Crimea, although they also were decimated by the cholera epidemic which Florence Nightingale was trying to fight in Scutari hospital to save the British troops.

To seal the peace, Franz Josef signed a concordat with Rome, surrendering much of the power won by his ancestors over the Church and education. He seemed to be seeking a dangerous truce at any price. He was occupied at home, dealing with the hostilities between his mother and his wife. Elisabeth only escaped from the Archduchess Sophie once with her husband and his entourage on a state visit to Bohemia and Moravia. There she became pregnant, but the Archduchess had already let her son know her opinion of Elisabeth, who should either look in her mirror or at him and at nothing else.

When the Empress gave birth to a daugher, she was named Sophie after the Archduchess, who was not mollified. There was no son and heir for the empire. Elisabeth was still being instructed as if she were a schoolgirl. The adjutant Weckbecker was told to sit next to her at dinner by order of the Emperor. 'She was still very shy and had to be trained in small talk.' The choice of the Mistress of the Household, selected by Archduchess Sophie, seemed unfortunate. The Countess Esterházy-Liechtenstein 'treated the young Empress in the manner of a governess'. She also regaled Elisabeth with gossip about the Viennese aristocracy, which was of no interest to the young Bavarian. Although Elisabeth won a battle about wearing a pair of slippers several times instead of once, she was dispirited and melancholy, sometimes spending all day weeping in her room. She ate so little that meals rarely lasted more than twenty minutes; her staff had to leave the table hungry. She also refused to eat with her gloves on, the fashion of the nobility. And when she was told that her bare hands were a deviation from the rule, she dared to reply, 'then let the deviation now be the rule.'

Motherhood improved Elisabeth's presence. She cut her sparse diet after her pregnancy in fear that her small waist might grow a fraction. She scandalised her mother-in-law by taking up her riding a month after the birth. She began to make a cult of her beauty, turning the washing of her hair into a ritual, yet she would not stand anyone gazing at her. She raised her fan or dipped her sunshade to people who looked at her face, as if the stare were a violation. The Emperor's valet Ketterl, who recorded his memoirs, considered the treatment of her long tresses as 'quite an affair of State, for in addition to a number of yolks of eggs, twenty bottles of the best French brandy were also used every time.' The brushing of her hair came to be another remarkable nightly performance. As her niece Luisa di Toscana later declared, a white cloth was spread over the carpet in her dressing-room. The hairdresser wore white from head to foot. He brushed and combed and arranged the long strands of her *coiffure*. Then he would carefully gather up every stray hair. 'Then they would be counted and the Empress would be told how many of her hairs had fallen out. If she thought there were too many, she would become disturbed.'

There was no escape for Elisabeth into the freedom of the café and the circus, where her father had taken her. Yet this was the time that Vienna was glorious with its musicians and its poets. Franz Liszt

had just written his *Mazeppa* on the theme of the poem by Byron
about the Cossack bound to his galloping horse, also an inspiration
to the romantic young Empress, stifled by the elderly and the critical.
She could not even shop on the Graben without a police escort.
Another poem of hers, written soon after the marriage, told of her
confinement:

> I am awake and I am in my cell.
> I see the chains that bind my hands too well.

The Archduchess Sophie took over the baby who bore her name
in a nursery near her rooms with a wet nurse and a doctor chosen by
herself. Although Elisabeth saw her daughter, she had to fight for
that right. The Archduchess wanted to remain in control of her
grandchild as well as her son. As Elisabeth soon became pregnant
again, she found it difficult to resist the envelopment of her mother-
in-law. They were becoming implacable enemies. And when the
second child of Elisabeth also was born a girl, named Gisela, her
failure to produce an heir to the imperial crown played even more
into the hands of the Archduchess.

Although Franz Josef had managed to stay out of the Crimean
War, the Peace of Paris which ended the conflict condemned Austria
for its failure to join the victors. Franz Josef had to evacuate the
Danube principalities. Piedmont had joined with France and Britain
against Russia, and so looked for its rewards in Austrian Italy through
the wily diplomacy of Cavour, who was the most brilliant bluffer in
the game of international poker. The assassination attempt by
bombing of the Italian Count Orsini on Louis Napoleon and his
wife Eugénie resulted in his execution, but also in the loss of nerve
by the French Emperor, who, as Disraeli had noticed, was alarmed
for his life and yet wanted to do something for Italy. A deal would be
hatched with Cavour to intervene on behalf of the oppressed citizens of the Duke of Modena, who was backed by the repressive
regime of the ninety-year-old Marshal Radetsky in Lombardy,
seething under the Austrian occupation after Radetsky's previous
victory over the Piedmontese. Some idea of the intensity of feeling

could be surmised in the satirical poem of the Tuscan Giuseppe
Giusti, 'The Steam Guillotine':

> The Emperor has integrity,
> A little mean and gruff and dry.
> Yet he loves the community
> And he has said he would supply
> For inventors initiatives
> > That he gives.

> In one of our duchies
> People were being fractious
> About duties and taxes.
> The thing from His Majesty
> Got rid without traces
> > Of long faces.

To counteract the French and Piedmontese encouragement of
Italian nationalism, Franz Josef decided to take his Empress on a
tour of the royal palaces at Venice and Milan. Her beauty and inno-
cence might put a gloss on his reputation for intransigence. There
was no trouble, although the Archduchess Sophie stated the truth
when she warned her son that Italy was more of an armed camp than
a health resort. Huge crowds came out to stare at the young couple,
but in silence at Trieste, where they first arrived. For thousands of
radical sympathisers and Italian nationalists had been put in prison
as a precaution for the course of the visit. A fire did start in the
Municipal Palace while the Emperor and the Empress were there
before they left for Venice by the royal yacht *Elisabetta*, escorted by
the Austrian navy. Yet the only fireworks were over the Grand Canal,
which was as cold as their welcome. The boxes of the Fenice Theatre
were empty of the nobility for an imperial gala performance of the
opera; the stalls had to be filled with the Austrian military. An
amnesty on political offenders issued by Franz Josef had some effect
on their frigid reception. They were cheered on another visit to the
Fenice, which was now occupied. And Elisabeth was allowed to meet

the people. Her watchdog, the Countess Esterházy-Liechtenstein, even complained to the Archduchess Sophie that the Empress had taken up the cause of the rabble and was compromising imperial prestige by being kind to every scoundrel.

The crowds on the progress through the cities of the Po valley were equally dour. And in Milan, Piedmontese propaganda encouraged the city to turn a cold shoulder and a blind eye to the imperial couple. Even the announcement of the retirement of Marshal Radetsky in favour of the Emperor's brother, the Archduke Ferdinand Maximilian, who was only an amiable twenty-four years old, provoked little warmth or response. Although the young were superseding the old in power, their coming could not assuage ancient wrongs. Most Italians merely wanted to see the back of every Austrian in their country.

Following the policy of appeasement in Italy, which had not altered the war plans of France and Piedmont, Franz Josef decided on another amnesty for the Hungarian revolutionaries, to be followed by an imperial visit by him and his wife. He believed that if conciliation followed repression, the fervent nationalism of his age might still find a place within the old dynastic structures. As on the tour of Venetia and Lombardy, Elisabeth now insisted on taking her elder daughter Sophie with her. No longer would she accept the determination and fears of her mother-in-law. In fact, she took the baby Gisela, too, although with the Archduchess's approved medical authority, Dr Seeburger. The reception for the imperial couple at Budapest was warmer. Already the young Empress had shown her predilection for Hungary and its horsemen. Her antagonism to the repressive Archduchess Sophie was also common knowledge. The Hungarian nobles were led by the pardoned Count Julius Andrássy, who had to flee to Paris after the rising for independence of 1848, and they showed off their gallantry and attributes to Elisabeth. She was offered horses and later a country estate, which would become a second hunting home for her, the Castle of Gödöllö. The way to her heart was known to be through the hoof.

She and Franz Josef set off for the country from Budapest; but they were recalled to the Hungarian capital. Their daughter Sophie was ill, probably of typhoid fever. Elisabeth stayed beside the bedside of the sick child for eleven hours until she died. She was inconsolable, thinking herself guilty for bringing Sophie along with her. Perhaps her mother-in-law had been right in trying to prevent the two little girls leaving the Hofburg, even with their ineffectual doctor. The first of Elisabeth's neurotic symptoms of withdrawal took place. She talked of suicide, would let nobody approach her, and went riding in the forests, lathering her mounts almost into the ground.

A memoir of her by de Burgh, which appeared soon after her death, testified that her general unpopularity among her German subjects was due to her dislike of the state ceremonials and entertainments at Court, and her inveterate love of field sports and *haute école*. 'From early morning to her *déjeuner* she spent her time at the imperial riding school, exercising horse after horse, and in the afternoon she could be seen daily in the Park riding on her private roads, generally using three or four horses in succession. So devoted was she to the sport that it was reported she learned to ride without a saddle, kneeling on horseback, and even standing, as we sometimes see done in a circus, for which reason she was nicknamed by the Viennese bourgeoisie "The Circus Rider"; and her infrequent public appearances, despite the charm of her extraordinary beauty and grace, were coldly greeted by the populace of the imperial city. This, combined with the behaviour of the nobility at the time of her marriage, brought about a feeling of dislike for Vienna, whose people she considered narrow-minded.'

A third young royal contemporary, whose fate would intertwine with hers, was married in the January of 1858 to the heir to the throne of the perennial rival of Austria. The Princess Royal of England, Victoria, was united with Prince Frederick Wilhelm of Prussia, whose brave military bearing made him appear to be another Franz Josef. His predicament was almost as complicated as that of the Austrian Emperor at his succession. His uncle, the King of Prussia, was slipping into insanity. His father was taking over state affairs, but had to tread warily and maintain the King's policies in case His Majesty recovered his wits. He was surrounded by reactionary courtiers and the spies of the Wittelsbach Queen of Prussia, the sister of Elisabeth's mother; but the architect of the future union of Germany, the Junker Count Otto von Bismarck-Schönhausen, was already a royal adviser and would soon become the ambassador to Russia. To Vienna, however, this Anglo-Prussian alliance between the eldest daughter of Queen Victoria and the future Crown Prince of Prussia was ominous, especially for Lombardy, the most vulnerable province of the empire.

The situation there worsened as Austria still found itself isolated after the Crimean War. Cavour was modelling his policy on Machiavelli's principles; he was a master of intrigue, who had put Austria in quarantine. Now, as he told Odo Russell, the British Minister in Rome, he wanted to force Austria to declare war on Piedmont. If that happened, France with her armies would back the small Alpine kingdom, while Britain and Russia would not intervene in memory of Sebastopol and Austria's duplicity. Prussia itself, with its recent royal alliance to Queen Victoria, would sit on its hands and watch the humiliation of its rival in Germany. The only thing would be the cause of the spark in the tinderbox.

Before the conflagration, Elisabeth did what was expected of her. She gave birth to the heir to the throne, Rudolf. She was admirable during the pregnancy, seeming tranquil and taking medical advice. Two of her sisters were to marry well, Hélène to the wealthy Bavarian Prince of Thurn and Taxis, and as she herself had done at sixteen, Marie to the Duke of Calabria, the heir to the kingdom of Naples. Nothing appeared able to stop the Wittelsbach talent in advantageous alliances by blood. The point, however, was to produce a male child for the future of the realms, to which their parents bound the young women. And Elisabeth fulfilled her duty in the August of 1858; the birth of the heir was followed by the sound of the *Te Deum* in all the churches of the empire. She was only twenty-one years old; her husband immediately wrapped the Crown Prince Rudolf in the Order of the Golden Fleece.

Overjoyed by the birth of his son, Franz Josef was listening more and more to his general staff and his paramount adviser, Count Grünne. That elegant reactionary was playing the role of a father to the Emperor with the approval of his mother, the Archduchess Sophie. Although he fell out of favour during the Crimean War, he asserted his influence again over Franz Josef in the Italian crisis. He pushed for the appointment of a new Commander-in-Chief in Italy, Field Marshal Gyulai, whose pride was only exceeded by his timidity. Grünne had fallen out with the Empress on the tour of Venetia and Lombardy, and he enjoyed the opportunity of proving his power over the Emperor and ending the policy of appeasement. Franz Josef's brother, the Archduke Ferdinand Maximilian with his fresh Coburg wife from Belgium, was not heeded when he wrote back to Vienna that Lombardy had cause for complaint, and recommended 'a just, wise, and mild treatment, wherever possible . . . We live here in utter chaos.'

Piedmont and France had already signalled their alliance through the scandalous betrothal of the raddled and notorious cousin of Louis Napoleon, known as Plon-Plon, with the fifteen-year-old Princess Clotilde, the eldest daughter of King Victor Emmanuel of Sardinia; she was sacrificed to the marriage market at the same age as Elisabeth. She agreed to marry the aged French rake 'with the sense of duty which marked the House of Savoy'. Now that Piedmont was mobilising its forces and the secret alliance with Louis Napoleon was known, Franz Josef would not listen to his brother, who begged that somebody would restrain Marshal Gyulai from a provocative show of force, for Austria had put in the field five army corps and a cavalry division, a hundred thousand men. The last hope of peace lay in English diplomacy. Queen Victoria had made it clear to Louis Napoleon that Britain would support no war, even in the cause of the unification of Italy. She believed that Prussia, where her daughter had given birth to a future kaiser, would be drawn into the struggle against France and begin another Napoleonic war in Europe. In point of fact, she had already been advised by her diplomats in Berlin of Bismarck's loathing of Austria. As the Prussian told her ambassador there, 'You can have no notion how we hate them. I do not think that any government we might have could ever bring our army to regard the Austrians otherwise than as enemies: – I am convinced that no sentry could stand on an outpost with an Austrian against a common enemy without the fear of betrayal!' Bismarck even thought that 'a downright serious war' with Austria could have its origin in Italy, where any British intervention would be useless, because ships would have little to do with the result.

The diplomacy of London in Paris and Vienna proved futile. Franz Josef refused the advice of the aged Metternich and issued an ultimatum to Piedmont to disarm within three days. This was rejected. The best strategy for Marshal Gyulai was to advance and destroy the inferior Piedmontese army before Louis Napoleon could reinforce it by sea to Genoa or across the Alps. Although Gyulai was a ramrod on the parade ground and his troops wore the most resplendent uniforms in Europe, some of them still carried flintlock rifles. He was slow in attack and quick to withdraw behind fortifications. He was not 'able to do', in Grünne's words, 'what that old ass of a Radetsky could to at eighty'.

Outflanking the sluggish Austrian army, Louis Napoleon struck at Milan from Genoa. Opposed at Magenta, his Imperial Guard fought their way over the canal bridges and compelled Gyulai to retire with his army. Milan lay open and was seized among the shouts of the jubilant crowds, so silent at the visit of the Austrian Emperor and Empress. Franz Josef had now reached Verona with Grünne, in order to take command of the campaign in a heatwave with the fighting men falling sick with malaria. He advanced towards the approaching French and Piedmontese: the armies met at the shambles of Solferino, a bloody exercise in mass disorganisation.

That June morning of 1859, Franz Josef was writing back to his Empress as he regularly did. She had begged to join him at the front, although later she was accused by the Grünne family of deserting him on the campaign. 'Women are out of place in the disturbed life at Headquarters,' he wrote, 'and I cannot set my army a bad example.' She was pleasing him by setting up a hospital for the wounded at Laxenburg and trying to persuade her sister Marie to bring in the kingdom of Naples on the Austrian side. Yet first he had to win one of the larger pitched battles of European history between two hundred and seventy thousand soldiers who had stumbled over each other.

In an intense heat, a series of engagements led to great courage and carnage. The French took the crests of the hills of Solferino and forced back the Austrian centre and left. On the right, the admirable Field Marshal Benedek held his ground and wept when his Emperor ordered the retreat in a thunderstorm. There was no pursuit. Forty thousand men were dead or wounded in a futile confrontation which had shattered the military panache of both commanders. 'I know what it feels like to be a beaten general,' Franz Josef wrote to Elisabeth. Louis Napoleon had also had enough. He had failed to smash the Austrian army, which had withdrawn in good order. He had done enough to get what he wanted in his secret treaty with Piedmont, the territories of Nice and Savoy. And Prussia was mobilising at last, moving its armies towards the Rhine. Much as it might want the humiliation of its rival power in Germany, a resurgent France was a greater danger.

Louis Napoleon offered an armistice in Lombardy, which was accepted by Franz Josef. The truce was followed by a meeting between the two leaders at Villafranca, although Franz Josef dreaded dealing with somebody he thought a scoundrel. Meanwhile, the old Marshal Prince Windischgrätz was sent to Berlin, where he told Prince Hohenzollern-Sigmaringen, as Princess Victoria reported to her mother in London: 'If we did not help them now, they would *never* forgive us – and *not* help us if they made peace now and we were attacked.'

The peace secured at Villafranca and signed at Zurich was a body blow to Prussia. Its mobilisation against France was futile, while Lombardy was conceded to Piedmont, although Austria kept Venetia. And although Franz Josef fought bitterly for the rights of his dispossessed cousins in Modena and Tuscany, he was unable to save their thrones. Prussia had lost credit in Germany and was exposed to a French attack. The Royal Archives at Windsor Castle show that Princess Victoria told her mother that feelings in Berlin 'were more kindled against Austria's perfidy than against anyone else's.' The peace with France was 'a dreadful crushing blow for us. Our position in Germany is gone.' As for Louis Napoleon, he was a man without principles. 'Every one is on the *qui vive* here, war is always thought of and talked of – God avert this calamity from us, I say.'

The royal women of Europe all thought the same. War between brothers and nephews and cousins on the thrones of Europe would always be a calamity. The problem was that women finally had too little influence, even when one of them sat on the throne, as Queen Victoria did. As for Elisabeth of Austria, her battle with her mother-in-law and the appointed Dr Seeburger was still being fought. He reported to the Minister of Police, as the best of her biographers Count Corti recounted, that 'she was unfit for her position both as Empress and as wife, although she has really nothing to do. Her relations with the children are most perfunctory, and though she grieves and weeps over the noble Emperor's absence, she goes out riding for hours on end, ruining her health.'

The débâcle in Italy led to the estrangement of the Emperor from Count Grünne, who was replaced by the Count de Crenneville, as Gyulai was by Benedek, who had proved at Solferino that he could fight. Grünne's son had been a page in Italy during the imperial visit there, and he told his heirs that Elisabeth refused every night to let the Emperor enter her bedroom. Certainly after his return from the disaster in Lombardy, she had the first of her nervous breakdowns. She had begun chain-smoking cigarettes, to the scandal of Vienna and Queen Victoria, who considered them the fuses of revolution. She usually refused to do what her husband asked her to do: 'Take hold of yourself. Show yourself occasionally in the city. Visit public institutions.' Instead she went out on her horses alone with a good-looking English riding master, Henry Holmes; her husband thought this was unbecoming.

After the birth of Rudolf, she had taken to a starvation diet. She stuck to her regime and would not appear at dinner with the Emperor, who began to give up the occasion and eat at his desk, trying to deal with his avalanche of paperwork. When she did appear at table, she ate practically nothing. And in private, she had no more than a jockey did so that she could keep her weight down. This punishment of her body was also a reproach to her husband. For something had shattered their understanding. One of her nieces, Marie

Wallersee-Wittelsbach, Countess Larisch, would later write in her memoirs that Elisabeth found out that her husband had an affair with a Polish countess and never recovered from the shock. More likely was that the Emperor had resumed his relationships with opera and ballet singers and peasant girls during her pregnancy with Rudolf and on his Italian campaign. As Princess Victoria wrote to her father, Prince Albert, 'The young Emperor possesses neither popularity nor confidence. This may be attributed to his private life. He is said to be very immoral. And to all this the terrible blow their military power has received . . .'

The greatest fear of most women in the nineteenth century was to get syphilis from their husbands. And when Elisabeth, already so passionate about her physical condition, suffered from hideous swellings at the wrists and knees and other internal ailments in 1860, she blamed Franz Josef. Dr Seeburger and unofficial medical advisers could not cure her; but she was told that she had contracted a venereal infection. The remedy for that disease at the time was a poisonous metal, a compound of quicksilver; as the saying went, 'One night under Venus, a lifetime under Mercury.' The horror of Elisabeth at the harm done to herself led to a hysterical demand for escape at all costs from the Viennese winter and the stifling Court. She was even more angered by Franz Josef's refusal to send Austrian troops to aid her sister Marie, now Queen of Naples, who was being chased out of her realm by Garibaldi and his redshirts.

In his remorse, Franz Josef could refuse her nothing. She wanted to go to Madeira to find the sun again and recover her health. He could provide no vessel, for the Austrian navy in the Mediterranean had been depleted during the war. At this time of trial, the royal network of Europe proved its value. Probably acting on her daughter's information about the Emperor's habits, Queen Victoria offered her royal yacht *Osborne* to take the distraught Empress to the Canary Islands. It would carry, as she wrote to her daughter in Prussia, 'the beautiful, fragile young Empress alone without husband and children to a distant land! May it not be too late.'

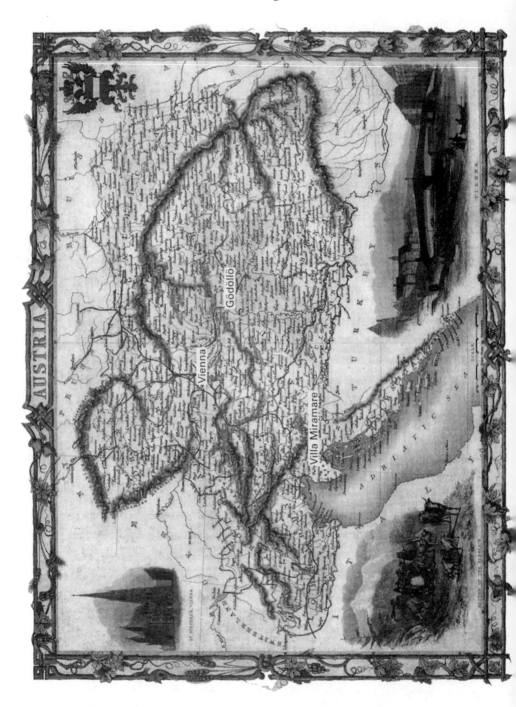

CHAPTER THREE

To Run Away

❖

ONE OF THE PARADOXES of the history of the nineteenth century was that the Mediterranean became a British lake. The age of steam so made it, after the wooden warships of Nelson had their day. Royal yachts had been a part of the British dynasty since the days of King Charles the Second, who had fled to France in one and ended by possessing twenty of them after his restoration to the throne. While still in her mother's womb, Queen Victoria had been carried by the custom-built *Royal George* across the Channel. Yet when she was crowned, she showed no gratitude towards the vessel, which was cumbersome and slow. She had the Admiralty commission her first yacht, *Victoria and Albert*, named after her husband. Still built in oak, the ship could be propelled by steam power through twin paddle wheels. When the Queen was at her Italianate villa at Osborne, she used two smaller steamers, the *Fairy* and the *Elfin*, to transport the royal mail from the Isle of Wight to the mainland. A larger *Victoria and Albert II* was built with twin funnels and with decoration in chintz and mahogany in the comfortable style preferred by Queen Victoria, particularly in the royal bathroom. Hearing of the Austrian Empress's wish to visit Madeira, the British royal sovereign commanded her original yacht, now given the name of the *Osborne*, to sail to Belgium and meet her wishes.

In her journal and her correspondence, Queen Victoria recorded the beginning of the voyage of Elisabeth from Antwerp to the Canary Islands. She had heard from a great gossip, King Leopold the First, King of the Belgians, that the Empress wished to travel 'in the strictest incognito . . . It seems the young Lady hurt her health really wantonly; she used to ride *jusqu'à 4 chevaux par jour* (up to 4 horses a day), and as hard as possible. The dancing was equally kept up with a sort of fury. She is very pretty . . . but without much mind or judgement. Father and Mother did not shine that way, and her grandfather Prince of Bavaria was a real idiot.' Captain Denman, in command of the *Osborne* when it docked at Margate, also described Elisabeth as 'very beautiful and interesting, but very imprudent about her health'. Everybody on board, however, appeared to be very pleased. 'The Empress had not suffered at all from sea-sickness,' although she was coughing a great deal.

During the storms on the Atlantic on the voyage to Madeira, Elisabeth was the only person in the imperial party not to be indisposed. She seemed to thrive on the frenzy of the ocean. Her health was almost restored. The chief proprietor of Madeira, Count Carvajal, offered her a large villa, which she would not take. She preferred a clifftop house on its own, far from prying eyes. A tropical garden of bougainvillaea and mimosa, palm and camellia trees, lay outside the veranda. At first, she was enchanted by the setting, but she soon relapsed into melancholy. She did not hear about the fate of her sister Marie, who had been ousted from Naples by Garibaldi and was besieged in Gaeta, where she became the heroine of the royal resistance, inspiring the garrison to hold out against furious attacks. She missed her children, left under the care of her mother-in-law at the Hofburg. 'She eats alarmingly little,' reported one of the Emperor's messengers, Count Rechberg, 'and we, too, have to suffer for this, for the whole meal, consisting of four courses, four desserts, and coffee, does not last more than twenty-five minutes. She is so depressed that she never goes out, but simply sits at the open window, except for an hour's ride at a foot's pace.'

She spent four months on the Atlantic island before she felt well enough to return to the confinement of the Austrian Court. She read Rousseau's *Confessions* and Lamartine and Heine. Her spirits improved because she had won over her three young ladies-in-waiting and her two handsome equerries, the Counts Mitrovsky and Imre Hunyády, who gave her Hungarian lessons and rode with her. His fate for his devotion to his imperial mistress was to be recalled to his regiment. He was never allowed to meet the Empress again because the Emperor's informants in Madeira had reported on his closeness to Elisabeth. She, however, had begun to become a brilliant linguist, speaking and reading in nine modern languages, as well as classical Latin and Greek.

The *Victoria and Albert II* took the imperial party home in the April of 1861 to Trieste. The royal yacht docked at Cadiz on the voyage, where the Empress tried to remain anonymous and see a bull-fight without fuss. The intrusion of the Duke de Montpensier, the brother-in-law of the Queen of Spain, with the full protocol of the Spanish crown annoyed her. She wanted to see the sights, not to show off. But the Austrian ambassador to Madrid reported on another triumph in public relations. The Empress had delighted everybody. 'Her gracious dignity and elegant simplicity could not fail to produce a great effect and impress people here, where stilted emotions alternate with the most unbecoming informality.' She sailed on past Gibraltar to Malta and to Corfu; the Ionian Islands were then a British protectorate. Her father's love of Greece made her, too, become enamoured of the Homeric island of King Alcinous and Nausikaa with its gardens and palaces. 'I love Corfu so much,' she said, 'that I would gladly give up all other travelling, and, if it were in my power, stay here for the rest of my life.'

She could not do what she wanted. Already the Emperor was sailing to meet her on the Greek island of paradise. He was on board the imperial yacht *Phantasie*, escorted by five battleships. He took Elisabeth back to the Castello Miramare near Trieste, the last palace of his unfortunate brother Maximilian and his young wife, the Coburg Princess Charlotte. After the defeat in Italy, Maximilian was no longer the ruler of Lombardy and Venetia. The pillars of the marble and sandstone palace by the sea could hardly support his disappointment, although the impossible dream of an empire in Mexico was awaiting his choice.

Franz Josef and his wife soon returned to Vienna, where Elisabeth found her children Gisela and Rudolf completely under the control of the Archduchess Sophie. In the recollections of the Emperor's aide-de-camp Count Paar, the absence of Elisabeth had been a good business for the Archduchess, who was always trying to force the imperial couple to separate. 'She was so successful that in the 'sixties the Emperor and Empress were virtually living apart and hardly ever saw each other for nearly seven years . . . She now had the Emperor's children also in her power. Her victory was complete. No one in Vienna gave another thought to the faraway Empress. The Archduchess Sophie left no stone unturned to make people forget her altogether.'

Even Gisela and Rudolf had been turned against their mother, who was only allowed to visit her children in their outdoor playground according to a rigorous timetable. The Empress herself had been committed to an interminable series of postponed state banquets and diplomatic soirées and Court galas and receptions. Yet these stiff and endless occasions had been the chief reason for her flight to the sun. At her husband's request, she had carried out some of her public duties at the opera and churches and hospitals and children's homes, while he was campaigning in Lombardy. A breakdown in her health had been the result. If she was now kept from her children by her mother-in-law, what was the point of her return?

A fanatic about health and hygiene, she had failed to improve conditions even in the Hofburg, where there were neither bathrooms nor lavatories nor even running water. The chamber pots were carried through long corridors, where anyone could see their contents. She had, however, installed a gymnasium in her dressing-room. Over the purple drapes, parallel bars were put in position, also two rings for swinging on ropes attached to the gilt ceiling. A heavy iron bath had to be carried in for her cold dip every morning. The walls were covered with pictures of her favourite horses and dogs. Her revolt from the strict order of Court life was her obsession with her own body. Exercise was her relief and her revenge on the conventions, which oppressed her. Without sexual satisfaction, she drilled her body into good shape.

Cured in Madeira and Corfu, Elisabeth fell ill again within a fort-night of her return to Austria. She had fever and intestinal com-plaints as well as her coughing. This did not come from smoking, as her husband had made her give up cigarettes because the habit did not become a lady. The Viennese doctors despaired of the condition of her lungs, if she did not change climate by a return to Corfu. The British ambassador reported: 'It is very sad to think of the state of the Empress's health and I fear that she goes to Corfu to die. Such at least is the opinion of the people immediately about Her Majesty.'

Franz Josef travelled back with her as far as the Castello Miramare near Trieste with his brother Maximilian, almost as restless a dreamer as Elisabeth was. Soundings from Paris had already been made of a great adventure in the New World. The Civil War between the North and South in the United States had persuaded Louis Napoleon that America was doomed to tear itself apart. That new nation was unable now to enforce the Monroe Doctrine and defend its supremacy over its continents. France might forge a Caribbean empire to recom-pense it for the cheap sale of Louisiana by the first Napoleon. Mexico was going through one of its frequent times of trouble. Nothing could stop French intervention there except the British navy or a retributory stab across the Rhine by the old enemies, Austria and Prussia. If an unemployed Habsburg archduke, however, was backed by French grenadiers and put on the Mexican throne, one who happened to be married to a Coburg princess related to the British and Prussian royal families, who would deny Louis Napoleon and his ambition?

Any discussion of this ominous diplomacy did not prevent the sick Elisabeth leaving for Corfu. The year of 1861 was to prove one of significant deaths for the royal houses of Europe. The King of Prussia had died on New Year's Day, making Queen Victoria's daughter, the Crown Princess, and her husband Frederick the heirs to the throne. The Queen's own mother, the Duchess of Kent, also passed away to the consternation of her daughter, who confided: 'To lose a beloved mother is always terrible, and the blank can never be filled.' Two young Coburg cousins, the King of Portugal and his brother, would be struck down by typhoid fever. And finally, the

Prince Consort Albert would also succumb to typhoid, probably caught from the insanitary drains of Windsor Castle, leaving the Queen inconsolable at the age of forty-two with eight unmarried children. 'What is to become of us all?' she would ask her eldest child in Berlin. 'Of the unhappy country, of Europe, of all?'

Determined not to follow her fellow monarchs to an early grave, the Austrian Empress sailed to Corfu. The British royal yachts were not available, as the Crown Prince and Princess of Prussia were to use them on a Mediterranean tour of their own. Unlike the sea-worthy Elisabeth, Princess Victoria would be sick twenty-one times in two days and feel more dead than alive. Feeling more alive just at the sight of Gastouri Bay, Elisabeth arrived at Corfu and displaced the British Consul there from his residence on the beach. Her medical adviser, Dr Skoda, had come with her; but he soon returned to Trieste with news of her miraculous recovery. She took long walks in the woods of laurels, and she bathed in the sea. She wrote back to her husband of sailing far out in the bay and swimming among the rocks as well as watching the moonlight on the waters with her dogs. Her life, she reported, was even quieter than in Madeira; she did not choose to return. The British ambassador in Vienna wrote to London that Dr Skoda should have delayed his report as it came 'a trifle abruptly on the heels of talk concerning a mental illness'.

Now Elisabeth's bugbear, Count Grünne, reduced to the role of Master of the Horse, was sent to Corfu to find out the truth about her state. She took him on long walks as far as the bleak Mount Pantokrator, ruining his breeches on the brambles. When he took to horseback to follow her, she drew caricatures of him as a voyeur with a nose like the beak of a hawk. She was developing her education and her irony as well as her sense of distance. On his return, Grünne could only inform the Emperor and the Archduchess Sophie that he was puzzled by the Empress's mood and good health. There was little reason for her to stay away.

She was escaping into a private world of fantasy, as her father still did and her cousin, Ludwig of Bavaria. With her Greek tutors, she was recreating an ancient dream of physical perfection and sweet music and poetry. Remote from Court life, she thought of making real her own vagaries. Her mother Ludovika knew of the Wittelsbach illusions and sent out her practical sister Hélène, the Princess of Thurn and Taxis, to see her sibling. Hélène found that Elisabeth had swellings around the cheeks and the eyes, perhaps a recurrence of the old illness which had sent her to Madeira. Yet her sister ascribed the malady to malnutrition, for Elisabeth was hardly eating and taking too much exercise. Trying to keep up with her, Hélène succumbed to swollen feet, although she did put Elisabeth on a diet of goat meat three times a day. Returning to Vienna at the end of September, Hélène was reunited with her husband and informed the Emperor that there was a hope of reconciliation with his wife, if he went to Corfu to negotiate with her.

Once again, the Emperor set out with the Austrian navy to rescue his marriage. The terms of his wife were stiff. She would return, but not to the Court, only within the limits of the Austrian Empire. She would live in Venice for a while, and her children must be taken from the Archduchess Sophie and sent to her there. Franz Josef had to agree because of his guilt over infecting her, and she sailed back on the steam frigate *Lucia* to the lagoon city. Again a mass silence met her arrival. Imperial troops guarded her safety. She could not go on her wanderings through the narrow streets, for her feet were now swollen with the mysterious malady, which was still passing through her body. She was even more besieged in her fortress of a palace on the Lido, while Elizabeth Barrett Browning fulminated from Florence against Italy's refusal to revolt from Habsburg repression:

> What! – while Austria stands at bay
> In Mantua, and our Venice bears
> The cursed flag of the yellow and black?

Elisabeth did, however, rebel about the running of her own establishment. She was insisting on her hard-won independence even more than the Venetians, who were relying on outsiders to gain it for them. The Countess Esterházy-Liechtenstein had brought Gisela and Rudolf down to the Lido with a curriculum and a daily programme. Elisabeth objected to her rules and dismissed her old adversary, to be replaced by Paula Bellegarde, a former lady-in-waiting who had married Count Königsegg-Aulendorf, who was now made the Controller of her Household. Her ankles and knees remained swollen in spite of the attentions of a Swedish masseur, who had joined her attendants. And she continued with her diet and her gymnastics, once telling a new Greek tutor who tried to help her on her leaps and bounds that she needed no aid. He would soon see that she could also have been an acrobat.

Her hair dominated her life. As she said, it was like a strange body on her head, a crown in place of the Austrian crown. 'If only *that* could be more easily got rid of than this,' was her sour comment on her tiara. Yet she kept her coils, for if she cut her hair, she thought the people would fall on her like wolves. The daily care of her braids, which now fell to the floor, was a mania according to the later description of another Greek tutor, Christomanos, as well as a routine. Like St Mary Magdalene, she seemed to wear only her tresses, although she put on a blue lace *peignoir* beneath the auburn cascade. The hairdresser with her white hands 'searched in the waves of her hair, lifted them in the air and palpitated them. She then rolled them around her arms as if they were streamers she had seized. She separated each wave into many others with an amber and golden comb, then parted every one of these into innumerable strands which were like gold in the sunlight. These were gently placed on her shoulders for brushing again . . . into new and pleasing waves, plaited into artful tresses which were transformed into two heavy magic serpents.' Then the hairdresser lifted the serpents and rolled them above the scalp of the Empress, interlacing them with silk thread in a magnificent crown. Any loose hairs were braided into place with a silver comb, while those which fell were preserved with the date of their loss. 'I always feel my *coiffure*,' the Empress said, and so she carried her crowning glory, erect and proud on her slender frame.

Another obsession now began. She wanted to be the most beautiful woman in the world. She had begun collecting photographs of her rivals, including those in Turkish harems, for her scrap-book. She would be lovelier than they were. Her mother Ludovika now hurried to Venice to rescue her daughter from her romantic desires. She was

wrathful enough, a valkyrie of judgement. She found her daughter
too lean, but well enough. She persuaded Elisabeth to come with her
gymnasium and her children to the spa at Bad Reichenau near to
Vienna. Another doctor called Fischer diagnosed her condition as
acute anaemia. She was in excellent form, in spite of her puffiness.
Unable to state that she was suffering from neurosis or a venereal
infection from her husband, Fischer persuaded her to go to the
mineral bath of Kissengen. There she met the aged blind Duke of
Mecklenburg; they talked of life and death on long walks. She wrote
a poem for him, which she had framed:

> If large or little, all that we have done
> At close of day is nothing when we've gone.
> How quickly is our vacuum now filled!
> What changes in the vastness of the ocean?
> A drop more, or a wave, when we are spilled.

At Kissengen, Elisabeth felt better, returning to her childhood
home at Possenhofen in July. Her eldest brother Ludwig had married
a comic actress, Henrietta Mendel, who had been ennobled as a
matter of propriety and was now the Baroness Wallersee; she had
recently given birth to a daughter. Her sister Marie, who had lost in
spite of her gallantry at the siege of Gaeta the throne of Naples, had
delivered illegitimate twin girls in the Ursuline convent in Augsburg;
the father was a Belgian officer in the Papal Guard. Even so, the
exiled King of Naples wanted his erring wife back. The Duchess
Ludovika had had quite enough of the scandals caused by both her
difficult daughters and packed them back to their husbands.

When Elisabeth returned unexpectedly to Vienna, she was
received with huge enthusiasm. 'Now we have her back in this
country,' a niece wrote, 'just as we had two years ago; yet how many
things lie between – Madeira, Corfu and a world of troubles.'
Although she looked well, 'her expression is not natural, it is forced
and nervous as it can be, her colour so high that she looks over-
heated, and though her face is no longer swollen, it is much thick-
ened and changed . . . How much she dreads being alone with *him*

and all of us.' *Him* was her husband Franz Josef, who could not make it up with his wife. Rumours had reached her of his liaisons with old flames including the Polish countess. Yet she settled at the Palace of Schönbrunn to bring up her children. 'It was hard for her, as I can understand,' her niece went on, 'to give up her recent travels. If one has no inner peace at all, one may think that moving is the answer to life, and she is now only used to that.'

That December her contemporary, Victoria, the Crown Princess of Prussia, returning from her Mediterranean tour with her husband, stopped in Vienna. She wrote back to her mother in Windsor Castle that she was quite charmed by the beauty of the Empress, which was surpassing. 'I never saw anything so dazzling or piquant. Her features are *not* so good as they are represented on most of her pictures – but the ensemble is far more lovely than any reproduction can convey an idea of.' Her skin was beautiful, her eyes expressive although not large, 'her mouth exceedingly pretty – and the sweetest softest expression possible. Her teeth are not good, but they hardly show at all. She has the most extraordinary quantity of chestnut hair I ever saw, perfectly loads of it.' She was intensely tall and wore very high heels. Her walk was very graceful, although she was 'laced dreadfully tight', which was hardly necessary with such a magnificent figure.

Her expression hardly ever changed, although she did pay Victoria a very long visit. 'Nothing could be more kind and more amiable than she was – it is impossible not to love her.' She seemed very shy and timid and did not speak much. Indeed, any conversation was difficult because she appeared to know very little and to take interest in very few things. She hardly spoke of her children, but she adored her sisters and was particularly fond of everything English. 'The Emperor seems to *dote* on her – but I did not observe that she did on him.'

This revealing report on the Austrian Empress from the Crown Princess of Prussia to the British Queen showed the effectiveness of royal contacts and intelligence in trying to keep the peace in Europe. Yet while Elisabeth made an effort to shed her fantasies and return to reality and some of her state duties, the Archduke Ferdinand Maximilian was following his delusions on to Mexico. The republican government of President Juarez had repudiated its international debts. Louis Napoleon had sent a French force across the Atlantic with nominal British and Spanish contingents to collect and to acquire a fresh dependency in the New World. He needed a romantic Habsburg figurehead to act as the king there and legitimise his ambitions. Was not the House of Coburg acquiring throne after throne, including the British crown by marriage? What of the proud record of the Habsburgs, who had once had the same facility?

'I do not underestimate', the Archduke Maximilian wrote in his journal, 'the advantages of my acceptance to Austria, to the splendour of my House which is now to be revived.' Jealous of his elder brother, he accused him of losing sovereignties in Italy. 'It has been the useful custom of great dynasties throughout the ages to place younger princes, living on allowances under the civil list, in advanced posts where they can do service.' The descendant of the Ferdinand and Isabella who had won the Americas, he would conquer it again for his dynasty.

He was warned against his rash attempt, and he had to have the consent of his brother, the Emperor. This was easily given, for Franz Josef wanted him far away. He was an embarrassment in Italy and a popular rival on home ground. Franz Josef gave his younger brother a miserable two hundred thousand florins for expenses and allowed him to recruit Austrian volunteers against the pledge of the throne of Mexico to the family, if Maximilian succeeded there. Although offered the alternative crown of Greece, from where his cousin Otto had been chased out by revolutionaries, Maximilian stuck to his otherworldly illusion. French forces took Mexico City and proclaimed him and his wife the imperial rulers in the June of 1863. Without the backing of the two powers interested there, Britain and Spain, and warned by the American President Lincoln to stay out of the hemisphere, he was then forced by his brother to yield his rights of succession to the Austrian throne. In spite of all this deterrence, the new Emperor and Empress of Mexico, Maximilian and Charlotte, sailed on the frigate *Novara* to their doom. At Gibraltar, he recanted his signed renunciation of the Austrian throne. He still imagined he could gain and retain all.

Franz Josef had more troubles with another friend and enemy, Prussia, over the vexed question of who was to lead Germany and who was to take the duchies of Schleswig and Holstein from the control of Denmark. The ruthless and scheming Count Otto von Bismarck-Schönhausen had been given power in Berlin by the new King Wilhelm the First in order to break the control of parliament over the budget of the army, which was being modernised with breech-loading rifles capable of rapid fire. A believer in the necessity of war with Austria so that Prussia could have the hegemony over Germany, Bismarck was open about his plans, telling Benjamin Disraeli in London: 'As soon as the army shall have been brought to such a condition as to inspire respect, I shall seize the best pretext to declare war on Austria, dissolve the German Diet, subdue the minor States, and give national unity to Germany under Prussia's leadership.'

Bismarck struck first by concluding a shameful treaty with the Tsar Alexander the Second, who was alienated from Franz Josef. The result was the effective suppression of Polish independence by Russia; Austria already held Galicia. Moving against this threatening alliance, Franz Josef cleverly called for a meeting of the German princes in Frankfurt in the August of 1863, where he would propose the revival of the ancient Habsburg role as Holy Roman Emperor, so restoring the power of Austria over Germany. The problem was the assent of the King of Prussia, who insisted to the British ambassador in Berlin that the bad relationship between the Hohenzollerns and the Habsburgs would persist until Austria had convinced herself 'that Prussia is her equal as a European Power, and her superior as a German one, and can never be forced to hold a subordinate position in the Confederation.' He would not attend the Frankfurt Congress. For that was, as Lord Clarendon reported back to London, a team of thirty horses – 'two great dray horses, who must be at wheel, and who are always kicking and biting each other – then a lot of half bred shambling vicious beasts of different sizes, and a dozen Shetland Ponies.' Without the presence of Prussia, such a team would collapse, as the Congress did.

In an effort to bridge the growing rift in Germany between her daughters and cousins spread among the two great Germanic powers and the princely states, Queen Victoria herself went to Coburg, where she was visited by King Wilhelm with Bismarck himself, and by the Austrian Emperor. When she stressed her earnest hope that Prussia and Austria would get together, the King replied, 'But how? It had been made quite impossible for him.' His visit was followed by that of Franz Josef, which Queen Victoria found '*very very* trying' for her in every way. She took care to say what her daughter, the Crown Princess, wanted her to say, that Prussia had to be put on a footing of equality. The Emperor assured her that this was his wish, there was no other wish in Germany, and Austria was very kindly disposed to that policy.

So the royal intelligence network again tried to serve the cause of peace. Yet ironically, the interests of the British dynasty in a rapprochement between the Germanic powers would result in a cynical alliance between them to harm the royal house of Denmark, into which the Prince of Wales had married. His bride was Alexandra – her brother had also been chosen to be the new King of Greece. The powerful British navy seemed to be gaining important bases in the Baltic and the Mediterranean, while blocking Prussian plans for expansion into Hanover and Schleswig and Holstein. The sudden death of the King of Denmark in the middle of November provoked an international crisis. The father of Princess Alexandra was proclaimed King Christian the Ninth and immediately signed a constitution incorporating Schleswig into his realm. The Local Assembly in Holstein appealed to the German Confederation to send as their ruler Duke Frederick of Augustenburg. Queen Victoria's peace policy lay in ruins. Prussian interests could not be reconciled with Danish or English ones, but they could be with Austrian and Russian ambitions. In return for support from Berlin and Vienna in the continuing repression of Poland, the Tsar agreed not to help King Christian in his time of trial.

On behalf of the German Confederation, Austrian and Prussian troops marched side by side into Schleswig and Holstein. Bismarck wanted annexation, so that Prussia would cut off Denmark and acquire access to the North Sea. Even England felt unable to support

the Danes with her navy, for Queen Victoria was adamant on neutrality, now that her family in the north of Europe were fighting with
one another. Both of her German sons-in-law were army officers
and had left for the front line. 'I had hoped that this dreadful war
might be prevented,' she wrote to the Crown Princess in Berlin, 'but
you all (God forgive you for it) would have it!' The Prince of Wales
and his wife Alexandra were frantic. Her father and brothers were
fighting against their German cousins. 'Oh,' the British Queen protested, 'if Bertie's wife was only a good German and not a Dane!'

In spite of a heroic resistance, Denmark had to sue for peace and
concede the two duchies, which were jointly occupied by Prussian
and Austrian forces. This was not so much an alliance of conve-
nience, but an increase of opportunities for misunderstanding,
which Bismarck might use to provoke a civil war in Germany. He
would lure Austria into agreeing that it should take Holstein, while
Schleswig should be annexed by Prussia. Then trouble would be
stirred up in Holstein, until the Crown Princess was forced to inform
Queen Victoria that Prussia was suspended midway between peace
and war, with Bismarck turning and twisting everything to serve his
purpose of aggression. 'Austria', as the Iron Chancellor said, 'was
only a question of time.'

Louis Napoleon had not intervened across the Rhine because the
German Confederation was united, and he was engaged on the
Mexican adventure. The Archduke Maximilian had arrived to be proclaimed Emperor with his Empress Charlotte. His French expeditionary force was winning victory after victory against the guerrillas
of Juárez, who held all the country outside the major cities. But the
Union was now beating the Confederacy in the American Civil War
and threatening intervention with its military resources. The French
commander, Marshal Bazaine, began to withdraw his troops, stating
that Maximilian could manage on his own. In the romantic dream
that was so often part of the Wittelsbach inheritance, Maximilian
refused to recognise the treachery and illusion which surrounded
him and Charlotte in his shining residences in Mexico. 'We live sometimes in the enormous Palais Nacional in the city,' he wrote back to
Vienna, 'and sometimes in Chapultepec, the Schönbrunn of Mexico.

This charming summer palace is built on basalt and surrounded by the giant trees of Montezuma. The view can only be compared to Sorrento.' Charlotte gave a ball every Monday. All the most beautiful women and leading diplomats came to these occasions. The Viennese chef had made the kitchen and the cellar among the best in the world, and the guests gorged themselves into grunting without speech.

The Mexican Emperor learned Spanish and imagined that he could create a constitutional monarchy in this strange new world. 'I live in a free country,' he wrote, 'where principles hold sway which you would not even dare to imagine at home in the night.' Even if Mexico were backward economically, in social thinking it was far ahead of Europe and Austria. 'A spirit of democracy is dominant here of such force and conviction that you Austrians may only have it after fifty years of dedicated struggle.' Maximilian did not know that the referendum which had elected him Emperor was a forgery. He was unaware of the hatred of European intervention by the republicans, who still supported the Indian Juárez. And he was offending the clericals, who had supported him, by his liberalism and wishes to establish a democracy in what was usually a tyranny. The victim of his illusions as much as Don Quixote, Maximilian believed only what he wanted to believe, and his fantasies were driving his ambitious wife Charlotte to the edge of madness.

Although Abraham Lincoln was assassinated, the Union won the Civil War. Its huge army would withstand any foreign incursion into its Mexican neighbour. The Pope was outraged with Maximilian's efforts at liberalism, while Louis Napoleon wrote off his Caribbean adventure and had his grenadiers recalled. Franz Josef still would not come to the aid of his popular brother in spite of the pleas of his mother, the Archduchess Sophie. Maximilian found himself with few European troops, an empty treasury and a disaffected local army. He gave up his policy of conciliation for one of intimidation. Nearly all the Mexican states were rebellious. He had only really held the areas protected by French bayonets, so he wrote out a statement of abdication. The game was over.

As at the siege of Gaeta, the wife proved stronger than the

husband. Charlotte insisted that her spouse cling to the imperial and colonial crown, while she returned to Europe to rally Paris and Rome and Vienna to his cause. Increasingly hysterical and distraught, she was shunned by Louis Napoleon and his Empress Eugénie. Charlotte then went to Miramare, expecting a visit from Franz Josef to see her along with his navy at Trieste. 'I prefer to remain here,' the Austrian Emperor wrote from the Hofburg to his wife, then in Hungary, 'rather than make the journey. Come back soon, my angel.' Elisabeth also did not venture to see Charlotte at Miramare, but returned back to Austria. She, too, divorced herself from the sorry mess across the Atlantic.

Forbidden to go to Vienna, the Empress Charlotte made her way to Rome. Pope Pius the Ninth received a weeping woman, who was falling into paranoia. She thought that her own household was trying to poison her on the orders of Louis Napoleon. Her nervous breakdown was so extreme that she had to be put up for the night on a ramshackle bed in the Papal Library. Her mind began to give way, and she relapsed into a coma. Often held in a straitjacket, she would spend her remaining fifty years in unoccupied royal villas or fortresses or mental homes.

Abandoned in Mexico City, Maximilian remained in the prison of his dreams. Again the example of Marie, the Queen of Naples, was followed in her last stand at Gaeta. Maximilian took refuge with the remnants of his supporters in the upland city of Querétaro, where he was soon captured by the victorious troops of Juárez. Although he escaped, he was seized once more. As the ultimate deterrence, the Mexican President put the Austrian prince on trial for treason. The Prussian King and the American President and even Garibaldi sent pleas for clemency and deportation. The execution of Maximilian might even interfere with the approaching coronation of Franz Josef and Elisabeth as the King and Queen of Hungary, which could reconcile the Habsburg Empire at last.

The coronation in Budapest took place. Eleven days later, on 19th June 1867, Maximilian was executed in Querétaro by a firing squad. He was brave and composed while facing the soldiers. He asked to be shot cleanly through the heart, but stray bullets disfigured his face and his yellow beard. Franz Josef did not hear of his young brother's death until ten days after the tragedy. He ordered a battleship sent to Mexico to collect the corpse, and Maxmilian would be buried with full military honours six months after his end. His wife Charlotte was insane, while two other family tragedies interrupted the mourning for him.

Smoking a secret cigarette had led to the death by burns of Mathilde, the eighteen-year-old daughter of another Habsburg, the Archduke Albrecht. At her father's approach, and frightened of his disapproval, she had stuck the smouldering tobacco behind the back of her muslin dress, which caught on fire. She expired in agony. And Elisabeth's sister Hélène, who had been intended as the wife of Franz Josef, suffered the burial of her replacement husband, the Prince of Thurn and Taxis. He died early, as would his son by Hélène at the age of twenty-one. With the loss of members of the family as well as the thrones of Naples and Mexico, the Habsburgs and the Wittelsbachs were not doing well in their dynastic marriages. Maximilian had turned the nightmare of the royal families into a fact. A Habsburg prince had been slain by a republican volley. Betrayed by his own family and the Napoleons, the wild imagination of the young Emperor had only led to his downfall in a far country.

Another doomed and romantic Wittelsbach prince went to meet his cousin, the Austrian Empress, in Bavaria. With the death of his father, partially from the worry of the Schleswig and Holstein crisis, King Ludwig the Second had ascended the throne at the age of eighteen, as Franz Josef had. They were far apart in character, for Ludwig worried less about the state of the army than the curls in his hair, much as his cousin Elisabeth did. He had chosen Wagner almost as a surrogate father because of his dreamland operas of *Lohengrin* and *Tannhäuser* and *Tristan*. The composer feared that the life of the young King 'must vanish like a fleeting godlike dream in this crude world of ours. He loves me with the fire and tenderness of first love.' His prophecy was correct, but if Ludwig's life was to be short and tragic, he would create Wagner's fame for ever. In three castles of fantasy, he would enshrine the sets of operas in murals and stones.

On Lake Starnberg across the water from Possenhofen stood the rural Schloss Berg, where Ludwig moved after his infatuation with Wagner, who was housed in the nearby Villa Pellet to finish *Tristan* and *Die Meistersinger* and complete the *Ring*. Of Ludwig, Wagner wrote: 'He is like a God! If I am Wotan, then he is my Siegfried.' Ludwig's love of clothes and cross-dressing, of poetry and music, had not made him yet aware of his repressed homosexuality. He did not see that he enjoyed the company of Elisabeth's brother 'Gackel', the Cock, almost as much as hers, when he spent a whole month with the ducal Wittelsbach family at the resort of Kissingen. Indeed, Elisabeth wrote back to her daughter Gisela in Vienna of a visit by the scented Bavarian King to her at Possenhofen. He had kissed her hand so many times that her young sister Sophie had asked her afterwards whether she had any hand left. Yet the Austrian ambassador in Bavaria informed her that the King took no pleasure in the company of ladies or in associating with the feminine sex.

For four weeks at Kissingen, Elisabeth and Ludwig became inseparable, riding side by side through the forests, looking on each other's related beauty as once Narcissus looked on himself in the pool of legend. She had a grey horse from Hungary, while he had a hunter from Ireland. She called him the Eagle, while he named her the Dove. He even ignored Wagner by Lake Starnberg, finding a superior romantic in his cousin, who also wanted to build actual castles of the imagination in Austria and Greece. Yet they were phantoms of the real world, living in the warm bath of mutual admiration. Their relationship had no hope of success, for if Ludwig had been interested in young women, the younger Sophie must have been and would be his choice. For a time, however, the Wittelsbach cousins escaped together into a paradise of their strange spirits, a Xanadu of their minds.

CHAPTER FOUR

A Certain Assertion

❖

'I T I S M Y W I S H that full and unlimited powers should be reserved by me in all things concerning the children,' Elisabeth declared to her husband, asserting her new confidence, 'the choice of those who surround them and of their place of residence, and the entire control of their education. In short, I alone must decide everything until they come of age.' She further required that everything to do with her personal affairs and domestic arrangements should be left to her to judge. This was her ultimatum to Franz Josef, if he wished her to continue in her duties as the Empress of Austria. The influence of his mother had to be curbed. Elisabeth had to be supreme.

The Emperor capitulated. The tutors of Crown Prince Rudolf were changed from bullying generals to liberal doctors. Moreover, King Ludwig of Bavaria had given the Empress the courage of her own artistic tastes. When Wagner put on a series of three concerts in Vienna, Elisabeth sent the composer a gift of a thousand gulden. She further became a patroness of Liszt and took up her father's talent of playing on the zither. Drawn by Ludwig's example, she also began to assert herself in the decoration of some of her fifty residences within the Habsburg Empire, particularly her apartments in the Hofburg and Schönbrunn and Laxenburg, as well as planning her own dream castles at Lainz near Vienna and in Corfu in the future.

She was showing herself a true Wittelsbach in her newfound passion for music and architecture.

In politics, however, she was still looking for her role, which she would find in Hungary – she was studying the Magyar language assiduously. But she could not stop her fellow soul Ludwig from diplomatic actions against her family, such as the recognition of the kingdom of Italy by Bavaria, which meant the end of the hopes of her sister Marie's restoration as the Queen of Naples. Even so, as she wrote to Ludwig, she could not feel bitter or angry at him, although all the ruling houses driven out of united Italy contained some member of the Bavarian royal family. The Wittelsbachs, indeed, had married into almost every duchy and principality from the North Sea to the Mediterranean.

Although Elisbeth was keeping her side of the bargain and staying near Vienna with her children, she still had recurrences of her old maladies, the swellings and the neurasthenia. When she was suffering, she would abandon Court life and abscond to her family in Possenhofen and Munich. On one flight at Christmas in 1865, she was accused by the Prussian ambassador of caprice rather than illness, 'something not too unusual in the princesses of the Bavarian ducal line'. Franz Josef, however, was in Budapest, still looking to pacify restive Hungary through the mediation of the moderate reformer Ferencz Deák. With his wife's sympathy for that country, he saw the hope of a solution.

In early January at the Hofburg, Elisabeth received a Hungarian delegation led by the charismatic Count Gyula Andrássy. Through an intermediary in the Household of the Empress, Ida Ferenczy, he had heard of the predilection of Elisabeth for Hungary after her visit there. She received the delegation of the Hungarian nobles and representatives, dressed in a national costume of an embroidered velvet bodice and white silk dress and lace apron and cap, crowned with diamonds. She replied to the official greeting in Magyar, saying that she would visit Budapest soon, which she did with the Emperor at the end of the month. For the first time on her official tour, she met with a warm welcome, although she complained to her children about all the official ceremonies and the endless dressing and undressing. She did, however, manage a visit to the riding school every day. Franz Josef even praised her diplomatic efforts to his mother, writing that she was a great help with her courtesy, tact, discretion and excellent Hungarian. And she, who was often seeing Andrássy, confided in him: 'If the Emperor's cause goes badly in Italy, it hurts me, but if it goes badly in Hungary, it is death to me.'

Although Franz Josef did not wish to grant Hungary much more independence, he was forced along a policy of conciliation. Bismarck was pushing the King of Prussia towards a quick war with Austria and the southern German states in order to force a unity on the country, as Piedmont had in Italy outside Venetia, which Austria was still holding. Bismarck could and would compel Austria into a war on two fronts by making a treaty with Italy; but neither Germanic power might afford an intervention against them by France or by Russia, which also had to be kept sweet. The conflict of the two dynasties of Central Europe would be the opportunity of their rivals on their borders.

Against the urging of Bismarck and the Chief of the General Staff von Moltke, the King of Prussia would not declare an immediate war on the Habsburg Empire. He would not permit an unjust war against fellow Germans. But the Austrians were provoked into taking elementary military precautions against a surprise attack. Their army needed seven weeks to mobilise, the Prussians only three. They felt obliged to reinforce their fortresses in Bohemia and Moravia. With intelligence sources reporting every detail of these troop movements, Bismarck could represent defensive measures as aggressive ones.

Unexpectedly, the King of Prussia responded to an offer of British arbitration between Berlin and Vienna. He declared that he did not want to push things to extremes. For the first time, he spoke to his son Frederick, the Crown Prince, about the political crisis, asking him to write to Queen Victoria and offer her the agreeable task of mediating between the two German powers. This was a strange change of face and a blow to Bismarck's methods of diplomacy. As the British ambassador said, the question for Bismarck was: Would he carry the King with him? If the British could get the wedge in,

Bismarck would find it more difficult. 'You again, dearest Mama,' the Crown Princess wrote in elation, 'may be the means of averting a European conflagration.'

Queen Victoria knew the limits of royal diplomacy far better than her daughter did. She told her Prime Minister immediately of the information in her daughter's letter, but she did not think an offer to referee between the two German powers would work. Yet she sent a personal letter to the King of Prussia as a private act, begging him as always to respect the family relationships between the dynasties of Europe:

Beloved Brother,

At this fearful moment I cannot be silent, without raising my voice earnestly, and in the name of all that is most holy and sacred against the threatened probability of war. It is in your power to avert the calamities of a war, the results of which are too fearful to be even thought of, and in which thousands of innocent lives will be lost, and brother will be arrayed against brother.

War is ever fearful, but when it is begun for mere objects of ambition, for imaginary affronts and wrongs, it is still more fearful. You are deceived, you are made to believe that you are to be attacked, and I, your true friend and sister, hear your honoured name attacked and abused for the faults and recklessness of others – or, rather more, of ONE man! . . .

Ever your affectionate and unhappy Sister and Friend.

Victoria R

Faced with this appeal from his sister monarch, the King wavered. If Austria would withdraw its forces from Prussia's borders, he would pull back his own. Now the secret pact of Bismarck with Italy saved his policy and restored the King's faith in him. He persuaded his ally to move most of her army towards Lombardy. The Austrians could not leave Venetia undefended against such a threat, and the Emperor felt obliged to declare a partial mobilisation of his southern army. This made it seem as if he had been deceiving the King of Prussia about disarmament and wanting peace. As Bismarck asserted, war was necessary. Austria could hardly commit her armies to an Italian campaign without first deploying defensively against a stab in the back from Prussia. Her slow process of deployment, twice as long as Prussia's, meant that she must make her preparations first. So six days after the partial mobilisation in the south, the Austrian Emperor reluctantly ordered the movement of the northern army to Bohemia. Even if this were to provoke a full Prussian response, there seemed nothing else he could do.

Bismarck had got what he wanted, an apparent Austrian threat against Prussia. His health suddenly and wonderfully improved. As he joked to the British ambassador, he would prefer to descend to posterity in the character of Attila. There would have to be a conflict to remove so dangerous a man — or an assassination. And indeed, a student from Tübingen, Ferdinand Cohen-Blind, fired five shots at Bismarck at point-blank range. The minister gripped his assailant and handed him over to a couple of passing guards. During the struggle, the revolver was pressed against Bismarck's thick coat, which was pierced by two bullets, one of which bruised his ribs without breaking the skin. The would-be assassin was the Jewish stepson of Karl Blind, a socialist revolutionary from southern Germany, then in exile in London. Bismarck's spies immediately linked the attempt to a secret society of republicans in Württemberg who planned to murder the King of Prussia and leading members of his government. The King was confirmed in his fears of revolutionaries and of his own political murder. Even the British were linked with the conspiracy. The identity of the assassin was a godsend, a Jew and a radical, connected with two opponents of Bismarck's diplomacy, Württemberg and England.

The sequel was extremely odd and made the attempted assassination seem even more spurious. Cohen-Blind cut his own throat in his cell. He was either murdered by police agents or had been given a razor and encouraged to commit suicide. He could never disclose the identity of those who had placed him in Bismarck's path, armed with a revolver so defective that it was little better than a popgun.

Everybody was arming against somebody — Queen Victoria recorded — and everybody declared they wanted to attack nobody. At least, she was on the sidelines of the war, involved only through her children and cousins. Her daughter, the Crown Princess of Prussia, was threatened with worse in this 'monstrous mixture of absurdity and horror'. Her own husband might have to try to kill her sister's husband in Hesse and her close relatives in Hanover and Coburg and the princely families in the south, which would necessarily side with Austria. Her sister Alice's husband, Louis, and his youngest brother, Wilhelm, would have to support the Grand Duke of Hesse-Darmstadt against Prussia. Yet the second brother, Heinrich, was in command in the Prussian Lancers and would have to fight with the Crown Prince, perhaps against Hesse. The family might be slaughtering one another.

Austria now made the mistake of repudiating the agreement to split the Danish border duchies with Prussia. In reply, the King sent Prussian troops into Holstein. The Austrian forces would not fight, but withdrew over the border into Hanover. Not a shot had been fired, and peace was still just possible. But Austria now called for the mobilisation of all the smaller German states against Prussia. Most of them wished to be neutral, but they were caught between the hammer and the anvil. They agreed to arm, but only to defend their individual frontiers. Their weak decision meant that Prussia could gobble them up piecemeal. Bismarck immediately sent an ultimatum to Hanover and Saxony: they must allow Prussian troops to march through their territory or be destroyed. The two states rejected the ultimatum and prepared to fight the war that was being forced upon them.

Reporting from Vienna, the British ambassador found confidence in the Austrian camp, which thought that a quick victory in Italy would be followed by another against Prussia, weakened in its wars against the states of southern Germany. Materially speaking, there was a fair chance if the two great countries really came to blows. What the unacceptable was Prussia's wish to take 'the Supremacy in Germany'. Indeed, the prospect of war seemed to calm the nerves in the Hofburg. Rather like the King of Prussia, as the Crown Princess Victoria found, the spirits of the Emperor were lifted at the thought of military action. 'I don't *think* he *wishes* war –' Victoria wrote to her mother, 'but his passion for soldiering puts other considerations into the shade. I fear it is a characteristic trait of the whole family, you know.' Hohenzollerns and Habsburgs stirred to the sound of trumpets.

With the worsening situation, Elisabeth had to leave Hungary to return to Vienna, although the Court did move to Schönbrunn, where she was more at ease. 'I am happy to leave the city and enjoy greater freedom,' she wrote to a Hungarian friend, 'especially as I have permission to go to the stables by myself when I like.' She fretted over the clouds of war, wishing that the King of Prussia might die and Ludwig of Bavaria would pay more attention to his threatened state than to Wagner. Indeed, when hostilities did break out, Ludwig retired to his island of roses in Lake Starnberg and left his troops to fight on the Austrian side without him. Her brothers would have to join in the Bavarian combat, while her job was again to set up a hospital at Laxenburg. For wounded there would certainly be, and she would prefer to be with the Hungarian soldiers.

On the southern front, the Archduke Albrecht defeated the Italian forces at Custozza, almost on the site of a previous victory by the late Marshal Radetsky. And yet Benedek with the main Austrian army would not move north from Moravia against the advancing Prussians, because he only had one railway line to bring up his supplies. Two days after Prussia invaded Bavaria and Hanover and Saxony, Benedek moved slowly into Bohemia. He took up defensive positions around the fortified town of Königgrätz near Sadowa. The Prussian Chief of the General Staff von Moltke planned a trident assault by three armies on the entrenched Austrians. Success depended on the Second Army led by the Crown Prince Frederick breaking through at the end of the day, as Blucher had done to defeat Napoleon finally at Waterloo. That was the strategy. Deployment meant even more than courage. Benedek knew that and requested peace at any price, telegraphing the Emperor that catastrophe was unavoidable. 'Impossible to make peace,' was the Emperor's response. 'I authorise a retreat in good order, if it is unavoidable.'

That was what he had had to do at Solferino; that would be the result of Königgrätz. Nearly half a million men were engaged in the struggle, a greater concentration of troops than in the Napoleonic wars. This was the herald of the triumph of the railway carriage over the horse-drawn wagon. It would decide the future of Germany, which had been so long confused with the Holy Roman Empire. The outcome would make the judgement on the rule of Germany by the Habsburgs, who had unfortunately looked more towards the Danube and the Mediterranean than to the Rhine and the Elbe. The battle would be the verdict on whether Germany was to be united at last by a greater Prussia, or whether the Austrian Emperor and the King of Saxony and the gaggle of minor German princes leading the Federal Army in the south-west would keep Germany as divided and impotent as Italy had been before the Austrian defeat there.

The Prussian attack by its First Army in the morning did not go well. The Saxons fought valiantly, led by the two sons of their king. Benedek's men checked the advance of the Prussian troops and put them on the defensive. The Austrian cavalry was massing for a charge which might might end in an enemy rout. Then, towards one o'clock, 'a line of grey trees' was seen advancing from the east. It was the Second Army making for the Austrian flank and rear, exactly where it should be.

Heavily bombarded by artillery, the Crown Prince of Prussia's advance guard stormed the village of Chlum and threatened Benedek's line of retreat to the south through Königgrätz. The Austrian commander sent in his reserve to retake Chlum, but the Crown Prince held on, pushing up more and more of his men. Benedek had to fall back or risk the loss of his whole army. Through the courage of his rearguard and the Saxons, he managed to escape with a hundred and eighty thousand men, leaving forty thousand dead or wounded or taken prisoner. The Prussian cavalry, which had hardly been used in the action, failed to charge in hot pursuit to break up the routed Austrians. Benedek still stood with a large army before Vienna.

Franz Josef was sitting with Elisabeth when the news of the defeat came to them. He wished to fight on. 'God grant that a peace is reached,' she recorded. 'We have no more to lose, so it would be best to meet our ruin with honour.' With the Prussians advancing on

Vienna, Elisabeth was sent to Budapest to prepare for the flight of the whole Court. On her arrival, she was met warmly by Deák and Andrássy. They warned her of what she knew. If the Hungarian reformers were not given what they wanted, the revolutionaries could overthrow the empire in its weakness. She took the Villa Kochmeister for herself and her children and returned to Vienna to advise her husband to take Andrássy for his Foreign Minister. Already jealous of the Hungarian Count, Franz Josef temporised, but he sent his wife and and children back to Hungary to pacify it with good intentions, if she could.

The paradox of the Habsburg Empire was that its greatest enemy Bismarck was its saviour from collapse at the time of its disaster. The Archduke Albrecht had now taken command of a combined Austrian army. Prince Louis Napoleon threatened Prussia on the Rhine. Russia might always enter the fray to seize the mouth of the Danube, or even attack Berlin. The forces of the southern German states were still in the field. The object was to unite Germany under the leadership of Prussia, not to destroy Austria, so useful a counter-weight in the politics of Central Europe. Yet King Wilhelm the Second wanted to march in triumph through the streets of Vienna. For three days and nights, the Iron Chancellor and the monarch were in deadlock. Then Bismarck got what he wanted, a figleaf to cover the forced Prussian unification of Germany, so that other major powers did not intervene against them.

The terms were merciful to Austria, which had to cede no central territory, but was to be excluded from Germany; Prussia was to acquire Schleswig and Holstein and a large indemnity; France would receive Venetia and hand it over immediately to Italy. Nothing was to be agreed about northern Germany. There, Bismarck and the King were to have a free hand. Prussia could swallow up the small states in due time; not at a gulp, but slowly, bite by bite.

The fighting was not yet finished. By making a separate peace with Prussia, Austria had left her German allies in the lurch. All the Prussian armies could now turn and crush the small states. The forces of the German Federation were only saved from annihilation because the various states began to defect from the common cause and submit to Prussia. Bavaria was the first to make a separate peace, followed by Baden. The other minor German states soon gave up the fight and trembled to think what their fate might be.

Queen Victoria tried to plead for her German relatives through her son-in-law, the Crown Prince. She expected he could do little and admitted that she wrote only to ease her conscience. She knew that such a total victory had given Prussia the power to annex by right of conquest. All kingdoms had been assembled by the Queen's method – royal marriage – or by Bismarck's method – war. Her feelings about Prussia's victory were ambivalent. She believed that Prussia should unify Germany, and she was influenced by her eldest daughter's pride in the success and example on the battlefield of her husband, the Crown Prince. It had not been so in Bavaria, where Ludwig had been graceful only in his surrender, while in Austria, Crown Prince Rudolf was growing up to be a nervous child in a troubled atmosphere.

Secure in the education of her children in Hungary, Elisabeth was insisting on her new political role to preserve the empire for her son Rudolf. She had an interview alone with Andrássy. If he were to be trusted, he could save not only Hungary, but the Monarchy. He would do all he could for them. Franz Josef must meet him at the Hofburg. Andrássy was a man of honour, she wrote to her husband. 'What he has – his sympathy and influence in this country – he will lay at your feet. For the last time, I beg you in the name of Rudolf not to lose this last opportunity.'

The motives of Elisabeth, as her husband knew, were not entirely the interests of her son, but also her own feelings for Andrássy and his country. According to the Grünne family, Franz Josef grew so jealous of Andrássy that he thought of challenging him to a duel, but he was dissuaded on the grounds that an emperor could not fight a subject. The imperial valet also confirmed that his master was largely excluded from the Empress's quarters, when he visited Hungary. If he arrived early or late, he was told that she was still sleeping. If he called during the day, he was told that she was out riding or walking. 'The Emperor would go to visit her ten days in succession, and yet never be received.'

Franz Josef did receive Andrássy and wrote to his wife that the

Hungarian wanted too much and offered too little. He was not definite enough in his views and lacked consideration for the rest of the Monarchy. Elisabeth continued to plead the Hungarian cause by letter; but she now wanted to buy the country estate of Gödöllö, where there was a hospital for the wounded as well as magnificent riding. Her husband pleaded that they must economise after the Prussian devastation of the imperial lands. Elisabeth would not concede his point and continued her campaign for reform and another territory in the place where she now felt so happy.

Her championship of Hungary was making her unpopular at Court. But she persisted in her policy that there should be a dual rather than a single monarchy. She would then become the Queen of Hungary as well as the Empress of Austria. Franz Josef gave way, the Hungarian Constitution was restored, and Andrássy was appointed the Minister President of the country. In return, Elisabeth was endowed by the grateful Hungarians with her favourite Gödöllö at no expense to Franz Josef as an imperial residence. A coronation was announced, at which both of Their Majesties would assume the Crown of St Stephen.

Meanwhile, the surprising news had reached Elisabeth that King Ludwig of Bavaria was betrothed to her sister Sophie. A slender princess with yellow hair, Sophie was an enthusiast for Wagner and could sing his music prettily. Her brother 'Gackel', also a friend of the King, had been sent to ask his intentions. Ludwig had jibbed at any close relationship with Sophie, but then had met her at a Court ball and told his mother that he would marry her. On her acceptance, they were frequently seen together and compared to Venus and Adonis. Even so, Ludwig wrote ominously to Wagner: 'I will be true to Sophie until death. But even in death, I will remain true to you, the lord of my life.'

Intimations of instability began at a ball given by Prince Hohenlohe, at which Ludwig left early to see the last act of a play by Schiller, without taking leave of Sophie. But such unconventional behaviour was typical of the artistic Wittelsbachs, as Elisabeth had already shown at Vienna. The date of the actual wedding kept on being postponed. Rumours at Court told of Ludwig saying that he would rather drown himself than marry, and asking the Royal Doctor to give him a certificate to declare that he was unfit to wed. When Duke Max finally insisted on a commitment for the ceremony, Ludwig came out of the throne room. Sophie had been a childhood friend, almost a sister, but there was no love on his side. 'The picture of gloom disappears,' he wrote in his journal. 'I longed for freedom to wake from this terrible nightmare.'

If Ludwig had ever loved a woman, it was Sophie's sister Elisabeth. As he had written to her after a railway journey together, his sincere love and reverence and faith in her made him see heaven on earth and could only be put out by death. They had frequently met on his isle of roses in the middle of Lake Starnberg, where there was a Roman temple to Mithras and sixteen thousand bushes of flowers tended by six gardeners, told to be always invisible. Yet Elisabeth was now conventional enough to be angry with her Ludwig. As she wrote to her mother, there were no words for such behaviour. Yet God knew that Sophie could never have been happy with such a man. She was aware of Ludwig's romantic and homosexual nature, sublimated to a degree in his worship of Wagner and his building of fantasy castles. Sophie would find another husband, the Wittelsbach princesses always did. Soon she was to marry Ferdinand, the Prince of Orleans and Duke of Alençon. France would be her fate.

Elisabeth was more preoccupied with her second coronation in Budapest. She was perfecting her knowledge of the Magyar tongue and politics, taught by a liberal Jewish tutor, Max Falk. In the May of 1867, she travelled with the Emperor to Budapest, where the reception was rapturous and unusual. They visited Gödöllö, which was already being rebuilt for their use with its marvellous facilities for riding. Then they returned to the Hungarian capital for the exhausting festivities before the actual ceremony. 'What a fearful burden it is,' Elisabeth wrote to her mother, 'to dress up first thing in the morning in a Court train and Crown and hold Courts and receive presentations all the time – and then this appalling heat!'

There were still tragedies in the family, the death of Mathilde from burns and the approaching execution of Maximilian by a Mexican firing squad. Mourning was the dress at Court in Vienna, but the coronation in Budapest could not be postponed or conducted in black. A pattern of lilac blossom and opals and other gems was sewn on to Elisabeth's brocade dress of silver and white, while she wore the black velvet bodice of her adopted land and a diamond crown. A state coach again drew her to the ceremony behind eight horses, while Franz Josef rode in the uniform of a Marshal of the Hungarian army. In the cathedral, Andrássy, dressed in all his glory of jewels and fur, put the crown and mantle of St Stephen on the sovereign's head and shoulders. Then he held the same crown over Elisabeth's piled tresses and made her Queen of Hungary. The Austrian Adjutant-General Count Crenville would have rather died than witness 'such a shameful display of weakness'. For him, Andrássy deserved the gallows even more than in the year of the Hungarian rebellion.

For her, a romantic dream had become a ritual and a fact. Through the love of a people, she had found a new power and home in another country. In a way, she was now wedded to Hungary. As Hélène Fürstenberg, one of the ladies-in-waiting of the Archduchess Sophie, commented, 'Her Majesty looked quite lovely and out of this world during the solemnities, so absorbed and feeling like a bride. I rather felt also as if, in *one* respect, she did interpret it as that.' For the first time in her marriage, she was defining her own role against its honoured conventions. She was the darling of the Hungarians. She represented their daring thrust for more independence. In opposition to her stood the massed conservation of the Viennese aristocracy and the Habsburg crown. They would confuse her wayward life with her emotional support for a whole people, pushing for too much liberty.

Now that there was a Dual Monarchy with shared responsibilities called Austro-Hungary, Elisabeth certainly felt herself the Queen of the eastern half. Using her beauty at the time of the imperial defeat by Prussia to subjugate her husband's intransigence as well as the hearts of his restless Magyar subjects, she had found herself a separate political role, which removed her from the hateful constrictions of the Hofburg and the Archduchess Sophie. She was the heroine of Budapest, not the pariah of Vienna. Her gratitude to Franz Josef at her victory over him and his Court made her agree to go with him to

Ischl for his hunting and become again his true wife. The supremacy was briefly hers, and so she gave herself once more to him for a time. Her new power led to a short surrender. Yet now with the split control of affairs, the Viennese talked of an 'empire under notice'.

With the piercing vision of the young, the eight-year-old Crown Prince Rudolf had described the coronation, and the two men and one woman who had figured in the ceremony. 'Mama sat on a kind of throne and Papa went to the altar where a good deal of Latin was said.' The sacred mantle was wrapped round Rudolf's father and the Primate gave him the sword of St Stephen to slash three times. 'After that there was a roll of drums and Andrássy and the Primate placed the crown on Papa,' who then took the orb and sceptre. 'Papa and Mama at this point went up to the throne and Andrássy walked out into the middle of the church and shouted three times, "Long Live the King."' Then Mama went to the altar for the crown to be held over her head, before Rudolf went riding with her in a glass coach. If the wise child did not say his father the Emperor had no clothes, he did notice that the crown of St Stephen appeared to be the gift of a Hungarian count, who also presented it to his mother.

CHAPTER FIVE

The Queen of Hungary

❖

A LAST IDYLL at Ischl with Franz Josef made Elisabeth pregnant once more. Yet the deaths in the family had continued with the sudden end of Hélène's husband, the Prince of Thurn and Taxis. And when Louis Napoleon and his wife Eugénie threatened a visit to Salzburg to improve French relations with Austro-Hungary, Elisabeth declared that her condition made the proposed meeting too depressing. She was so miserable, she wrote to the Emperor, that she could cry all day long. 'I take no pleasure in anything, I do not want to ride or go for walks, everything in the world has no flavour.' Not feeling at her best, Elisabeth did not relish a comparison with Eugénie, who was her only rival in the beauty stakes among the ruling women of Europe. Yet diplomacy triumphed over intimacy. The encounter at Salzburg took place with a cool courtesy. Without stressing it, Franz Josef still considered Louis Napoleon a scoundrel and an adventurer, who had robbed the old Austrian Empire of Lombardy. Only the fear of an attack by Prussia could bring the two powers loosely together. As for Elisabeth, she was a head taller than Eugénie, who was pretty enough, but obviously inferior in birth as well as height. The two couples did not mix well in their guarded truce.

Although Franz Josef did do his duty and pay a return visit to the World Exhibition in Paris, which he found surpassing in its beauty,

Elisabeth prepared to return to Gödöllö to have her child and reign over the hearts of the Hungarians. She was happy enough that her husband was enjoying himself elsewhere. 'After all,' she wrote to her mother Ludovika, 'everything is so much easier and simpler for gentlemen.' The Exhibition was only marred by another assassination attempt, this time by a refugee Pole on the Tsar and Tsarina of Russia. She cried all the evening, he was white as a sheet – so the Crown Princess of Prussia reported to her mother Queen Victoria. The imperial Russian couple both regretted that Louis Napoleon had not been touched, while they had faced murder.

The policy of a Habsburg entente with France against the ambitions of Prussia was not working. Italy would have to join a triple alliance so that Franz Josef might be sure that he would not have to fight another war on two fronts as before. The problem was that French troops now maintained the independence of Rome and the Papal States, thus preventing the final unification of Italy. And so, with the other powers divided against him, Bismarck could pick his occasion for an advance on the Rhine and the remaining independent German states in the south. Louis Napoleon made a mistake in not pressing for an alliance. Austria-Hungary would remain neutral, particularly as Bismarck had now a supporter in Andrássy, who depended on Prussian threats against Vienna to guarantee the hard-won liberties of Budapest.

In politics as in love, it is difficult to know who uses whom. Andrássy certainly used his relationship with the Empress Elisabeth to gain limited powers for Hungary, while she used her enticement of the Magyar Court to gain her own release from the confines of Vienna. If through her influence Andrássy won a kind of independence for his country, she gained a kind of independence from her country and an influence in his. Her choice of Gödöllö as her regular residence and the birthplace of her new daughter Marie Valérie offended Austrian opinion, particularly at Court, where such conduct was seen as a form of treachery. The Emperor had to travel from the Hofburg down the Danube to see his wife, who was the leader of Hungarian society – a role she had shunned in Vienna. She dismissed the last survivors of her entourage appointed by the

Archduchess Sophie; even the Controller of her Houshold was now the Hungarian Baron Francis Nopsca. She had embraced her new land with a passion, which was matched by its people. When she declared to the radical poet Jókai that she understood nothing about politics, he replied that the highest point of policy was to win the heart of a country, 'and Your Majesty understands perfectly how to do that.' To him, she was not the Queen, but the genius of the land.

To Andrássy, she was the saviour of the land, and he was her devoted admirer. He took her to racecourses at Alag and Pardubitz. He rode with her through the wild woods without an escort. Yet he respected her independence, as she respected that of Hungary. Both needed protection in their solitude from the packs of wild dogs and wolves, who might attack and pull them down. Andrássy bought for the Empress a lady's revolver engraved in gold with his name. The gun fitted into a small holster on a smaller belt, which was buckled round her slender waist. However far she rode alone, she could defend herself.

The forests and heaths of Gödöllö spread over thirty thousand acres, where the horses could gallop to exhaustion. There were marshes for shooting snipe, if the Emperor ever came to stay. There was also fox-hunting almost in the English style with the Kinskys and the Liechtensteins and even the Esterházys whose family was now forgiven by Elisabeth. She hated the press and the first of the photographers, who came to the meets. She hid from their intrusive eyes and lenses behind a small leather fan, which hung from her saddle-bow.

Most of those who knew her as well as her observer de Burgh did thought that she spent her happiest days at Gödöllö. 'Here all pomp and show was dispensed with; here she kept her hunting stud and kennels; here she was entirely her own mistress, unrestrained by Court ceremony, surrounded by her favourite ladies-in-waiting, equerries and servants; and here she indulged in the life she loved. The Magyars simply adored and worshipped her. It is certain that she fully returned their affection with a heartiness the sincerity of which was never doubted in the Kingdom of the Five Rivers. She shared their field sports, to which she imparted a prestige and an impulse of unprecedented force; her knowledge of their national history and literature was complete; and she won the love of all, high and low, and the admiration and appreciation of such renowned scientists as Ferencz Pulsky and Vambéry,' also the Abbé Liszt and Count Majláth, Tiska and the wise Deák. She flourished in their admiration.

In the opinion of the perceptive Count Corti, Elisabeth was a compound of a spirit of revolt with a mutable melancholy, which would suddenly burst into an impish joy. 'At times her mood would be deeply serious, critical, ironical, and even cynical, and then again she would be thoroughly childlike. Her love for her little daughter absorbed her utterly, and with her she became a child again.' The two of them were surrounded by gypsies and zithers and even a tame bear, so that Elisabeth's mother had to remind her, 'My dear Sisi, you are becoming exactly like your father with your passion for trick performers.' And as for Valérie, she was said to be reared like the daughter of a Hungarian king.

Strangely, the Emperor now went on his travels to the East, and not his wife, who was bound to remain with her children. The occasion was the opening of the Suez Canal, the waterway to India; and although it was strategically important to Louis Napoleon, he sent his wife Eugénie in his place, feeling that the situation in Europe was too menacing for him to leave for the Near East. Franz Josef visited the Sultan and his stables at Constantinople with his eight hundred splendid Arab horses, then the Holy Places in Palestine, and then Jaffa and Suez. Andrássy accompanied him, leaving Elisabeth in Hungary, although she declared she was jealous of her men falling under the spell of Eugénie in Egypt. She herself had to go to Rome for the birth of a daughter to her sister, the dispossessed Queen Marie of Naples, before her return to her realm.

'We could now fight France and beat her too,' Bismarck declared early in 1870. 'But that war would give rise to five or six others.' He was waiting for his opportunity to make France seem an aggressor. Time and custom delivered that chance into his hands. The throne of Spain was vacant; as usual, a German prince was the traditional choice to fill it. The Spanish parliament and its leader, General Prim, asked for a Hohenzollern prince to accept their crown. To France, this overture appeared to be a Prussian plot. In the event of war, Louis Napoleon would have to divide his armies to guard against a stab in the back from across the Pyrenees. But how could he protest against the offer? How could a civilised modern country still go to war for dynastic reasons?

To Bismarck, a new war of succession in the nineteenth century was ridiculous. Yet he had certainly protested enough when one of Queen Victoria's children and relatives made a marriage or took a throne that seemed to threaten Prussia's interests. He knew that there would be a furore in France with a Hohenzollern prince on the Spanish throne. A plebiscite had confirmed Louis Napoleon's tenure by a huge majority. As his new Foreign Minister, he had chosen the Duke de Gramont, who mistakenly believed that he could count on Habsburg support in a war against Prussia. When, at the end of June, the French discovered that General Prim had asked the Spanish parliament to 'elect' Prince Leopold as King, all hell broke loose in Paris. And when the chosen Hohenzollern accepted the offer and the King of Prussia gave whatever consent he could, de Gramont's fury was even greater than the national anger. He made an inflammatory speech in the French parliament, threatening war if the Hohenzollern candidate did not refuse the Spanish throne.

Austria-Hungary could have prevented the war or ensured a Prussian loss. Yet because it was now a Dual Monarchy, the second part induced a compromise on the first. Andrássy and his nation had all to lose in another war between the German powers; for only the Prussian victory had given them some freedom, while a Prussian defeat might mean the revival of Viennese autocracy. At a ministerial council, Andrássy pointed out that Russia posed a greater threat to the Dual Monarchy and would press forward in the Balkans and the lower Danube, if they were not defended. 'Austria's mission remained, as before, to be the bulwark against Russia.' Already the loser in two European wars, Franz Josef inclined towards caution and suspected a fresh trap. As he had observed to his mother about his last disaster against Bismarck's diplomacy, 'Everything was fixed between Paris, Berlin and Florence. As for us we were very honest, but very stupid.' He did not intend to be a third time unlucky.

Contingency plans, however, had already been made by the Archduke Albrecht with the French, who believed that the Habsburgs were on their side against a Hohenzollern on the Spanish throne. The Archduke had concocted a war plan with the French General Staff in the event of a conflict with Prussia, based on a triple alliance with Italy. If the French could advance on Nuremberg and hold the German forces for the six weeks needed for mobilisation, the Austrians could permit an Italian march on Bavaria, while they put two armies into Bohemia and Saxony. Count Richard Metternich, the Austrian ambassador in Paris, was assured that Austria-Hungary considered 'the cause of France our own' and would contribute in every way possible to the success of French arms. 'Our neutrality is only a means towards the true end of our policy: the sole means of completing our armaments without exposing ourselves to a premature attack from Prussia or Russia.'

When Paris was provoked into sending its ultimatum to Berlin, the speed of Prussian mobilisation and the enthusiasm of the southern German states to join in the fight against their old French enemies across the Rhine took Louis Napoleon by surprise as it had Franz Josef three years before. A preliminary success by the French at Saarbrücken caused pleasure to the Empress Elisabeth, who thought they had made a good beginning against the Prussians. 'If this sort of thing goes on, they will soon be back in Berlin again.' Yet then reverse followed reverse at Weissenburg and Wörth, and defeat came after defeat at Spichern and Mars la Tour. There was a certain bitter satisfaction for Elisabeth in the bravery of her own Bavarian soldiers. She told her son Rudolf that she was delighted that they had so distinguished themselves in the field, but as one of their blood, she could only regret that they had not done so when opposing Prussia three years before. 'Now they are fighting and shedding their blood like true Germans for the utter ruin of their independence and autonomy.'

To her as to her husband, a Prussian victory would be even worse than a French one. With that triumph, Bismarck and the Kaiser could engulf the remaining German states and so exclude Austro-Hungary for ever from the ancient Holy Roman Empire.

Intervention was still possible. Or else, as Elisabeth wrote to Franz Josef, 'We may possibly vegetate for a year or two more before our turn arrives.' Yet even if the Emperor had sought to interfere, the rapid capitulation of Louis Napoleon after the defeat at Sedan, where he surrendered his sword to the King of Prussia, made anything but neutrality quite impossible. Three days later, a Republic was proclaimed in Paris, and the Empress Eugénie became a refugee. The only surprise for Franz Josef was that this revolution had not happened long ago. While the French capital was put under siege, a German Empire was proclaimed in the Hall of Mirrors at Versailles, excluding only the Habsburg lands. For that dynasty, this was the deluge.

For once, Elisabeth's cousin, King Ludwig of Bavaria, had acted more positively than her own husband. Struck by indecision at first as the Austrian Emperor had been and lying on a *chaise-longue* demanding if there was any way of avoiding war, Ludwig had come to the right and distasteful decision. He had ordered the mobilisation of the Bavarian army on the side of Prussia against France. This had been his 'good deed' before he wrote to the Crown Prince of Prussia that he hoped after the war the independence of his country would be respected. The Crown Prince was not impressed, finding a great change in Ludwig, who had lost his front teeth and his good looks. He was pale and nervous and restless. He never waited for his questions to be answered, but he asked further questions about other things before he listened to any reply. He did not visit his army, which was led to success by the Prussian Crown Prince at Weissenburg and Wörth. He remained in his fairy castles of Hohenschwangau or Linderhof, escaping all involvement. He was in Munich when the French capitulation at Sedan was announced; but he would not appear at the celebrations, pleading a headache.

Ludwig had correctly foreseen that the declaration of a German Empire was the prelude to the loss of Bavarian independence. When his presence was demanded at Versailles, he claimed that he had to stay at home because of toothache as well as migraine, for which he was sedated with chloroform. Under pressure from Bismarck, he agreed in a *Kaiserbrief* that the King of Prussia should become the

Emperor of Germany, if he respected a limited measure of Bavarian independence, rather as the Austrian Emperor had been forced to do in Hungary. When Paris also capitulated and punitive terms were inflicted on France including a huge indemnity and the loss of Alsace and most of Lorraine, a victory parade was held in Munich with the Crown Prince of Prussia again in charge, handing out Iron Crosses to Ludwig's soldiers. This display of military power reduced the King of Bavaria to absolute despair. 'I have come to hate ruling, to hate people,' he wrote to his brother Otto, who was as disturbed as himself. 'And yet to be a king, to govern, is the finest and noblest thing on earth.' He regretted that he was born at a time when every pleasure in life was taken from him.

The defeat of Louis Napoleon also led to the final unification of Italy. For the French troops which were guarding the Papal lands and Rome were driven out by Garibaldi and his redshirts, and with them, the disinherited King and Queen Marie of Naples. She now had to imitate her sister Elisabeth and begin a wandering life of exile, beginning with a visit to the Austrian Empress at Merano in the south Tyrol before she returned to Budapest. There Elisabeth was to acquire her closest lady-in-waiting, the Countess Marie Festetics, who admired the Empress to distraction in spite of disliking those around her. She was persuaded to serve by her fellow Hungarian Andrássy, who told her that Elisabeth was good, clever and pure. 'They abuse her because she loves our country, and for that they will never forgive her. For the same reason, they will persecute you, but that is not important. In this way, you will be able to serve both the Queen and your homeland.' And her imperial mistress told her again not to listen to the abuse against them. 'If you want to say anything to me, say it honestly and frankly. If you want to know anything, ask *me* and nobody else.'

Elisabeth had reverted to a policy of keeping her husband away from her. Her pretext was that if Franz Josef came to visit, he might bring with him infectious diseases such as scarlet fever and chickenpox, which would afflict her adored Valérie. When asked what she would like on her birthday, she replied in the manner of the Wittelsbachs, a strange mixture of oddity and prophecy. She wanted a royal Bengal tiger or a locket or a fully equipped lunatic asylum. This triple request was a revelation of her nature and her fears. She loved wild things, she was nostalgic for the past, she was afraid of the mad streak in her family. Her concern for the insane, however, was to remain as important as her concentration on gymnasiums, as if she thought the mind and the body both needed a regular correction.

The triumph of Prussia in its war against France led to another change of heart and policy by Franz Josef. The power of a Germany united under the policy of Bismarck threatened the very survival of Austro-Hungary. The recent enemy must become the future guardian. There were two meetings between the German and Austrian Emperors at Ischl and Salzburg, before the extraordinary announcement by Franz Josef that Andrássy would become his new Foreign Minister, although a rival in his wife's affections and the political leader of Hungary. This was an accommodation with a vengeance.

With his gypsy face and mercurial temperament, Andrássy had not been the favourite of the Emperor; but his political astuteness made him a necessary choice. What the Hungarian Count could teach the autocratic Franz Josef was the art of constitutional rule. Brought up as an autocrat, Franz Josef had to learn the niceties of governing through a parliament. With his extraordinary finesse, Andrássy gave the Austrian Emperor and King of Hungary a sanction in advance of all the legislation which he proposed. If Franz Josef disapproved, his ministers in Budapest tended not to proceed, although they had the right to do so. This pre-emption avoided another crisis in the Dual Monarchy, as well as warning the Emperor that in the modern state, there were limits to his decisions. This was the lesson which Bismarck had taught the Kaiser in Germany.

In spite of his preferment of Andrássy, Franz Josef could not win his way back into the graces of Elisabeth. She was withdrawing more and more from the social world. One day she asked Marie Festetics whether her lady-in-waiting was not surprised that an empress should live like a hermit, when she was still so young. She had no choice, she declared, for she had been so misjudged and slandered, hurt and wounded in the great world. 'God looks into my soul. I have never done what was evil.' She was compelled to turn to nature, for the forest could not hurt her. Hard as it was to be alone, she had become used to some solitude and now enjoyed it. 'Nature is far more grateful than men.'

These were the beginnings of a persecution mania, which would bedevil the rest of her life. She continued to brood on the unkindness of a Court society which condemned her. The cancer of her existence, the Archduchess Sophie, was in decline, yet this was not enough. As with many of the Wittelsbachs, her delusions often overcame her capacities to do something about them. When she was not striding and riding, she tended to fall into melancholy and intellectual indolence, as Marie Festetics noted, combined with 'a craving for freedom which makes any restraint terrible to her'.

Her daughter Gisela seemed set to follow her mother in her romantic morbidity. Just sixteen years old, she became engaged to another Wittelsbach cousin, Prince Leopold of Bavaria. Elisabeth thought that this proposed marriage would be too soon and too close in blood, but there were few Catholic princes available, and the Habsburgs and the Wittelsbachs had a long history of intermarriage. In these frequent mergings, the Countess Marie Larisch Wallersee would notice, 'with the Habsburgs insanity usually shows itself in depravity, self-effacement, and common marriages, while, in the case of the Wittelsbachs, it transforms the sufferer into a romantic being who is quite above the banalities of everyday life, but who occasionally deteriorates . . .'

Elisabeth was summoned to the dying of her mother-in-law. Her chief concern was that she would not be there. For if she missed the passing of the intransigent mother of her husband, she would never be forgiven by Viennese society. She spent many nights at the bedside of the Archduchess Sophie with other members of the dynasty; but when the death throes began, she had retired from Schönbrunn to the Hofburg. The old lady survived in her agony long enough for the return of her daughter-in-law and Marie Festetics, who thought that the great should be allowed to die in peace. Beggars were allowed to do so, but not the imperial family, who made a Court ceremonial of a going away. The Empress agreed, saying that she felt that all this form put an end to feeling. Yet she stayed at the bedside without food for ten hours until the Archduchess breathed her last in a terminal forgiveness.

After the funeral of her mother-in-law, the Empress left for Ischl and the summer. She wore black on her long walks, but Marie Festetics did manage to keep up with her and found it a joy. Elisabeth was fine and noble in everything, a lily and a swan as well as a queen. Yet she found no pleasure in living, although she kept her calm. 'Her voice is generally tranquil and soft, only rarely excited. Now and then, when she speaks of the lack of mercy in the way others treat her, there is a small quiver in her throat. How can anyone hurt a person looking like her?'

Although she was devoted to the shy and dependent Valérie, Elisabeth had little to do with the education of her precocious and nervous son Rudolf. Due to her influence, he was taught as the future King of Hungary to speak Magyar along with German and French and Czech, Polish and some Latin. Elisabeth insisted on his taking physical exercise, riding and swimming and walking. He was also trained in fencing and shooting, which he loved with a sort of blood lust, clearing with his shotgun the branches of the trees around Laxenburg of all the birds. 'He was a gifted boy, quick of perception, vivid of fancy, of insatiable curiosity,' the biographer Eugene Bagger wrote of him. 'But he disliked continuous effort; he could not concentrate; restraint of any description was to him like poison – it literally made him ill; and he was subject to violent moods, swinging from exuberance to utter dejection. An authentic little Wittelsbach – Elisabeth's son.'

She returned to Gödöllö, where she would spend many months annually. She took up hunting with a pack of hounds, usually leading the field on one of her twenty-six hunters. From one meet on the racecourse, she had a particularly fine run, as she wrote to Franz Josef. One horse was killed at a ditch, four of the Hungarian nobles were thrown. 'But the fox ran to earth; they dug all round the spot for a fearfully long time, but in the end they left the poor creature in peace.' Another story had her stag-hunting until the exhausted beast plunged in the river; she had the hounds whipped off to 'give the brave stag his life'. Sometimes she rode for seven hours on the trot, either outdoors or in the rebuilt riding school at her new home. She had an instinctive rapport with her mounts. As the instructor of the *haute école* in Vienna later wrote, 'She has the knack of pulling herself into immediate and almost mesmeric communication with her horse. She far outshines any rider of her own sex.'

The Hungarian baroque castle of Gödöllö had been constructed in the middle of the eighteenth century by Count Grassalkovich, an intimate of the Empress Maria Theresa. During the Hungarian revolution, Prince Windischgratz, the Commander-in-Chief of the Austrian army, had made his headquarters there, as did Kossuth, when his freedom fighters won a brief victory. Presented to Elisabeth and Franz Josef, Gödöllö became in Hungary what Schönbrunn was in Austria, the royal palace near the capital of the country. Elisabeth developed the riding school and bought four special horses, which had been schooled in *haute école*. The daughter of the equestrian showman at her marriage celebrations, Elisa Renz, was installed to teach the Empress to be a trainer and put the steeds through their paces. They were made to wheel and circle, rear and fall on their knees. They followed the commands of their mistress, who felt herself back in the circus again with her beloved father. Wherever she went in Hungary, particularly in the hunt, she was irresistible in the saddle with her erect beauty and slender grace. 'How enthusiastic the young people are when they see her,' Andrassy confided. 'Sometimes they express this feeling too closely, like dolphins round a ship.'

Yet when she returned to Vienna, she fell back into her aversions and mild paranoia. She wore a thick blue veil on her walks, or hid her face behind a parasol or a fan. She imagined that everybody was gossiping about her behind her back. There was some sense of guilt in this suspicion of hers, for she knew that she was not fulfilling her role as the Emperor's consort as well as she should. She would and could not become the slave of the Court fashion and etiquette. 'She will do less and less,' Marie Festetics prophesied. 'People will attack her more and more, and for all her riches she will become poorer and poorer, and no one will recall she was forced into this loneliness.'

Two important occasions, however, reconciled her to her imperial life in Vienna. The first was the marriage of her daughter Gisela to Prince Leopold of Bavaria, the second was a World Exhibition to rival the previous ones in London and Paris. At her daughter's wedding, Elisabeth looked like a sister. On the waves of her piled hair, a crown of diamonds shone, while silver embroidery fell in cascades over her dress. As a mother should, she wept when her child accepted another man as her own. Shakespeare's *A Midsummer Night's Dream* was chosen as the play for the gala performance at the celebrations. Knowing the Wittelsbachs of Bavaria, Elisabeth wondered whether there was an allusion in the drama, for the Queen of the Fairies fell in love with a man with the head of an ass.

The World Exhibition in Vienna was a prolonged and resplendent occasion. Its significance was great, for it was meant to show off Austro-Hungary as another European power in the industrial age. Franz Josef was transforming Vienna and promoting capitalism in the restricted Habsburg Empire. Already, he had begun the construction of the Ringstrasse and the Opera in a huge horseshoe extending from the Danube Canal to curve upon the Hofburg. Imposing palaces and museums and residences flanked the magnificent approach, while a model aqueduct brought Alpine water to the citizens. Now an immense Rotonde, which looked like an iced cake topped with cream, was built on the Prater, while hotels and restaurants and cafés sprang up to welcome the seven million visitors, who were transported there in the new railway cars. The crowned heads of Europe joined the tourist throng. In the spring of 1873, Vienna appeared to be the centre of the civilised world of the future.

The continuing ill fortune of the Habsburgs would scupper the grand occasion. Yet most of the crowned heads of Europe came to visit. Elisabeth did consent to see the Tsar and Tsarina of Russia, but she refused to meet King Victor Emmanuel of Italy, because he had helped to chase her sister Marie from the throne of Naples as well as her husband from Lombardy and Venetia. He had to do the honours, although the officers around Victor Emmanuel sported so many coloured feathers that they looked like a pack of parrots. She did meet the heirs to the thrones of Britain and Prussia, Denmark and Belgium, who were all in attendance with a panoply of foreign princes, described by the young Sigmund Freud as 'made up exclusively of mustachios and medals'. She also did her duty when the other sovereigns arrived, the Kings of Belgium and of Greece, the Shah of Persia and even the German Emperor in person, forcing Franz Josef to don for a parade the uniform of a Prussian Grenadier, which made him feel like Shakespeare's Richard the Third, an enemy to himself. The Shah, however, told Andrássy that the Empress was a goddess and the most beautiful woman he had seen. 'Such dignity, such a smile, such tenderness!'

Again Elisabeth struck a special chord of sympathy in the Crown Princess Victoria of Prussia, who worked like she did on hospitals and asylums. She presented the daughter of the British Queen with her portrait, a particular mark of affection. The two royal women were drawn together by their views on education, particularly of their difficult sons. For Victoria's child Wilhelm had been born with a withered arm, and only his mother's insistence on exercise and mastering his infirmity by vigorous discipline had schooled him into suppressing his tendency to self-pity. She had also set up a *Victoria Schule* and *Lyceum*, where young women went in for gymnastics and sports – the passions of the life of Elisabeth. She wrote back to Queen Victoria that the beauty of the Empress seemed more marvellous on each sight of her. The impact came from Elisabeth's 'picturesque and striking ensemble . . . The complexion and colouring, the figure and the extraordinary hair.'

The Exhibition was now plagued by a strike of cab drivers, then an epidemic of cholera which killed twenty-five hundred people, and then the collapse of the Viennese stock exchange on a Black Friday. A hundred traders in the Bourse were insolvent, dozens of major companies were bankrupt, and corruption in dealing in stocks and shares extended up to ministers in the government. The causes of the collapse were speculation and the building boom, but the financial panic spread overseas as far as the United States, proving that an international market had already been created. The World Exhibition itself lost fifteen million gulden, another money pit.

Perhaps Elisabeth was right in her scepticism about the great show, when she became jammed in her carriage in the crowds along the Ringstrasse and told Marie Festetics that she could not go on, she was quite seasick already. Indeed, there was stormy weather ahead.

CHAPTER SIX

Hunting

❖

'I NEVER,' Queen Victoria wrote to her eldest daughter in Berlin, 'never shall be able to bear that dreadful weary, chilling, unnatural life of a widow.' Her remedy came to be a strange relationship with her Highland servant John Brown, which would cause almost as much international scandal as the vagaries of the Wittelsbach family. The Scotsman's gruff courtesy and total devotion made the British sovereign relish his company, as Elisabeth did that of the gypsies at Possenhofen and Gödöllö. Brown cleaned the Queen's things and did odd jobs, put her on her pony and took her off, fussed over her welfare and shielded her privacy – and even interposed his body between her and attempted assassins.

The Queen's Highland servant was five years younger than she was, a handsome brawny man with a curly beard and bright blue eyes. He had a trenchant manner which could offend; he was liable to call the Queen 'Wumman' and tell her how to behave outdoors. The Prince of Wales thought him a boor and an intruder. Yet Brown could be so tender, particularly about the Queen's grief for her dead husband, that she was touched to the heart. In her most illuminating story about her new relationship, she told the Crown Princess of Prussia about Brown's first visit to the Mausoleum at Frogmore near Windsor.

When he came to her room later, he was much affected. He looked at the Queen with pity, while tears rolled down his cheeks. In his simple expressive way, he said, 'I didn't like to see ye at Frogmore this morning. I felt for ye – to see ye coming there with your daughters and your husband lying there – marriage on one side and death on the other. No, I didn't like to see it. I felt sorry for ye. I know so well what your feeling must be – ye who had been so happy. There is no more pleasure for you, poor Queen, and I feel for ye but what can I do for ye? I could die for ye.'

The Queen was deeply moved by this emotional speech from her blunt hardy man, her child of the mountains. She grew to depend on his care and judgement. His constant presence by her and her continuing refusal to make public appearances led to rumours and jokes that she was 'Mrs John Brown'. She would try to dismiss these insinuations as ill-natured gossip among the aristocracy, because she would not be forced out of her seclusion. But she could not stop the deterioration abroad of her image of strict morality, particularly where viperous tongues were stinging the ears of the Austrian and the German Emperors.

Queen Victoria's character and dignity made it unbelievable that she could be John Brown's mistress or his secret wife. She wanted security and devotion, no more than that. But her fierce defence of Brown's position so close to her person, her refusal to listen to the wise advice to shed him for the sake of her reputation, damned her in the eyes of gossips and intriguers against any English alliance. What Queen of England could complain of immoral behaviour by foreign royalty when she was so close to a body-servant? Those who lived in glass palaces could not throw stones.

Actually, at the celebrations for his Silver Jubilee as Emperor of Austria, Franz Josef would see for the first time the love and solace and scandal of the last thirty years of his reign, a young blonde comic actress, Katharina Schratt. She was playing the lead in Shakespeare's *The Taming of the Shrew*, and some impression must have been made on the Emperor, for he thanked the director Laube of the Stadttheater with the words: 'It was very beautiful and gave me much pleasure.' And yet Elisabeth was with him in Vienna, suffering from recurrent gastric flu and shock, when she was nearly crushed to death by an enthusiastic crowd in the Ringstrasse. She would soon become a grandmother at the age of only thirty-six years, for Gisela was about to give birth to another Elisabeth, to be named after her. The Empress was not too pleased at seeing the baby, finding it ugly and lively, rather like its mother. She seemed to prefer to visit the cholera hospital in Munich in her chosen and dangerous role of mercy, even touching the skins of those with the sweat of death upon them. If she did destroy her gloves later, she never considered the risk to her children as well as herself.

Her sister Marie, the exiled Queen of Naples, was also in Munich and fanned the flames of the wanderlust of Elisabeth by saying that a queen on the retired list could do exactly what she wanted. She had leased a hunting box near Althorp Park, the family home in Northamptonshire of John, the fifth Earl Spencer. He had been a young Lord Lieutenant of Ireland, where he was known as the 'Red Earl', because of his bad temper and lust for blood sports and pride in his lineage, which led him to despise Irish society. Fox-hunting was his consuming passion, and the Queen of Naples assured her sister Elisabeth that the chase in the Midlands of England was even more dashing than on the Hungarian plains.

King Ludwig visited Elisabeth frequently, although she no longer relished his company, for he was puffy and morbid. After he had finally left her, saying, 'One forgets all about time here,' she confided to Marie Festetics that she was fonder of her bed than her cousin. She was, however, very sorry for him and admitted to a certain resemblance between them, including a tendency to melancholy and a love of solitude. 'God forbid,' the Countess answered boldly. 'Your Majesty simply wants to excuse everything on the ground that it is a family idiosyncrasy for which nobody is responsible.' This reply made Elisabeth laugh, but she was hardly at her best when the Queen Mother of Bavaria took her to an actual lunatic asylum. The displays there of mental illness had a terrible effect on her, as she told Marie Festetics. She was astonished at the behaviour of the Queen Mother, who seemed almost to be amused. 'But of course, the poor thing is used to it,' having watched the antics of the Wittelsbachs for far too long.

Soon after Elisabeth's return to Vienna, Franz Josef left for the first time for St Petersburg to visit the Tsar. The great game of imperial encounters was in full swing. To Bismarck, the intention seemed to be the encirclement of Prussia by royal alliances. For now Queen Victoria's son, Prince Alfred, was engaged to the Tsar's only daughter, the Grand Duchess Marie; her children seemed to be trying to surround Germany with their blood. Even the Crown Prince accused the Prince of Wales of working to populate northern Europe with anti-German marriages. Ever since the defeat of the French and the founding of the German Empire, Bismarck had been aiming to preserve the peace of Europe, and to consolidate the new nation. His greatest fear was a conflict on two or three fronts. France might combine with Austria or Russia in a war of revenge, leading a combination of Catholic and Orthodox powers against the Protestant north, unable to secure an alliance with the natural ally England. Indeed, Franz Josef did succeed in striking up a good relationship with Edward, the Prince of Wales, while they were both bear-hunting in Russia. As the Prince was a strong supporter of an entente between England and France, this was no good omen for Germany.

As her daughter Valérie later reported, Elisabeth went with Ida Ferenczy during her husband's absence to the masked ball at the Musikverein in a wig and a yellow silk domino with a long lace veil over her face and shoulders. There she noticed an elegant and solitary young civil servant, Fritz Pacher, who was brought up to her, as she sat in the gallery above the dancing. Elisabeth in her disguise asked the handsome official what he thought of the Empress. And what did other people say about her? He suspected her identity, and so he replied that he had only seen her on horseback in the Prater. Yet she was gloriously beautiful. In fact, people complained that they did not see enough of her. Only her horses and dogs did. Elisabeth was amused by this answer, but tried to dismiss him. He would not go so easily and ended by escorting her round the festivities for a couple of hours. She trembled on his arm when anyone bumped into her in the crowd, yet she seemed to want to be among the public, to know what was said about her. She talked more and more openly to the young Pacher; but she reacted strongly when he tried to lift her veil. Ida Ferenczy in her red domino pulled down his inquisitive hand and took her mistress away in a carriage.

Elisabeth had taken Pacher's address, and she wrote from Munich to her 'dear friend' a week later, telling him that though he might think he had found the princess of his dreams, he had lost her for ever. Unlike Cinderella, she was never to be discovered again by her Civil Servant Charming. Her letters, signed by 'Gabriele', and his replies were sent and received through the main post office in Vienna, where they were collected by unseen messengers. She believed herself to be incognito, a delusion she often had on her travels under assumed names. The episode was a romantic folly rather like her first girlish illusions of love at her childhood home at Possenhofen.

The justification for her new escape overseas was that the sea air might help the bronchitis of her youngest child Valérie as well as allowing her to try chasing the fox in the shires. Travelling under the pseudonym of the Countess von Hohenembs, she reached the mock-Gothic battlements of Steephill Castle on the wolds above the terraces of Ventnor on the Isle of Wight. She drove over to Osborne to visit Queen Victoria, who was there with the notorious John Brown. 'The Queen was very kind,' Elisabeth wrote back to Franz Josef, 'and said nothing that was not amiable, but she is not sympathetic to me.'

In point of fact, Victoria was impressed by Elisabeth. 'She is very tall and slight,' the Queen wrote in her journal, 'with a most beautiful figure, only almost too thin.' Although disappointed a little in the beauty of the Empress's face, Victoria recorded her 'lovely dark brown eyes, eyebrows and eyelids, a pretty mouth and expression. Her manner is very quiet and gentle and she speaks rather low, and not very much.' The British Queen, however, thought Elisabeth less shy and silent than expected in her simple dress of silver and grey. The Empress wanted to leave after five minutes, but the Prince of Wales and his wife took her out on to the terrace. On two following visits, the Empress was more forthcoming and talkative, 'looking very lovely, like a beautiful picture, with her magnificent hair, in which there is a rich tinge of auburn, braided all round her head and framing as it were a diadem. Her waist is smaller than anything one can imagine, and her walk most graceful.'

Much to the surprise of the British royal family, Elisabeth declined their subsequent invitations, because, as she told her mother, 'that sort of thing bores me'. She had come to England to be quiet and cure her little daughter. When she went bathing in the sea, a sport Queen Victoria had made popular, crowds watched her from the cliffs with field glasses. Marie Festetics and another decoy had to put on flannel bathing-gowns and come into the water to deceive the viewers. In spite of her own reclusiveness, Elisabeth did ask her husband to help in improving relations with England. He should come over for a fortnight, see London, dash up to Balmoral where Queen Victoria had now gone with John Brown, and then return for some hunting in the Midlands with her new aristocratic friends. Franz Josef could not come, and England would never help to close the gap with Catholic Austro-Hungary by royal gatherings.

With her Hungarian entourage, Elisabeth went to Belvoir Castle as the guest of the Duke of Rutland. At her first cub-hunt, her sister Marie, Queen of Naples, introduced her to Earl Spencer, who had ridden across from Althorp Park. He fell under the spell of Elisabeth in her green velvet and black habits, and he invited her to return to hunt with him during the full season. Another fateful introduction was to the dashing Levantine and Hungarian Baltazzi brothers, whose sister Baroness Hélène von Vetsera was climbing her way higher and higher in society in Vienna. Presented with both an English hunter by Lady Dudley and a new groom Allen to take back to the Prater and the steeplechase course on the Freudenau, Elisabeth resolved to return to the Midlands as soon as politics permitted.

After a winter of Court festivities in Vienna, which Elisabeth called going 'into harness', she persuaded her husband to allow her to try sea-bathing again in the June of 1875, this time at the château of Sassetôt-les-Mauconduits in Normandy. Franz Josef feared for her safety, because there were so many anarchists in France. 'Something will happen to you there,' he declared; 'and besides, they

will not be exactly delighted in Berlin.' Royal holidays still appeared
to have a diplomatic significance. That year, there was a war scare with
the General Staff in Berlin keen on another strike against France to
prevent an alliance of all the European powers against Germany. The
Austrian Emperor had to warn his German cousin not to fight the
Third Republic, which had superseded the rule of Louis Napoleon.
The Tsar had to travel to Prussia to repeat the same message; he was
bolstered by a letter from Queen Victoria, urging him to use his
influence on the Emperor Wilhelm. As all the monarchs of Europe
said they wanted peace, why should Germany have to fight?

Actually, the next scene of conflict would not be in the Rhineland,
but in the Balkans, where Bosnia and Herzegovina were rebelling
against Turkish rule. Franz Josef paid a visit with the imperial navy
to the ports of Dalmatia on the coast to scout the situation. The
Eastern Question would dominate European politics for the rest of
the decade, allowing Russia and Austro-Hungary to prise territories
from the ailing Ottoman Empire on the pretext of a last Christian
crusade against Islam. With their interests in the Suez Canal and Asia
and Africa, France and Britain were equally interested in controlling
Egypt, although not at the price of Russia taking Constantinople and
breaking into the Mediterranean from the Black Sea. Turkey was to
be the loser in the new age of European imperialism.

The death of the aged and abdicated Emperor Ferdinand in
Prague made Franz Josef wealthy at last. He himself went on living
like a soldier, sleeping on an iron bedstead with a cover of camelskin,
and starting each day with a splash of water from a cold water basin,
for he disapproved of proper bathrooms. He tripled, however, the
allowance of the Empress to three hundred thousand florins a year
and gave her another two million florins as capital for indulging her
tastes in art and architecture and fine horses. Her entourage was
always a great expense, comprising up to ninety people from her
household, such as Baron Nopsca and Ida Ferenczy and Marie
Festetics, her doctor Widerhofer and hairdresser Frau von Feyfalik,
and her grooms Bayzand and Allen. To have so many travelling
companions was paradoxical in somebody who sought solitude
wherever she went.

The young Elisabeth　　　　　Franz Josef showing Vienna to his bride

Elisabeth's country home in Bavaria, Possenhofen

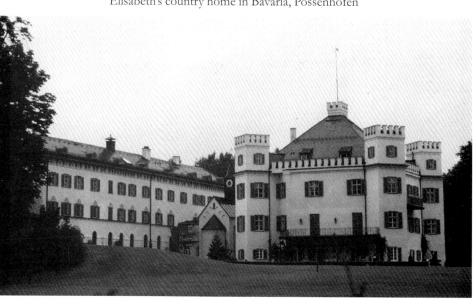

The wedding of Elisabeth to Franz Josef in 1854

Her wedding dress with her ladies-in-waiting

A memorial
of the wedding

Elisabeth in her boudoir

The Emperor and the Empress with their family at Gödöllö

The Empress *en tenue* at Gödöllö

The Empress Elisabeth at dressage

The Empress Elisabeth relaxing with her wolfhounds at Gödöllö

The Hungarian coronation, June 1867

Elisabeth leads the hunt at Gödöllö

(Left) Elisabeth with her ladies in Hungary, 1865

(Below) A lithograph of the Empress Elisabeth, 1867

(Left) A medallion of the Emperor Franz Josef and the Empress Elisabeth, 1879

The Austrian Emperor and Empress are crowned as King and Queen of Hungary, 1867

Elisabeth, Queen of Hungary

(Above left) The Emperor Franz Josef with his family at the engagement of his elder daughter. (Above right) Crown Prince Rudolf with his
wife Stephanie and his daughter. (Below) The Empress Elisabeth riding
in the Prater with Crown Prince Rudolf in 1876. (Right) A signed
photograph of Crown Prince Rudolf given to his mother, 1878

(*Above left*) The Archduchess Gisela, daughter of the Empress. (*Above right*) The Archduchess Valerie, with her husband and family. (*Left*) The Emperor on horseback. (*Below*) The Palace of Lainz

The Schönbrunn,
Vienna

The gardens of
the Schönbrunn

The new Burgtheater,
Vienna

(*Above*) A statue of Lord Byron in the garden of the Achilleion in Corfu. (*Left*) The statue of Achilles there. (*Below*) A statue of the dying Achilles with the palace of the Empress Elisabeth in the background

Crown Prince Rudolf

The Duchess of
Alençon, the sister
of the Empress

Marie Vetsera

One of the few unauthorised photographs of the Austrian Emperor and
Empress, taken shortly before her
assassination. She used her fan and
parasol to ward off viewers

Lucheni murders the Empress Elisabe (from a contemporary French illustrat magazine)

Lucheni is arrested in Geneva

(Below left) The lying-in-state at the Hotel Beau Rivage. (Below right) The last rites performed over the coffin in the church of the Capuchins

Mater Dolorosa. A vision of the Empress Elisabeth at the lying-in-state of the Hungarian statesman, Franz Deak, 1876

A photomontage of Elisabeth mourning the death of King Ludwig II of Bavaria in the lake

A music sheet and a film poster

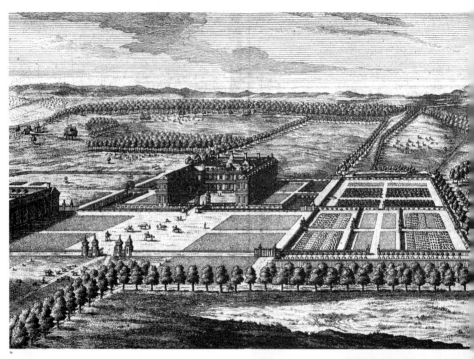

(*Above*) Formal gardens laid out beside the
Spencer family seat at Althorp, engraving by
Pierre Van der Aa, from *Les delices de la Grande
Bretagne, et l'Irelande*, 1707. Two royal women,
both martyred by their celebrity, rode and
lived here, the Empress Elisabeth of Austria,
also Diana, the Princess of Wales. (*Below and
right*) The tributes to Diana outside the palaces
in London were a brief garden of paradise.
She was buried by her brother, Earl Spencer,
on a flowering isle in the lake at Althorp.

DIANA OF LOVE

Elisabeth did not like Normandy, where she found the people 'more pushing than in any other country'. She also had a bad fall, which broke the pommel of her saddle and left her unconscious with slight concussion. Franz Josef was ready to rush from Vienna to her bedside, but she soon recovered, provoking a touching letter from King Ludwig of Bavaria to her son, the Crown Prince Rudolf. 'She should curb her impetuosity in riding. Never in my life should I recover from my grief if any accident were to happen to her. God forbid such a thing! And may He preserve you and me from such an appalling experience!' The two royal cousins, however, would not be preserved from even more violent endings.

With her sister hunting with the Grafton in the winter, Elisabeth arranged to rent Easton Neston, the seat of the Earls of Pomfret. The stately home had been designed by Hawksmoor and lay near Towcester in Northamptonshire. Accompanied by her extensive household and a retinue of aristocrats, including the Chief Lord High Steward, Prince Rudolf Liechtenstein, the Baron Orczy and the Counts Larisch and Prince Ferdinand Kinsky, the Empress found a new squire to lead her over the fences. William George Middleton was born into a Scottish sporting family: his uncle had been Master of the Fife Foxhounds. He became a Captain in the 12th Lancers, then quartered in Tipperary. Stocky with short sandy hair and a military moustache, Middleton had a sure seat in the saddle and leapt easily over hedge and ditch. He was made Master of the regimental Harriers and Draghounds, and then began racing in Cork. He took his nickname 'Bay' from a Derby winner. Although he was slightly deaf and abrupt, his blue stare and air of command made him attractive. Oddly enough, he collected Dresden china and could show a strange delicacy with horses and women. But above all, his instinct on the hunting field led him to the right jumps. He seemed a part of his steed, a Centaur astride, although he might punish his mounts severely if he thought they jibbed or tired at the chase.

The Emperor Franz Josef made two requests about Elisabeth's hunting. The first was that her doctor Langyi should always be nearby, in case she had another fall. The second was that her stud-groom Bayzand should ride beside her. Yet his role was soon superseded by 'Bay' Middleton, who became her scout. At first, he had refused to lead her. 'What is an empress to me?' he asked Earl Spencer. 'She'll only hold me back.' Yet at the Pytchley meet, Elisabeth flew after Middleton over the fences until she fell in a ditch, having matched him jump for jump. Stitched into special under-clothing of chamois leather, she was decorous even in her tumble. After that display, she held her horseman with his blue eyes and sharp moustache in her gloved hand. She hunted daily, writing back to the Emperor that she had not known 'a moment's fatigue'.

Earl Spencer entertained her and Middleton at Althorp Park, and she returned the favour at Easton Neston. On her arrival in England she had been put off by Queen Victoria, who did not find the time for a flying visit from the errant Empress, who had come to the country and taken a place in Northamptonshire 'merely for the hunting!' The proud Spencer family thought itself more English than the Saxe-Coburg-Gotha and Hanover dynasties which now occupied the throne, and just as aristocratic. One branch of the Spencers had married into the Churchills and the Marlboroughs. The other side chose wealth and beauty. The wife of the first Earl Spencer was Georgiana Poyntz, whose daughter Harriet turned down the Prince of Wales to marry the Earl of Bessborough. Her sister Georgiana wed the fifth Duke of Devonshire and campaigned for the Whig cause and American independence by kissing all the Cockney voters. Rather liberal and artistic in their tastes, and generally opposed to the Court, the Spencers appeared to have much in common with the Wittelsbachs of Bavaria, especially a sporting and generous instinct. Elisabeth's host, the 'Red Earl', supported the Liberal Prime Minister Gladstone, and he would even present Wimbledon Common to the people to match the creation of the royal parks for the public.

Yet Elisabeth could not wholly ignore her imperial duty in order to hunt daily with her aristocratic English and Hungarian courtiers and admirers. Her sister Queen Marie was looking for a subsidy from the Rothschild family, which earnestly wanted recognition and con-tacts at the highest level in Vienna. Elisabeth was persuaded to combine a visit on a Sunday and a Monday to both Windsor Castle and Baron Ferdinand de Rothschild at Leighton House and his stud at Mentmore. Queen Victoria was not pleased at Elisabeth breaking the sabbath on her duty call. The Empress arrived in a violent snow-storm just after the service in chapel had ended. 'She was looking very well and handsome, in black, with fur,' so the Queen wrote in her journal. 'She spoke with delight of having hunted each day since she arrived!! and of how civil everyone was.' Queen Marie of Naples had not accompanied her, but was remaining in England to hunt. 'The Empress so regretted the Emperor had not also come over.' In spite of every offer, Elisabeth would not stay to lunch or take any-thing to eat or drink. After presenting 'her very numerous suite', the displeased British Queen recorded, 'we took her down again to the door.'

When she did fulfil her imperial obligations, Elisabeth seemed to offend more by her casualness than if she had ignored what she should do. Indeed, Queen Victoria referred in a private letter to 'the extraordinary visit of that foolish Empress of Austria'. The British ambassador in Vienna reported on the public indignation there that the Empress had gone to hunt in England at all, while Count Andrássy was prepared to advise his imperial mistress never to pay an official visit on a Sunday again. She did not do so, but she went on hunting in the counties on borrowed local hunters. She even scolded her husband because none of his imported Austrian horses were up to the mark. 'They are slow and spiritless; one wants quite different material here.'

Moreover, she defended her excursion to him. She was continu-ally being asked when he would join her. 'After all, everybody has the right to a holiday from time to time.' She established a steeplechase prize under her pseudonym, the Hohenembs Cup, which was won by 'Bay' Middleton. He also accepted her invitation to visit her after her return to Gödöllö. Although he was rather deaf, she hardly minded because she could listen to him and did not have to reply. Her husband paid the expenses of her trip of more than one hundred thousand gulden, on hearing from Baron Nopsca of her triumphs in the saddle, where she had become freckled and tanned and healthy. 'Not in England or anywhere else in the world was a lady who could ride like Her Imperial Highness, and very few men either.'

To save her youthful looks from all of this outdoor exposure, Elisabeth used special eccentric beauty treatments. As a remedy for the freckles, she sometimes wore a silk face mask, packed with slices of raw veal, rather like boxers trusted to a bloody steak to relieve their black eyes. Otherwise, she would cover her cheeks with purified honey for a couple of hours, followed by a protective ointment of fresh strawberries crushed into vaseline. For her massage, a special lotion was used of alcohol and glycerine and ox-gall. At night, she slept in hot wet towels, knotted round her small waist of twenty inches – she was so proud of it that she had herself sewn into some of her riding costumes just before the meet. She now added pressed onions and Peruvian balsam to the cognac in her shampoo. She would bathe in hot olive oil after the manner of Cleopatra; she had noticed on Corfu how the Greek girls treading the harvest in the tubs for the presses kept their golden and soft complexions. To keep herself slender, she added to her strong meat juice extract from game a drink of the whites of eggs, mixed with salt. So obsessed was she with the purity of the milk she drank that special Jersey cows were added to her household on her travels. She used their fresh cream as a skin lotion, along with mixtures made from lily bulbs. In her way, she anticipated the modern preoccupation with natural beauty products in an age when arsenic was still being used in compounds to bleach the skin.

Her good influence in Hungary had helped to bring some stability to that restive country within the Dual Monarchy. Koloman Tiksa had formed a Magyar government which would persist for the next fifteen years. Moreover, since her admirer Count Andrássy was serving as the Foreign Minister of the whole Habsburg Empire, the Hungarians could feel that they ruled at home and were well represented abroad. Supported by the Empress when she was in residence at Gödöllö and increasingly by her son, the Crown Prince Rudolf, the Magyar people felt secure within the imperial framework of the Habsburg Empire. Largely through her influence, the Emperor had accepted devolution in order to prevent another revolution, and so preserve and even expand his sovereignty.

Before leaving for Gödöllö, Elisabeth had to submit to 'unbearable and horrible' Court ceremonies including the hallowed Corpus

Christi festival. She met the adventuress Baroness Hélène von Vetsera and asked her to Gödöllö, as Marie Festetics noted. One of her last opponents, Count Grünne, was removed from his post as Master of the Horse, while Andrássy was still managing foreign affairs. Although her political influence was waning, her enemies were fading and her friends were being promoted. Whenever she did choose to intervene, she could still achieve what she wanted. She took the imperial yacht *Miramare*, a paddle steamer with twin funnels which allowed her to exercise on deck, for a trip to Corfu and Athens before going to Gödöllö for more sport. She would play, while the Habsburg Empire turned towards the east.

Still devoted to her daughter Valérie, she was becoming closer to her son Rudolf, who now came to Gödöllö with her, freed from Court discipline because he had reached his majority. He was good-looking and precocious and rebellious, 'opposing for the sake of opposing' in the words of Prince Kinsky's son; his chief joy was shooting eagles. Also at Gödöllö was the Empress's niece Marie Wallersee, the daughter of her brother Ludwig and the comedienne Henriette Mendel; she was intriguing and deceitful, and Rudolf was averse to her, although, like Baroness Vetsera, she would have a role in his fate. 'She is not genuine,' the Empress wrote, 'not sincere, as though she had a talent for acting.' She had to be married off to one of the Empress's admirers, Count Georg Larisch, in order to keep her from the Crown Prince. She was trying to captivate the heir to the throne for her own ambitions.

At Gödöllö, Elisabeth was the umpire among all the Hungarian aristocrats and the English gentleman competing for her promotion. As she observed, everybody wished to be Master of the Hounds, just as in a ministry, everybody wished to be President. The position of 'Bay' Middleton was a wonder to all. He was not a noble, but he was not a groom such as Allen or Bayzand. The easy passages of English society, where army officers or squires were the equals of the earls and the dukes and came from the same schools, were unknown among the rigid castes of the Habsburg Empire, where good breeding was held to be on the quarterings of the family shield. The Emperor Franz Josef placed Middleton in a cottage well away from his wife in the Hungarian palace. The terrible efforts at German speech and practical jokes of the English rider made him into a court jester, a Fool to kings who was forgiven for being so damnably smart over fences. Yet Elisabeth treated him as her leader in the chase and gave informal dinners without her husband, where Middleton was the guest of honour. The Baltazzi brothers, who had recently won the Derby with their horse, came out to join them and befriended Middleton against the increasing jealousy of Count Nicholas Esterházy, whose passion was to pilot the Empress in the hunt himself. For a while, he resigned from the Mastership in a temper, leaving Elisabeth the mistress of the field.

At that time, the Empress was not having an affair with 'Bay' Middleton. She was cold and reserved and apparently not interested, after her infection by her husband, in any sexual relationship. Yet like any reigning beauty, she loved to control and order and even inflame her many admirers. As the princesses in her childhood tales, she wished to remain beloved, but too far to touch. Certainly, within the vicious gossip of Court circles, she could afford no liaison with somebody the Austrians thought a servant, any more than Queen Victoria would dream of consummating her relationship with John Brown. Empresses were empresses, and grooms were grooms, and never the twain might meet except in the informality of the hunt, where the rules worshipped the rider, and not his pedigree – only fancied in horses.

Elisabeth showed off to her adorers not only in the saddle, but also fencing in the gymnasium. There she wore a body costume more suited to a circus or a music-hall than to a Court. Yet her head and her expression were masked, as she displayed the moving grace of her figure with the *épée* and the foil. She tantalised and remained at a distance. When Middleton escaped her to spend the night at a casino in Budapest where sex was on sale, Elisabeth sent the police force to find him and was furious, after his return to her country palace. Yet he was pardoned for his stupidity and his spree. As the story went, the Empress was surveying a painting of *A Midsummer Night's Dream*, in which Bottom with his ass's head was being cosseted by the Fairy Queen Titania. She was heard to say, 'Bay and I.'

Meanwhile, the Balkans had burst into flames. The revolt of Bosnia had been followed by another rising in the Rhodope mountains of Bulgaria. There were fearful atrocities committed by the rebels and the Turkish militia, followed by a coup against the Sultan in Constantinople. Serbia and Montenegro declared war on the Ottoman Empire, leaving the three interested European powers in their loose triple alliance, Austro-Hungary and Germany and Russia, to co-ordinate their response. In the secret Reichstadt Agreement, a partition of European Turkey was settled, if the Serbs and the Montenegrins won. They were soon overrun, however, making Russia keen to intervene on behalf of its persecuted Orthodox and Slavic brethren. In another secret agreement, the Tsar offered Franz Josef a free hand in Bosnia and Herzegovina, if he were to remain neutral in a Russian attack on Turkey. Although held at Plevna, the Russian armies advanced on Sofia and approached Constantinople, causing a capitulation by their enemies.

The subsequent peace treaty of San Stefano, however, was unacceptable to Vienna, for a huge satellite Bulgaria was to be created within the Russian orbit, while Austro-Hungary was to receive nothing. Andrássy persuaded the imperial parliaments to vote sixty million florins for a war against Russia or the occupation of Bosnia. At the later Congress of Berlin, Andrássy worked well with Bismarck and the British Foreign Secretary, Lord Salisbury, to achieve his country's aims – a small Bulgaria, a mandate to take over Bosnia and Herzegovina, and independence for Serbia and Rumania, while Austro-Hungary had the power to guarantee safe passage along the full length of the Danube. By diplomacy rather than battle, Franz Josef seemed to have won the day.

As the Greeks and the Romans and the Normans and the Venetians and the Turks had discovered over the past two thousand years, a hard time was given by the local peoples to any invaders from strongholds on the Adriatic coast. To march inland into the mountains was no picnic. The Bosnian capital of Sarajevo would prove again and again the jinx of the policies of western Europe. An additional subsidy of twenty-five million florins and an Austrian army of nearly two hundred thousand men were necessary to subdue the

Balkan provinces. Franz Josef wanted to annex his new conquests to the dismay of Andrássy, who complained to the Empress Elisabeth that her husband did not understand the Eastern Question and never would. If the mainly Muslim areas were annexed, Turkey would become an enemy and offence would be given to Germany and Russia as well as to Britain and France, still the guarantors of the Ottoman Empire. Eventually, Franz Josef accepted a mere mandate over the Balkan provinces, and Andrássy's last service to his Emperor before his resignation was to arrange with Bismarck a formal Austro-German alliance, which would endure for forty years until the collapse of the Habsburg and Hohenzollern Empires at the end of the First World War.

The bugbear of the rulers of Europe, an assassination by an anarchist or a lunatic, had caused a crisis in Germany. First, a socialist plumber named Max Hödel had fired two shots at the Emperor, as he was driving down the Unter den Linden in an open victoria carriage with his daughter Louise, the Grand Duchess of Baden. His shots were high and missed their target. But later, Dr Karl Nobiling, a radical journalist, fired both barrels of a shotgun at the passing Emperor from the top window of a house in Berlin. Twenty-seven pellets lodged in the Emperor's arms, five in his neck, and six in his left cheek and brow. One lead slug penetrated his jaw, another nicked an artery in his wrist. Torrents of blood flowed over the upholstery of the carriage, which was driven at snail's pace back to the palace. The old man insisted on walking unaided inside before fainting from loss of blood.

Unbelievably, the old Emperor made a slow recovery. His son, the Crown Prince Frederick, was a brief Regent in name, for Bismarck still ran the state. He had only the responsibility and agony of deciding on the execution of Hödel who was probably mad. For weeks he would not sign the death warrant, but he did so finally because of the need to deter future assassins. The Emperor thanked his son for sparing him the ordeal of taking another man's life; the Crown Prince had done right and God was pleased with him. Hödel refused all religious help before his head was struck off. Like Cohen-Blind before him, Dr Nobiling died of self-inflicted wounds before he could stand trial. He was reported as having said that his reasons for trying to kill the Emperor were political and that he had accomplices. A continual conspiracy appeared to stalk the crowned heads of Europe.

The Empress Elisabeth feared death neither in the streets nor in the field. She took a winter Palladian house, Cottesbrooke Park in Northamptonshire, and she rode desperately day after day with the Pytchley in pursuit of the stag and the fox. Two pictures, still at Althorp Park, showed her at the chase. Both were painted by John Charlton in 1879; in the first, Elisabeth rode Merry Andrew with the Pytchley Hounds; in the second, she set out from the Falconry with the fifth Earl Spencer and Will Goodall, the huntsman. Her sister Marie had tried to recruit 'Bay' Middleton as her scout in the absence of the Empress; but he had made an enemy of her by telling her envoy that he was damned if he would pilot every damn queen who came to England. He and Earl Spencer had been at the station to meet Elisabeth on her arrival, and he bought her a whole stud wisely and well, including an incomparable hunter named Bravo. Led by him on his splendid Minotaur in a series of hunts, the Empress was followed by her Austrian and Hungarian 'colony' of aristocrats. They fell almost as often as the soldiers in the Bosnian war. Count Clam-Gallas broke his jaw and tore his face open, while Elisabeth found the ditches 'peopled' with thrown ladies and gentlemen. As the hunt journal recorded: 'Space is wanting to give a full list of the wounded.'

Yet the Empress went on jumping faultlessly on her Bravo, which 'flew and was full of fire', as she told her husband. She declared that she did not mind the falls, but she would not like to scratch her face. Even when Middleton took a toss, she proved herself capable of taking her own line and being in at the kill. And the daily prayer of Marie Festetics was answered: 'God grant that my beloved Empress return home safe and sound.' Her exploits were even celebrated in a local ballad:

> 'The bright star of Europe' her kingdom has left,
> And Austria mourns of its Empress bereft.
> Firm seat in the saddle: light hands on the reins,

As e'er guided steed over Hungary's plains:
She has come – with her beauty, grace, courage and skill
To ride, with our hounds, from old Shuckburgh Hill.

The Crown Prince Rudolf had travelled with his mother, to explore not the mud of the shires, but the delights of London and British technology. He had told her pompously that he would not hunt. 'Our people here do not see any great glory in breaking one's neck, and my popularity means too much to me to make me throw it away on things like that.' He was initiated into the pleasures of the city by the Master of his Household, Count Bombelles, and by the rakish Marlborough House set around the Prince of Wales; he even courted the actress Lily Langtry. He did, however, secure a diplomatic triumph in his interview with Queen Victoria, who was most taken by his looks and his acumen. As her secretary reported to her cabinet, she considered Rudolf one of the most intelligent young princes she knew. 'He is *extremely* English in his views and feelings and *much* distressed at the "old policy" at Vienna, but said that his mother's return at *this* moment would have the best effect, for that *she* had *immense influence* and *if* Austria *acted* with *us soon* it would be *owing to her.* She has always supported Count Andrássy and first discovered his talents . . .' Austria he said had *quite* the same interests as England and *ought* to be her best ally.'

The young and unfortunate Prince Imperial Eugène, the son of Louis Napoleon the Third who had died from a gallstone operation in exile in England, was now a sacrifice to his horse and the British Empire. To fill in time, he became an observer with the expeditionary forces in South Africa, fighting against the formidable Zulus. On a cavalry patrol near the Tshotshosi River, he was ambushed by black spearmen. The Lieutenant-in-command galloped away with the rest of the scouts, abandoning the Prince Imperial, who was unhorsed and died of fourteen stab wounds from the Zulu assegais. As with the suspicious death of the young 'Aiglon' at the Habsburg Court after the defeat of his father, Napoleon the First, so the killing of Eugène after the funeral of his father terminated all hopes of any third Napoleonic restoration in France. Only the widowed Empress

Eugénie was left to moulder in the English countryside, hardly visited by the imperial families of Europe, an embarrassment to her hosts.

Hunting rather than hunted at Cottesbrooke, Elisabeth was spending several of the more fulfilled weeks of her life. She was surrounded by male admirers and excused the formalities of the Court. There was even little publicity, although she still dressed for the occasion, stitched into her leather underwear and into one of her sixteen riding habits for each meet. 'Bay' Middleton led her over the fences and ditches, although he was so keen that he often rode on top of hounds, even being told by Earl Spencer that he hoped 'Bay' broke his neck, if he ever did that again. Yet Elisabeth always asked for her friend to be forgiven for her sake. And so he was, while the Empress sang the praises of Earl Spencer to her husband Franz Josef, telling him how much they would like each other. So supreme was she in Northamptonshire that she was often likened to the *White Lady* painted by Gainsborough, which hung in the hall at Cottesbrooke in elegant composure.

However happy she was, Elisabeth kept her male admirers at a proper distance. Only 'Bay' Middleton, who was beginning to treat her with the rough familiarity that Queen Victoria accepted from John Brown, caused a rift between her and her son Rudolf. Because of jealousy at Middleton's refusal to pilot her while he would protect her sister with his life, Queen Marie retaliated by tattling to Rudolf about the closeness of his mother to the rude cavalry Captain. At a ball given by the German ambassador in London, Rudolf stared in silence at Middleton, when the Captain was presented to him. Then he turned away, cutting the other man dead. This public humiliation of her escort by her son hurt Elisabeth deeply, once it was reported to her. She felt vulnerable, where she had felt so safe. She knew that the news would reach Vienna and be used against her. She had to return, her idyll spoiled. Yet in a week's time, there were the steeple-chases for the Pytchley, in which she would present the prizes, and one of the winners was likely to be her 'Bay'. She could not spurn him, too. Also Earl Spencer was entertaining Alexandra, the Princess of Wales, and Elisabeth had promised to give a dinner at Cottesbrooke for their party.

Her refuge was to have a nervous attack and go to bed. Pope Pius the Ninth had just died, and so she had another pretext to leave the hunting field and seclude herself. She fell out with Rudolf over his discourtesy. The rift over 'Bay' would never be healed any more than Queen Victoria could persuade her son Edward, the Prince of Wales, to tolerate John Brown. Elisabeth did manage, however, to ride on the last hunt before the races, where her exquisite horsemanship on Bravo was watched by Lady Spencer and the Princess of Wales. The dinner engagement at Cottesbrooke also took place. Rudolf came with Count Bombelles, while 'Bay' Middleton was not among the guests. Ceremonial had triumphed over personal emotion. Yet Middleton won two of the steeplechase races on the following day, and he was given her Hohenembs Cup by the Empress. Rudolf watched the presentation without a word. Immediately afterwards, his mother left for Paris and Vienna, never to return and hunt in the Midlands again.

The friendship of the Austrian Empress with Earl Spencer would have uncanny echoes in the next century, when Lady Diana Spencer would marry Charles, the Prince of Wales. The two women were both reared in a wild country freedom and a hatred of formality, one at Possenhofen, the other at Althorp. Their royal marriages would end in long separations from their husbands. Princess Diana would be beset by male admirers and one particular cavalry officer, whom she would not keep at a full distance like the rest of them because he taught her to ride. She would be obsessed by her figure and her beauty, her diet and her appearance. She would visit those who were most unfortunate, struck by madness and plagues, an angel of gracious mercy. She would be hounded by journalists and photographers as she sought a shy celebrity. She would be called what Elisabeth was called, 'the queen of hearts'.

CHAPTER SEVEN

Clouds Gathering

❖

THE CROWN PRINCE RUDOLF shot himself in the left hand by mistake to the distress of his mother, and he soon wounded a beater, whose family was compensated for fifty gulden. As Marie Festetics commented, every creature that breathed or had wings was doomed to death from Rudolf's trigger finger. 'Such men become possessed by a sort of lust for killing, and it seems so unnecessary to me. Even as a child – and a charming little boy he was – he would shoot bullfinches from his window.' The question was when he would transfer the target of the gun in his hand from beasts and birds to human beings.

While Rudolf was following his father in the massacre of the chamois and the bear and the eagle and the quail, his mother was planning another season in Ireland to hunt down the fox and the stag. She had done her duty at Schönbrunn, visiting the soldiers who were wounded in the Bosnian campaign. Now, as in Hungary, she was riding into a political morass. The astute politician Parnell had brought together Irish opposition to the Protestant landlords in a demand for a measure of the Home Rule which Hungary had achieved. The previous Lord Lieutenant of Ireland, Earl Spencer, should not have advised the Catholic Austrian Empress to hunt there, although he would be in attendance. As a spokesman on Irish affairs for the Liberal Party, Spencer should have known the trouble which might be caused by her sporting visit. Yet he had met Franz Josef at Ischl and Gödöllö, where he had told the Emperor to ignore Queen Victoria's warning that her troubles in Ireland were similar to his in Hungary. As Elisabeth had pacified the Magyars, perhaps she would mollify the Irish as well. She did try to assure Queen Victoria by letter that she would keep to the strictest incognito while hunting in Ireland, but who could believe such a thing?

Travelling under her celebrated alias of the Countess of Hohenembs, the Empress was met by cheering crowds on her railway journey to Summerhill in Meath, where a private chapel for saying Mass was constructed for her use. A telegraph was installed with a separate line to the Continent, bypassing any attempt of England to monitor her messages. An additional block of stables was built to accommodate the Irish hunters which 'Bay' Middleton was borrowing and buying for her, Domino and Cameo, Hard Times and Doctor and St Patrick, Ashtown and Timon and the Widow. The cost to the imperial purse was almost sufficient for another Balkan campaign, nearly one hundred and sixty thousand gulden, enough to inflame the critics in Vienna at a time of floods on the lower Danube.

The Meath country had big banks rather than fences and great ditches. Elisabeth and 'Bay' Middleton and Bayzand were all unseated in accidents in the first week in the field. Nowhere had Marie Festetics heard so much about broken limbs and necks. Every day somebody was carried off to have their bones mended. Yet it was no use worrying about Elisabeth. 'She was a most thoughtful and judicious rider,' in the opinion of another lady riding with the Royal Meath, 'and eminently considerate for her mounts. I have seen her jump off with the lightness of a fawn when a check or a wait at covert side permitted, and almost unassisted shift her saddle slightly, always taking care that it was well clear of the play of the shoulders, and then from the pocket out would come sundry dainties ... Her hands were the smallest I ever saw, and her hair the longest – it fell around her like a cloak when unloosed.'

A friend of de Burgh's gave an account of the Empress out hunting that was equally full of admiration:

The Empress had an exquisite figure, and her riding-dress was the admiration of every field which she graced whilst visiting in Ireland. So closely did her well-cut skirt cling to her form that it was a common saying among ladies that she must be 'sewn into it', and that they did not believe she could dismount; while her jackets, of absolutely perfect build, were fitted to a twenty-inch waist of exquisite and natural rounding. She either wore a high silk hat or a small Tyrolese hat of pliable felt, dented slightly in the centre of the crown and furnished with one little up-standing wing. I never saw her wear a flower or a neck-bow, or a pocket handkerchief protruding from the front of her bodice. Her dress was simplicity itself, and its only noticeable adjunct was a black-and-yellow fan, very light and portable and about as plain as it was possible for it to be. This was carried either in her hand or in a little slip strap in front of her saddle, and it always came out at covert side, and very frequently when trotting along the roadway. 'Afraid of her complexion', the Irish ladies said; but it was not so . . . She had an absolute dread of the itinerant photographer and of the sketcher, ever on the watch to snatch impressions of her truly lovely face.

Taking her picture, indeed, without her consent did seem to her a theft, if not a rape. As for Earl Spencer, he merely referred to the press as 'you scum'.

Her diet was as extraordinary as her riding to hounds. She followed the regime of an English jockey. At six in the morning, she had a cup of tea and a biscuit, followed by her long toilette. At ten o'clock when not in the saddle, she took a mug of bouillon with an egg, and nothing more until dinner, when she might have chilled milk and the whites of eggs whipped up in port. If she found herself a pound or two overweight, she lived on an extraordinary game and beef broth, a distilled mixture of the meat juice from beef and venison and partridge and hare, strong enough to rejuvenate a Queen Victoria. Her strength of will in her exemplary eating would hardly be matched until modern times.

There was no way to avoid the presence of the Empress leading to a political disturbance in Ireland, even if it was a coincidence. A part of the brick wall surrounding the Catholic seminary at Maynooth College had collapsed. An exhausted stag leapt through the breach and turned at bay in the shrubbery. The hounds followed in hot pursuit with the Empress on Domino behind their paws. With her came 'Bay' Middleton and Earl Spencer, who knew that they were riding on dangerous turf. The President of the college, Dr Walsh, came out to invite the Empress inside. He wrapped his gown round her shoulders, for she was soaked to the skin after a previous fall. He then took her in to tea, where she charmed the priests. Six days later, Elisabeth returned to hear Mass at Maynooth with Marie Festetics and Count Rudi Liechtenstein and the stern Presbyterian Middleton. A red carpet was laid out for her; the Vicar Capitular of Dublin arrived for the ritual. A tour of the college followed, hailed by the cheering seminarians. All was widely reported in the pictorial papers. Although Queen Victoria herself had urged the financial support of Maynooth, no act of the Catholic Empress of Austria could have done more to inflame religious and nationalist feelings in Ireland, where the situation was becoming more explosive because of another potato blight afflicting the poor, as at the time of the Great Hunger.

The Whig Earl Spencer stayed away from this second visit and returned to his twenty-six thousand acres in Northamptonshire. Yet he had advised the action. He had been ambitious to be appointed Lord Lieutenant of Ireland for a second term; but the post had gone to the Duke of Marlborough, who was deeply embarrassed by the arrival of the Empress of Austria under a pseudonym, accompanied by Spencer and her notorious companion Middleton. The Duke could not receive Elisabeth with her false identity as a countess for political and social reasons; yet he could not ignore her escapades. He had been informed that the Empress was in touch with revolutionary Hungarians such as Kossuth, who had pledged his personal support to the Fenians and other rebel groups. Although this report was exaggerated, Elisabeth was well known for her sympathy for Hungarian independence within the Habsburg Empire. Her apparent seal of approval on Maynooth appeared to extend to the struggle of the Catholic masses against their Protestant rulers.

Yet Elisabeth could also offend where she was most beloved. By hunting unofficially on Ash Wednesday, when a stag was taken after a hot chase of forty minutes, she further alienated the powers that were. Things had gone so far that the Duchess of Marlborough was forced to take the train to the Royal Meath Hunt in order to be presented to the Empress, who told her coldly that she was anonymous, on holiday, and would attend no Viceregal Balls in Dublin, nor allow the Marlboroughs to visit her at Summerhill, where her intimacy was reserved for her three hunting companions, Captain Middleton and the two Counts, Heinrich Larisch and Rudi Liechtenstein.

In one sense the Counts were the guardians of the Empress, however attracted she was to her bold 'Bay' over the banks and ditches of Meath. They owed a duty to the Emperor as did Elisabeth, who rarely allowed any personal interviews with any of her admirers. She was surrounded by a huge household as well; some of them inevitably reported back on her behaviour to Vienna. However much 'Bay' was in love with Elisabeth, he would hardly have dared to overstep the limits of what he might do. His ruin would then be inevitable. With his debts piling up because of the huge expenses of maintaining his own stable in Ireland, Middleton was also casting round for a rich marriage. When the Empress was away, he was courting a Charlotte Baird, who was said to have twenty thousand pounds a year at her disposal. Dancing attendance on Elisabeth was a path to penury and might lead willy-nilly to a parting.

Leading a charmed life with only one fall, the Empress saw Bayzand carried off on a makeshift stretcher. 'There is only *one* opinion,' Marie Festetics wrote of her mistress, 'that she is incomparable as a rider and as a woman. But I suffer a thousand deaths!' The Empress and 'Bay' went on to jump the full course of the Irish Grand National at Fairyhouse, soaring over the Ballyhack double. She now wore a shamrock on the breast of her hunting habits, and crowds and triumphal arches met her on the roads near Summerhill, especially when she announced that she had to return to her own country. A special train took her to Dublin, where she had her only meeting with the Viceroy at the Shelbourne Hotel. The courtesies with the Duke and Duchess of Marlborough were brief and formal. She reserved her last supper in Ireland for 'Bay' Middleton alone with a single chaperon, for the sake of decency. Fortunately, for the Empress, Queen Victoria was abroad, and so Elisabeth had only to accept a call from the Prince of Wales for a quarter of an hour on her swift passage through London. She had all but escaped ceremonial on this blessed flight to Ireland and its green. She may have won over the people there, but she had worsened the relations between Austria and England.

Elisabeth had informed Franz Josef that she was only returning because of a flood disaster at the town of Szegedin, which was inundated. 'It is the greatest sacrifice I can make,' she wrote, 'but in such conditions it is necessary.' Her foreign trips were costing fortunes, which many of the Viennese thought would be better spent on the victims at home – and so did she, in her heart of hearts. Her compassion was as important to Elisabeth as her reckless and purging enjoyment of the hunt. Moreover, she would have to return for the Silver Jubilee of her marriage, an occasion which she was neglecting. All that publicity, and all those people. She was looking forward to it, she confessed, rather like the widow of a maharajah anticipated her *suttee*. When she appeared at a state reception at the Hofburg, her green satin gown and loose hair were sprinkled with drops of diamonds, so that she looked more like the water nymph Ondine than an imperial grandmother.

On the anniversary, the heavens opened. So much rain fell that the state procession was postponed. The artist Makart had planned the show, rather as Michelangelo and Leonardo da Vinci had done for the Medicis and the Sforzas in Renaissance times. All the guilds and the crafts of the capital city were represented in the pageant, giving the occasion a medieval flavour and adding to the popularity of the Empress, who would make the conditions of working women in Vienna an important one of her causes. As she would write to the responsible minister, 'My heart bleeds when I think of the misery of those poor women and girls, who work like the slaves of ancient times, without ever being able to earn enough to feed themselves properly. The vessel entrusted by God with our birth and posterity should at least be above want. The gratitude of all of us demands as much.' The implication was that if there were young women who did not earn enough to survive they would end on the streets of Vienna, servicing the arrogant men of power, such as the males in Elisabeth's own family.

Although the pageant for the Silver Jubilee did take place in glory and splendour in front of a million people, the gap between the rich and the poor in the Habsburg capital remained an abyss, especially for women. 'Apprentices usually work three years without any payment,' Elisabeth's report continued. 'At carnival times the girls sometimes work the whole night; and during several months the time allowed for them to sleep is very short.' Pageants and jubilees were staged by the exploitation of the young women; so was the reconstruction of Vienna as an imperial city to rival Berlin and Paris. There was intense competition in the embroidery trade, which was harmful to the eyes of the girls, forced to sew for two florins a week. 'Liver and lung diseases are very common in this industry.' Yet the hardest labour performed by women was in brick-making and house-building. 'They are obliged to draw carts filled with great loads of mortar, to carry heavy buckets up the scaffolds, and to endure cold and heat during a working day of sixteen to seventeen hours, labour-ing away as true martyrs up to a motherhood that brings them no joy and allows them no rest.' Many working women died prematurely, few had healthy children. That was the price paid by the imperial city.

As in so many areas of behaviour and health for women, Elisabeth would raise almost a lone voice. She was often a prophet of what her sex might demand and achieve in the next century, particularly in independence and fitness and sport. After another celebration of the Silver Jubilee in Budapest, she returned to hunting at Gödöllö, which she was making into an overseas British stud with a pack of hounds. 'When visiting her establishment,' de Burgh noted, 'one would hardly have imagined it to be in Hungary. All her grooms and stablemen were English or Irish, and everything was done as she had seen it in Meath and the Shires. The rooms of the Castle, which were given up to the paraphernalia of the hunt, were filled with brushes, spurs, crops, and hunting-fans, as she called them,' the many mementoes of her various experiences in the field. She went on practising *haute école* at Gödöllö, until she could change legs while threading her way in and out of the benches at a gallop. She was, indeed, not only the most beautiful princess and celebrity in Europe, but also supreme in the saddle.

The Silver Jubilee in Budapest had shown that Elisabeth was fêted even more there than in Ireland. Her natural rebelliousness seemed to speak to peoples who believed themselves oppressed, whether they truly were or not. In her most astute analysis of the character of her mistress, Marie Festetics wrote of the good and the bad fairy, who had come to the cradle of Elisabeth. The good one had brought her virtues – beauty and sweetness, grace and dignity, simplicity and kindness, nobility and profundity, wit and penetration. And yet the bad fairy had deprived her of moderation in all things. Nothing would bring her happiness, even her beauty would bring her sorrow. Her noble intelligence would lead her too deeply into things, so that she would despise humanity. Elisabeth would lose her 'faith in goodness and love, and your trust in those who are best, and give it to those who will abuse it. And so your soul will be full of disgust and bitterness, until you never find peace.'

During a second visit to hunt with the Royal Meath at Summerhill with her host Lord Langford, Elisabeth continued to find a strenuous peace. Her son Rudolf regretted that now she only cared for sport, and not for being the sole conduit of liberal influences to the Emperor, since Andrássy had retired from being the Foreign Minister. The Empress had again avoided visiting Queen Victoria in London, but she was welcomed by cheering mobs when she arrived at Dublin in the spring of 1880 with her forty tons of luggage and ninety staff and riding companions. 'Bay' Middleton was still her lead and inspiration, but there were more accidents during the hunting season, even to the Empress. For the Irish rebels, she seemed an example of liberty and daring, more a Queen of Ireland than Victoria, while Parnell, then collecting funds in America, was the uncrowned King of Eire. He would invite her through the Austrian

Embassy in London to come again to Ireland for its quiet. As Lord Granville informed an amazed Victoria, Parnell conveyed to Elisabeth that there was no reason why she should not hunt there, and a hearty welcome was assured. 'It is *rather* too much!' the Queen observed.

The Empress was, indeed, untrammelled and free in the chase. 'The great advantage of Ireland,' she said, 'is that it has no Royal Highnesses.' She was flattered by trainers and not grandees: a mare, named Empress after her, won the Grand National. As if she knew that this might be her last Irish season, she hunted behind her 'Bay' Middleton with even more determination and dash. The casualty list grew daily, and she was suffering more and more heavy falls. Her groom Tom Healey now took the place of the injured Bayzand, and even headed 'Bay', who was plunging into one disaster after another. As Elisabeth wrote back to Franz Josef, Middleton's mare pitched over into a watery ditch, leaving him hanging downwards with his foot fast in the stirrup. The Empress and her groom had to save him from drowning. Two days later, the same thing happened, so the Empress informed her husband. They had been invited to hunt the fox with the Kildare, but her gentlemen had decided to chase the stag elsewhere. The change of plans was agreed:

> . . . if only to give the slip to all the inquisitive persons who come out in crowds by special train when I am expected anywhere at a meet. All the evening and early this morning Middleton and Lord Langford were laughing at the thought of taking them in like this. A lady named Miss Hussey fell in front of me, and she and her grey simply rolled over and over. Later on she fell into the water too, but for all that she was in at the death. Middleton had another fall . . . and remained with his foot caught in the stirrup again, in a way that was almost more alarming than the other day, for his horse wanted to go on, but my Tom saved him again.

To avoid publicity, another lethal accident had nearly taken place. Yet 'Bay' Middleton recuperated so quickly that he appeared at supper at Summerhill on the same night to huge applause. A rhyme was even recorded in *British Hunts and Huntsmen* to celebrate the exploits of Elisabeth that day:

> The Queen of the Chase!
> The Queen! Yes, the Empress!
> Look, look, how she flies,
> With a hand that never fails
> And a pluck that never dies.
> The best man in England can't lead her – he's down!
> 'Bay' Middleton's back is done beautifully brown.
>
> Hark horn and hark halloa!
> Come on for a place!
> He must ride who would follow
> The Queen of the Chase!

Elisabeth could not stay overlong on this visit, and precautions were taken by the Viceroy to prevent Irish crowds seeing her departure on the steamer *Shamrock*. She had to pay her respects in London, where she met the Prince and Princess of Wales once more, and even the Queen was charmed against her inclinations with Elisabeth. 'She looked very handsome in a black velvet coat trimmed with fur,' Victoria conceded, 'with a black beaver hat on her head. She was very pleasant and unaffected.' Yet her charm did not mend the damage to diplomatic relations already done in Ireland.

Elisabeth was shocked to hear in London that Rudolf had become engaged at the age of twenty-two to the fifteen-year-old Coburg Princess Stéphanie of Belgium. This was the tender age at which she herself had been selected for a diplomatic marriage. Catholic princesses were thin on the ground, and Rudolf had not been attracted by offers of a partner at the Courts of Saxony and Spain. Stéphanie was no beauty, but she was blonde and tall. On a brief visit to Brussels, Elisabeth found that she did not approve of the character of Stéphanie, who was also clumsy and stupid, obstinate and jealous. Only heaven, in her opinion, would prevent a disaster. As her secretary later wrote, Elisabeth thought chiefly in terms of equine pedigree. She would never harness a racehorse and an Irish hunter to the same carriage, or an over-bred son to a thick-boned Flanders mare. She warned Rudolf that he was being pushed into the marriage by his father, who considered the political aspects of the affair in his capacity as the ruler of an empire. She desired Rudolf's happiness and concluded, 'after mature consideration, that Stéphanie is not at all the wife for you and can never be so'.

What was worse for the Empress was that her son's betrothal was a copy of her own. In the glass and golden imperial coach drawn by eight horses, she now had to process with Stéphanie at her side over the Elisabeth Bridge into Vienna to watch another wedding ceremony at the Church of St Augustine. Unfortunately, Stéphanie had not yet reached the age of puberty, although Elisabeth had at sixteen, when she had married the Emperor. Equally foreboding was the fate of Stéphanie's aunt Charlotte, who had married the Emperor's brother, the Archduke Maximilian executed in Mexico. After being rescued from a fire in the castle of Tervueren, where she had refused to leave the blaze and the battlements, shouting, 'We cannot abdicate!," Charlotte was confined as totally insane in the fortress of Bouchout. Although Rudolf had avoided a further Habsburg and Wittelsbach alliance, he appeared to have exchanged one family with a mad streak for another.

If Rudolf married in haste, he certainly repented at leisure, soon leaving his poorly educated wife for his artistic pursuits and affairs with the demi-mondaines of Vienna. Before his marriage, he had been pursued by the Baroness Vetsera with her two exquisite daughters. Even the Emperor had noticed how sly and glad Vetsera was to make use of everybody to advance herself and her family in Court circles. Other young women were procured for Rudolf by his entourage of dandies led by his Master of the Household, Captain Bombelles. They exploited his lack of interest in his wife, who was following in her loneliness Elisabeth's preoccupations with her *toilette* and a circle of admirers. Stéphanie did, however, reach maturity and spend enough time with Rudolf to produce a child, unfortunately a daughter, also to be named Elisabeth. She would have no male heirs in line for the Habsburg throne.

Because of the disaffection in Ireland and the new diplomatic alliance by blood between the Habsburgs and the Coburgs, the family of Queen Victoria's dead husband Albert, the British monarch won a victory against the Austrian Empress, who had to forego any more trips to Meath. England would have to replace Ireland as her happy hunting ground. Elisabeth chose Combermere Abbey in Cheshire as her base, a huge pile that was again installed with a Catholic chapel and a telegraph and a gymnasium and even with live turtles for her game soup. 'Bay' Middleton had suffered a fracture of the skull, but with his incredible stamina, he had recovered to lead her over the fences. She was more nervous and worried about her condition. Yet she was still wearing out three mounts during the course of the day. Even when she arrived back at Combermere in the evening, she worked out in her gymnasium on the bars. If she complained that the obstacles in Cheshire were small against those in Ireland, she had forgotten her own daring. Of a hundred and fifty riders who started the chase, only twenty were ever in at the kill along with herself. Elisabeth managed to hunt on twenty-two days in a month, generally riding a triple named Quicksilver and Sunflower and Butterduck; she said that everyone there wanted to sell her a horse. Her error was to admire the riding of the devious Marie Larisch-Wallersee too much. She transferred some of her rare intimacy from Marie Festetics to her tricky niece, who reported that she was the chaperon when 'Bay' Middleton spent a great deal of time alone with the Empress in her rooms at Combermere. Such royal gossip was explosive, if it was true. But as the displaced Marie Festetics observed of her rival Marie, 'She is not sincere, not straightforward, she is always acting a part.'

For Middleton had become engaged to Charlotte Baird and her money. One of her brothers was Master of the Cottesmore, another was shortly to be elected to the Jockey Club. In the enclosed world of British hunting, scandal was raising its horns. Elisabeth was nine years older than her 'Bay'. Although she looked younger, her body was beginning to give out after all the punishment which she inflicted on her poor flesh, what was left of it. She was driving herself too hard and suffered from insomnia. She was beginning to suffer from sciatica and swollen joints, so that tanks of Welsh seawater were delivered daily for her brine baths. Whatever exotic creams were applied to her face, the cold winds were inducing wrinkles and lines. Her love of her body and her beauty stood against riding so hard to hounds. Yet she did write back to Ida Ferenczy of one extraordinary hunt, in which she had fallen, but had remounted to be in at the kill. 'I received a superb fox's brush.'

On either side of Rudolf's wedding she spent two seasons at Combermere. Her considered renunciation of her chosen sport would be, in effect, the renunciation of her by Captain Middleton, who had decided to marry Charlotte Baird and pay the debts run up during the years of his devotion to the Empress of Austria. She arrived for her final hunts to find herself with a new pilot, the reserved Major Rivers-Bulkeley, who was embarrassed by his new role. Elisabeth announced sometimes that she was too tired to reach the meet, and sent a message through Marie Larisch-Wallersee, to summon Middleton from his Charlotte Baird back to his post beside her. He responded immediately, booking into a neighbouring hotel to lead her over the fences for the last time. Yet his Empress was now riding poorly, either because of her health or because of her disappointment at losing her 'Bay' to a younger woman.

Listless and irritable, the Empress cut her season short, but she summoned Middleton to a last sentimental dinner with her and Marie and Heinrich Larisch and the faithful Rudi Liechtenstein. She wore a blue and lilac gown of crêpe de Chine, and Marie Larisch-Wallersee sang 'The Last Rose of Summer'. Then she watched the Empress dissolve into tears and say that there would be no release now from her confinement. 'Why can't I break my neck at a fence and end all of it?' There was an ultimate private meeting with 'Bay', which was prolonged until Elisabeth nearly missed her train for an adieu at Windsor Castle to Queen Victoria. She gave him a ring to remember her by, yet she showed nothing of her emotion. She was, as she said, used to play-acting, for she sadly wore a crown. Victoria thought Elisabeth looked aged for the first time in her life.

In memory of her hunting in the British Isles, the Empress created a shrine to her horses in a riding chapel in the Hofburg. The equine artist Richter was commissioned to paint the hunters which came back to the Austrian Empire with her, Ashtown and Cameo, The Doctor and Domino, Hard Times and St Patrick and Summerhill, although her favourite mount was now named Nihilist. Many of her horses, she said, had gone to their deaths for her. No men had done that, they would rather assassinate her. This was not true of 'Bay' Middleton, who would die young at the age of forty-six of a broken neck, as he would have wished to go. In a steeplechase, his mount would rear its head and hit his chin and break his spine, killing him. He would end as had so many of the horses which he and Elisabeth had ridden together.

Another gory assassination bled in these troubled years. The Tsar Alexander the Second, who had recently married his mistress and the mother of four of his children, had his legs blown off by a Nihilist bomb. His death shocked the Empress, who said that she would rather be hunting in England than in his terrible country. Few of the rest of the European royalty dared to attend his obsequies, although the Crown Prince of Prussia was sent there by Bismarck. Police precautions were stringent, the funeral passed without incident. 'I felt sure it would,' the Crown Princess wrote to her mother Queen Victoria, 'as there would be no object in attempting the life of so many Foreigners at once.'

That was not so. Murder remained the terror of all royal persons. Voltaire had called Russia a despotism tempered by assassination, which it was. The Crown Prince was now convinced that all sovereigns would be murdered by Nihilists or Socialists. And the Grand Duchess Vladimir told the Empress that none of the Russian imperial family was safe any longer. The anxiety about her family was killing her. 'Whenever my husband goes out, I am forced to wonder whether he will return to me alive.'

That was the fear of Elisabeth, when Franz Josef set out on a visit to the disaffected lands of Trieste and Dalmatia. She insisted on accompanying him, as Italian anarchists were trying to murder the Austrian Emperor. Although the chief conspirators were arrested by the secret police, Elisabeth would sit on the pavement side of the imperial carriage to shield her husband from possible bullets. Even he would only take a small and indispensable suite with him. 'Here one really is in danger everywhere,' he said. A cruise on the gunboat *Luzifer* ended in flashes of lightning and a gale. Elisabeth was furious and rebuked the Minister President Taafe for his lack of security for them. 'We owe it to God, and God alone, that it went off well.'

She had begun, however, to be reckless about her own safety. Although she had almost given up hunting, she took to walking at a furious pace. This was a relief to Franz Josef, who had written in the margin of the expenses of her final hunting trip to England: 'If only you had never seen a saddle.' Hiking cost little outside boots, for she strode naked under her dress without stockings. Marie Festetics was almost the only one who could keep up with the Empress, who left her bodyguards panting in her wake. When the aged Emperor of Germany visited Ischl, he excused himself from her walks because of his advanced years. She raced along mountain paths for four to eight hours, covering long distances. When Prince Alexander of Hesse visited her, he thought she was too slender because of her excessive physical training and diet. She was living mainly on her special milk from her Jersey cows and eating very little. Her feet began to swell again, but she pushed on. She worked at her fencing, partially for the art and exercise, and also because the tight grey habit showed off her figure to perfection. Her dedication to fitness was also to her vanity.

With her absences, both her husband and her son took up with other women. Franz Josef had a long affair with the young wife of a railway official, Anna Nahowski; this plump and shrewd blonde extracted enough money from the Emperor to buy a town villa and mountain retreat. Crown Prince Rudolf's frequent liaisons were more like dalliances, although he appeared to have contracted some venereal infection as his father had. Certainly, his wife now banned him from her bedroom, ending any hope of a male heir. She had already been advised that she should not attempt to have another child. Elisabeth had put up the same barrier herself against Franz Josef after his Italian campaign, but she later relented after the usual mercury cure, although this remedy so badly affected her teeth that she kept her lips tight over her smile for most of her life. Often when she was amused, she looked as secretive as the Mona Lisa. Worse for Rudolf had been a fall on his head from a horse; he was not as good a rider as his mother. Taking morphia against the pain, he was becoming an addict, severely affecting his looks and his manner.

Already the Wittelsbach strain of outrageousness was corroding Rudolf as it was his cousin, Ludwig of Bavaria. The death of Richard Wagner in Venice in 1883 led the King nearer to the brink of sanity. 'Frightful! Terrible!' he cried out at the news. 'Let me be alone!' He insisted that the coffin of his composer be brought through Munich to Bayreuth. At the station, Siegfried's funeral march from *Götterdämmerung* was played. Ludwig remained in one of his extravagant castles, Hohenschwangau, where he ordered all the pianos to be covered with black crêpe. He felt that he had made Wagner, who had now deserted him. 'It was I', he declared, 'who saved him for the world.'

The influence of Wagner's operas was always the inspiration for the building of Ludwig's fantasies in architecture, as Ancient Greece was for Elisabeth of Austria. In one sense, the misfortune of the Wittelsbach cousins was to have enough resources to make their dreams come true. Both of them could have their myths turned into facts and fresco, bricks and stucco. Both shared a luxurious and childish taste, although Ludwig preferred opulence to recreation. The Bavarian Commission would be correct in declaring him unfit to govern before he completed his last masterwork on the island at the Herrenchiemsee. For his kingdom had already been beggared by the building of his castles at Linderhof and Neuschwanstein, which he had described to Wagner as sacred and inaccessible, although it has become since the Disneyland of Bavaria.

Elisabeth's classical follies were beginning with the planning of the Villa Hermes at Lainz, which she wanted to be 'Titania's enchanted castle'. To modern taste, this mock Renaissance villa designed by the architect of the Vienna Burgtheater is pompous and heavy with its décor overdone by the fashionable Makart, who pictured the Empress as Shakespeare's Fairy Queen in the frescos. The

ceiling of her ornate bedroom showed Zeus in his chariot appearing
from fleecy clouds. Even her gymnasium with its bars and weights
and scales and vaulting-horses was decorated in the Pompeian style
with two centaurs springing above the pediment of the door. Yet in
that period, the palatial villa in its game park seemed a paradise, at
least in the eyes and words of one of the last of the Emperor's aides-
de-camp, Baron von Margutti, remembering this original creation of
his dead mistress:

> Only a being with a rare feeling for Nature could have conceived
> the idea of making a country-place in the centre of the
> magnificent and extensive woods of the Lainz Tiergarten, woods
> completely cut off from the outside world by a wall miles in length
> and roamed at will by deer, stags, ibex, wild boar and other game.
> The villa itself, which was a masterpiece by virtue of its contents
> as well as its unity of style (Renaissance), showed in its most trivial
> detail that a woman of artistic gifts, exquisite taste and profound
> knowledge had reigned there. The wonderful peace, remote from
> the bustle of life, the splendid view over a delicious park which
> gradually merged into the dense and ancient woods which shut out
> the horizon on every side, the internal equipment of the château,
> which comprised an exquisite collection of choice *objets d'art*, – all
> this continually inspired me to reflection on the rare personality of
> the murdered Empress.

Such contemporary flattery and the continual indulgence of her
husband as long as she condoned his liaisons persuaded Elisabeth
that she had a rare taste for art, and indeed, the brothers Gustav and
Ernst Klimt did add some elegance to the Villa Hermes. But the
construction of her fairy palace did not satisfy her wanderlust, even
though Vienna was living out its golden age in music and dance, literature and the theatre, in which Franz Josef would soon find the
lasting involvement of his long life. His peace policy of the triple
alliance between Austro-Hungary and Germany and Russia with
Italy supporting them had allowed for peace and prosperity at home.
The French and the English had taken Egypt and the Suez Canal off

the wounded Ottoman Empire, which appeared to be in terminal decline. Only in the ungovernable Balkans were the dogs of war always baying at the throats of each other as well as of any invader. The sun of the Habsburgs was sinking in the east.

CHAPTER EIGHT

Royal Mistresses

❖

U NTIL THE NINETEENTH CENTURY, royal mistresses had been
a national institution and a political reality. The Queens of England
had to recognise the Kings' mistresses and often have them as Maids
of Honour or Women of the Bedchamber. When Queen Caroline
was dying, she had begged King George the Second to marry again.
The King had burst into tears and said, 'No – I will have – mistresses.'
'My God,' the dying Queen had said, 'marriage doesn't stop that.' The
British Kings had been particularly fond of actresses, as had the
Kings of Bavaria. Charles the Second had preferred Nell Gwynne
even to his principal mistress, Louise de Kerouaille, the Duchess of
Portsmouth. So when a mob attacked Nell in Hyde Park, she was able
to shout to them, 'No, no, good people, I am the English whore, not
the French one.' And when the King refused to ennoble one of his
sons by her, she held the child out of a high window and threatened
to throw him down till King Charles looked up and cried, 'God Save
the Earl of Burford!' and later made him Duke of St. Albans.
Preferment came from lying down in bed.

While he was heir to the throne, King George the Fourth had a
long liaison and a kind of marriage with Mrs Fitzherbert, who also
produced children. Her successor at the Royal Pavilion at Brighton,
Lady Conyngham, was dull and devastatingly described by the
Princess Lievens: 'Not an idea in her head; not a word to say of

herself; nothing but a hand to accept pearls and diamonds with, and an enormous balcony to wear them on.' The future William the Fourth had been hailed by his father on his return from Hanover as a 'Fine stud! Fine stud!,' but he had not enjoyed it much when he was there, writing home, 'I hate being in this damnable country, smoking, playing at twopenny whist and wearing great thick boots. Oh, for England and the pretty girls of Westminster; at least to such as would not clap or pox me every time I f...ed.' He had so many bastards including four sons, some by the actress Mrs Jordan, that he could not find enough titles for them when he did eventually reach the throne. Their presence at Court, however, made life livelier in a way that legitimate princes and princesses could not.

In spite of the scandal of her relationship with John Brown before his premature death, Queen Victoria could not extend her respectability to her eldest son Edward, who was known for his love of horses, women and the good life. He was the only Prince of Wales ever to give evidence in a divorce case. When asked by his counsel, 'Has there ever been any improper familiarity or criminal act between yourself and Lady Mordaunt?', the Prince of Wales replied, 'There has not.' There was a burst of applause in court. Edward took care to keep his many mistresses – aristocrats and actresses – under cover, although his love letters to Lady Warwick – he called her 'my own adored little Daisy Wife' – had to be suppressed by his son King George the Fifth. Like the Austrian Crown Prince Rudolf, Edward also liked low life when he travelled abroad, and the Moulin Rouge dancer, La Goulue, was heard to shout to him, '*Ullo, Wales, est-ce tu vas payer mon champagne?*'

The prolonged affair between the Emperor Franz Josef and the actress Katharina Schratt was actually encouraged by his wife Elisabeth, who felt almost grateful to her rival for consoling her husband when she continued to leave Vienna on her extensive travellings. Katharina had married a Hungarian, Nicholas Kiss, who had fled from his debts, leaving her and her son Anton or Toni. She petitioned the Emperor for a restoration of the lost revenue from the Kiss properties, which had been confiscated for twenty years after the Hungarian revolution. Yet she excused her plea, saying that she did not want to be there and make it: the Emperor must have thought he was seeing a ghost. Although the petition was not granted, Katharina met Franz Josef again in the February of 1885 at the Industrial Ball in the *Redoutensaal* of the Hofburg. The Emperor monopolised the actress in a long conversation; she had returned from America to act again at the Burgtheater, where she had been restored to favour with the help of Count Hans Wilczek, a wealthy explorer and patron of the arts. Franz Josef followed the encounter by frequent visits to the Burgtheater, where Katharina was promoted to leading roles. Knowing of her husband's interest in the actress, Elisabeth took her daughter Valérie to see Katharina perform and then put an extraordinary seal of approval on the projected liaison. She commissioned the Court artist Heinrich von Angeli to paint a portrait of Katharina as a present for her husband, and she came with him to approve the picture and the new imperial mistress at the final sitting in the studio. No wife could be more complaisant for her own good. Three days after the meeting, she became the mistress of the completed Villa Hermes, a gift for a gift.

At the begining of her marriage with Franz Josef, Elisabeth had been jealous and possessive. If he paid attention to any other woman, she made her feelings obvious. Her pregnancies, however, had separated the couple. She retired into seclusion, hating the temporary loss of her figure. Her husband looked elsewhere for his satisfactions. Yet all had been gossip about his infidelities until she had become infected after his Italian campaign. That hurt had driven her into an almost obsessive purity and concentration on preserving her beauty. Her delight after her coronation as Queen of Hungary had led to a reconciliation and the birth of Valérie; but still the Emperor could never excuse himself to her for the past corruption of her body. Their separate lives were now a fact of state. She would never return to him for long, but she would keep up a necessary and decorous façade. In a way, her stamp of approval on a discreet and established Viennese mistress would prevent any more wildness from him. Elisabeth could trust Katharina Schratt to watch over the Emperor's escapades more successfully than she had done and could not do with her son, Rudolf, the increasingly erratic heir to the throne.

Katharina hired a villa for the summer of 1886 near Ischl, where she knew that the Emperor also went for hunting and walking in the mountains in his Tyrolean costume of leather breeches and Alpine hat and thick boots. She had also become fond of hiking up the slopes and was able to join him on his expeditions. He came over to visit her for breakfast, as he would for the next thirty years. She was neither as beautiful nor as original as Elisabeth was. A good mother and cook and housekeeper, an amusing gossip and a devout Catholic, she was the antithesis of the Empress. She was the best of companions and the most comfortable of friends. The five hundred letters of the Emperor to her prove almost beyond doubt that they were sexual partners. Extracts from his correspondence reveal a jealous and committed lover:

> You must know that I adore you. You must sense it at least. My feelings grow all the time, ever since I experienced the great happiness of knowing you . . .
>
> Your conscience is hurting you again and making you very afraid that I consider you a seducer and could become angry with you. I could not do that, and as for seduction, it is true that you are so beautiful and lovely and good that you would be a danger to me, but I stay strong . . . And now I am saved from my stupid jealousy which pricks me so often . . .
>
> I torture myself often with the thought you love me no longer, not even a little bit . . . I think of you constantly and I long for you without pause . . .

The letters of the Emperor to the actress also proved the extraordinary compliance of his wife in the domestic triangle. Franz Josef wrote to Katharina in the November of 1887 from Gödöllö that he had eaten alone with the Empress and Valérie and was astonished to see champagne glasses on the table, 'as usually we do not allow ourselves the luxury of this wine'. Elisabeth had ordered the champagne so that they could all drink the health of Katharina. 'This was a successful and fine surprise.' The following summer, the Empress invited Katharina to Ischl to climb with her the Jainzen, which Valérie called 'Mamma's magic mountain'. Later, she apologised for leaving the Burgtheater because of the heat in the interval of a Schratt performance, to which the Emperor took the Kaiser Wilhelm. She even used the apartment of Ida Ferenczy in Vienna to conduct the actress personally to the imperial residence for a *rendezvous à trois*. And the two women exchanged advice on dieting and slimming pills, while the Emperor praised Katharina for wearing her hair in one play in the style of the Empress when she was young.

The health and neuroses of Elisabeth were taking a turn for the worse. Her punishment of her body from her hunting seasons had given her such pains that she had decided to take a cure by the sea in Amsterdam from the famous Dr Metzger, who prescribed massage for her headaches and her swollen and aching joints. She continued to ride and fence and stride along the shore, forcing herself to her limits. Yet Metzger bullied her into eating regular meals by telling her that she would become an old woman in a couple of years if she went on starving herself. For once, her vanity overcame her strict regime.

She remained shy and withdrawn from society, although not from her large travelling entourage and her young daughter. Valérie wrote that she and her mother shared the same stubborn and erratic character; both of them were uncompromising, yet impatient, and capable of wild enthusiasms for different reasons. Valérie did not approve of her mother shrinking from contacts with other people. 'If Mamma only wished it, how she could be adored!' But the Empress wished it less and less.

Yet Elisabeth was extraordinarily kind and sympathetic to those whom she wanted to work for her and trusted. When her sister Marie had recommended to her Mary Throckmorton as a governess for Valérie, the Empress wrote that her only wish was that Miss Throckmorton would devote her life to her child. 'Have I any chance of seeing this, my fondest wish, fulfilled?' It was for some years, with the Englishwoman serving as a devoted guardian to Valérie. For Elisabeth could always keep her houshold with her, if she wanted to do so. She was also most generous to her own family, paying for the upkeep of her sister Mathilde and her little daughter, when her husband Louis de Bourbon, Count of Trani, expired. Yet any trespass on her privacy or overfamiliarity by a friend was severely punished. The intruder was excluded. The slight smile was replaced by the cold face hid behind the fan. Elisabeth chose who was in favour and who was out.

She was losing touch with Britain. Earl Spencer had become Lord Lieutenant of Ireland for a second term, when Gladstone became the Prime Minister. Tragedy greeted his accession to office. His two secretaries were murdered in Phoenix Park near the gates of the Viceregal Lodge. Even so, he continued to support Home Rule for Ireland, and so he antagonised any last traces of favour by Queen Victoria, who had never forgiven him for taking the Empress Elisabeth to Ireland. He was even attacked by Rudyard Kipling for betraying his country in 'The Ballad of the Red Earl'. In fact, Spencer was merely being enlightened and anticipating the inevitable. Ruined in the agricultural depression at the end of the century, Earl Spencer would live on beyond Elisabeth until the death of King Edward the Seventh, who would himself have to wait until old age to succeed his mother on the throne.

More and more, Elisabeth took to literature as her escape. Her enthusiasm for Heine and Homer grew all the while. She was touched when her estranged son Rudolf unearthed some of the German poet's letters in manuscript and presented them to her. She was devoted to the *Iliad* and had a copy of a statue of the dying Achilles set on the seashore at the Villa Miramare. Stimulated by her daughter, she took to poetry again, resolving to build her own palace by the Mediterranean. As Ithaca was for Odysseus, her palace would be the refuge from her wanderings over the waves:

> Over you as your seagulls
> I'll wheel without rest.
> For me there's no corner
> To build a sure nest.

Her thoughts strayed back to her cousin Ludwig, whose increasing insanity was threatening his hold on the throne of Bavaria. She remembered the days at Possenhofen and on his island of roses in Lake Starnberg, when she was the Dove to his Eagle, and she wrote:

> Eagle, on your throne on the mountain snows,
>   This swift seagull circling here,
> Sends from the crests of the billows
>   Greetings to your kingdom far.

If Elisabeth was no Heine, she knew it. She felt guilty of writing poetry and consigned many of her verses to the sea, which had inspired them. She had heard of Schliemann's excavations at Troy and Mycenae and longed to visit the sites of his discoveries. She managed a trip on the royal yacht, the paddle steamer *Miramare*, to Corfu, which the Austrian consul had identified as the realm of Odysseus. She visited a small offshore island, which was said to be a ship turned to stone by Neptune; on it now stood a Greek church in a cypress grove. She then sailed past Santa Maura, where Sappho was meant to have died, and on to the Dardanelles. Because of bad relations with Turkey, she was not allowed to traverse to the Black Sea. Yet she did visit the ruins of Troy and stand by the mound which was traditionally the grave of Achilles. Her poem to the Greek hero claimed that the sun and the moon and the stars also stopped on their circuits to honour him. Sending out decoys, Elisabeth managed to wander through Smyrna and Rhodes almost unnoticed. Yet by the time the *Miramare* had docked at Cyprus and Port Said, even the Empress had tired of her odyssey and ordered the voyage home to Trieste. She returned to a crisis in the Balkans, where Serbia had invaded Bulgaria. The conflict ended with a Bulgarian victory, but threats of intervention by Vienna led to no territorial gains.

So terrible was the sciatica in Elisabeth's feet that she began to talk of suicide and of living in a hell on earth. She managed to survive through the Court balls of the winter, when her daughter Valérie was courted by the Archduke Franz Salvator, a Habsburg from Tuscany, although her father wanted her to make a political marriage with the Crown Prince of Saxony. Elisabeth's state of mind grew worse and worse, as the Master of her Household, Baron Nopsca, informed the retired Count Andrássy, who was himself ailing. 'She has a diseased mind,' the Baron wrote bluntly. 'And she leads a life of such utter isolation that she becomes even more ill.'

The Wittelsbach inheritance of instability was also unbalancing King Ludwig. The most eminent mental physician of the day, Dr Bernhard von Gudden, was asked by the Minister President of Bavaria to collect evidence on the state of the royal mind and to prepare a report. Members of Ludwig's household were the main witnesses to his strange behaviour. He feared human society even more than his cousin Elisabeth. His brother Otto had already been confined in a padded cell for fourteen years in Fürstenried Castle. Ludwig had spat at a bust of his uncle, the German Emperor, in the Linderhof, and he had ordered a gang of villains to take Crown Prince Frederick prisoner and manacle him and feed him on bread and water. Like the Roman Emperor Nero, he wanted to burn Munich to the ground and execute all the people of Bavaria – if they had only one neck. More violently, he struck and abused his servants, nearly throttling one of them and beating another so badly that he died within the year.

The summing-up of the report by von Gudden had three conclusions. The first was that King Ludwig was in an advanced state of the mental disturbance known as paranoia. The second and the third analyses were:

> Suffering as he does from this form of disease, which has been gradually and continuously developing over a great number of years, His Majesty must be pronounced incurable and a further decay of his mental faculties is certain.
>
> By reason of this disease, free choice on His Majesty's part is completely impossible. His Majesty must be considered as incapable of exercising government; and this incapacity will last, not merely for a full year, but for the whole of the rest of his life.

The report allowed for a *coup d'état* to place the nearest sane Wittelsbach relative, the sixty-five-year-old Prince Luitpold, on the throne. Staying at Ischl, Elisabeth received information about the conspiracy. She did not believe the evidence against her cousin, the Eagle. She asked Franz Josef to intervene and save Ludwig and his throne; but he checked the facts with his daughter Gisela and the Austrian ambassador in Munich, and he found that all was true. Ludwig was as insane as his brother Otto and his aunt, the Princess Alexandra. His dreams were of smashing a bottle on his mother's head and stamping on her breasts, also dragging his father from his coffin and boxing his ears. Elisabeth still would not believe that the King was a madman, 'only an eccentric who lived in a world of ideas'.

Given the situation, she moved to be in the vicinity at Feldafing, near her childhood home at Possenhofen. The first act of the tragedy was a farce. A cabinet deputation went with a writ to Neuschwanstein to apprehend Ludwig. He had the deputies seized by his guards and locked in the servants' quarters of the castle. Enraged, he threatened to put out the eyes of the prisoners and have the skin flogged off their backs. His commands were not carried out and the captives were released. Ludwig was, however, advised to go to Munich and show himself to the people, who would drive out the traitors. Yet his phobias prevented him from leaving Neu-schwanstein and his realm of fantasy. He succeeded in reaching Bismarck with an appeal for help. The German Chancellor gave him the same advice, that he must go to Munich. As he declared later, Bismarck had argued to himself: 'Either the King is sane, in which case he will do as I suggest, or he is really mad, and then he will not be able to overcome his fear of appearing in public. The King did not go to Munich. He took no decision. He no longer had the strength of will. He abandoned himself to his fate.'

The officer in charge of Ludwig's guards was recalled to Munich. Before he left, Ludwig asked him for some poison, as he could not go on living. The officer refused and departed, then Ludwig denied a plea from some loyal peasants to escort him to safety over the Austrian border or to Feldafing and sanctuary with the Empress Elisabeth. He was paralysed with premonition and thoughts of suicide by drowning in the Alpsee or throwing himself from the tower of the fortress. His enemies were, anyway, hurling him down from the highest summit into nothingness, as he told a servant. They were destroying his life. 'While I live, they call me dead and that I cannot endure.'

A medical commission, led by Dr von Gudden and protected by policemen, was now sent to restrain the abandoned monarch. Warders seized Ludwig by his arms. He was told that a Regency under Prince Luitpold had been proclaimed. He asked the doctor why he had been declared insane without an examination: there was no convincing answer. Ludwig then said that there was no need for the Regent to be so crafty. He would have abdicated and gone abroad rather than suffer treatment by von Gudden. How long would that last? When told that a period of more than a year had to pass before a Regency could be confirmed, the King replied that it would take less time. 'They can do what they did to the Sultan. It is quite easy to end a man's life.'

The arrest of Ludwig by von Gudden was the death warrant of both men. What followed was described in full to Queen Victoria at her command by Victor Drummond, the chief of the British Legation in Bavaria. The King had arrived at the Schloss Berg and had passed a quiet night. He had walked out the following morning with some keepers and a policeman. When he asked von Gudden why he was being followed, the doctor replied, 'It is to protect Your Majesty.' 'What,' replied the King, 'are there any Socialists here?' He was perfectly gentle and quiet and dined alone, before ordering von Gudden to take an evening stroll with him down to Lake Starnberg. He was so rational in his talk that the doctor sent the single keeper with them back to the Schloss.

When the pair had not returned by eight o'clock, a search was made of the grounds. Two hours later, their hats and cloaks were found on the water's edge, then their bodies floating with their faces downwards in four or five feet of water. 'The struggle must have been desperate and fearful . . . The body of Dr Gudden showed marks of great violence, his throat and forehead giving proofs of this, as the "combat" was in the lake itself in shallow water not more than two to three feet deep.' In Drummond's opinion, Ludwig must have rushed into the lake with von Gudden plunging after him.

Then the Dr must have seized the King who I imagine retaliated by striking the Dr a terrible blow on the forehead and by seizing his throat, and in fact mortally injured him. By so disabling his strength that falling in the water he was drowned, the King fulfilling at the same time his determination of suicide. It is a too fearful tale of tragedy.

Later theories of an attempt by Ludwig to escape or of a heart attack following his killing of Dr von Gudden or of a double murder by German or Bavarian political agents have not replaced Drummond's immediate opinion of the tragedy to Queen Victoria. As for the lying-in-state, Drummond wrote:

The bed upon which lay the King's remains was surrounded with palms and ferns and at the foot of the bed were some wreaths of white and red flowers, and upon the blue silk coverlet of the bed was a single bunch of white flowers. His Majesty's countenance was most beautiful, a smile upon his lips and an expression of heavenly repose, with no signs of a violent death . . . All the peasants, who could, came from the surrounding country to Berg to look their last upon their King, all deeply afflicted, men and women in their holiday dresses with their little children weeping as they walked along.

Elisabeth came, too, across the lake in a rowboat to pay her last respects. She stood in silence by the corpse of her cousin and left a wreath of water lilies. She was shaken by fears of her own mental stability and withdrew to take a cure at Gastein, where she encountered Bismarck and the aged German Emperor. Her pallor and the marks of suffering in her face shocked those who saw her. She told Valérie that she now accepted God as a God of vengeance as well as of grace and wisdom. She found Ludwig's end a judgement as well as a confirmation of the 'black clouds' that hung over the Wittelsbachs. The thought of death was always with her. It cleansed the soul as a gardener pulled out weeds. She had to be alone with that thought. No curious eyes should look into her garden where death was working. 'I hold my sunshade and my fan before my face so that it may do its work without interference.'

After several meetings with Elisabeth, the shrewd Carmen Sylva, Queen of Rumania, formed an incisive opinion of the Empress, who was incapable of veiling the truth with even the smallest shred of convention. She had no desire for the recognition of the world, which she utterly despised. If she was famous, it was in spite of herself. Yet there was 'a prodigious force latent in the Empress, which has to work itself off somehow. This excess has to find an outlet in riding and walking, travelling and writing, and she has to do everything with all her might, if only to escape the crushing pressure of circumstances.' When the Queen asked the Empress if her beauty was not a help to her in curing her shyness, the reply was: 'I am not shy any more, only bored! They dress me up in fine clothes and all sorts of jewels, and then I go out and say a few words to people for hours on end, till I can bear it no longer. At last, I hurry back to my room, tear it all off and write, while Heine dictates to me.' The Queen refused to condemn the Empress for her inspiration and hatred of convention, considering that fashions existed for women without taste, etiquette for people of no breeding, the Church for people with no religious belief, and the treadmill of society for those with no imagination or sympathy.

The Empress had been worried about another sister, Sophie, the Duchess of Alençon, who had caught scarlet fever and could have infected Valérie, but did not. She was showing signs of the Wittelsbach strain of madness by threatening to divorce her noble husband in favour of a medical practitioner; her brother Karl Theodor or 'Gackel' would become, indeed, a celebrated ophthalmic surgeon and found eye hospitals. Fortunately, Sophie's madness turned out to be only the after-effects of the infection, which was cured in a sanatorium. By now, Elisabeth was telling Valérie that the whole of the ancient stock of the Wittelsbachs and the Habsburgs was rotten and diseased. She feared the prophecy that the empire had begun with a Rudolf and would end with a Rudolf, the name of her son.

There were more family catastrophes to come. Elisabeth's

extravagant and deluded brother-in-law, King Francis the Second of Naples, would also commit suicide, in Zurich. One of her nephews, the Archduke Ladislas, was to be killed out hunting. And her beloved and erratic father, the Archduke Max, would die of a stroke, while she was away from Bavaria. Fatality seemed to be stalking her House at home. Perhaps the best way of eluding age and death was to run away from it in a frenzy. Movement was all.

CHAPTER NINE

Mayerling

❖

THE CROWN PRINCE RUDOLF and the Prince of Wales both thought that they would never reach the throne. The Emperor Franz Josef and Queen Victoria appeared able to live beyond eternity, depriving their issue of real power. Yet the even more aged German Emperor did finally expire in 1888 at the age of ninety-one. Unhappily, the Crown Prince Frederick was already condemned to die of cancer of the throat. He would reign with his wife Victoria for only three months. 'People in general consider us a mere passing shadow,' the new German Empress wrote from Berlin to her mother at Windsor Castle, 'soon to be replaced by reality in the shape of William!!'

The new Kaiser Wilhelm the Second only had to wait for ninety-nine days before taking over the German Empire and condemning his mother to virtual seclusion and retirement at her Friedrichshof, a mock Renaissance and Palladian house in a park near Kronberg and the Rhine below the forested Taunus hills. The widowed Empress felt her life had been wasted with all the preparations for playing a liberal and a reforming role, which had presented itself too late. 'I am only a powerless and useless relic of the past –' she confided to Queen Victoria, 'a shadow – of what once might have been – and never came – and who is to gather up the broken threads of the slender web we had been YEARS weaving – only to see it torn up – and trampled under foot in the most ruthless manner – I know not!'

Although a stripling of thirty beside the widowed German Empress Victoria, the Crown Prince Rudolf felt much as she did. He was consulting with liberal thinkers. He had his plans for the reform of Austro-Hungary. He was jealous over the accession of the new Kaiser, who was his contemporary. They had been friendly, until the righteous Wilhelm had reproved him for his dissolute habits. Now he foresaw only a tragic future for Germany in the hands of a ruler who would soon dismiss Bismarck himself 'like a dog'. As Rudolf wrote: 'Wilhelm the Second is unfolding himself. Before long he will start an awful confusion in the old Europe; he is just that sort of a person. His mind is limited by the grace of God; he is vigorous and stubborn like a bull, and regards himself the greatest genius – what more do you want? In a few years he will probably land Hohenzollern Germany in the ditch where it belongs.'

The Balkan crisis of the year before had pushed Rudolf towards political intrigue. Only the diplomacy of Bismarck had prevented the breakdown of the League of the Three Emperors and a possible conflict between Austro-Hungary and Russia, which instigated a military conspiracy to force Alexander of Battenberg off the Bulgarian throne in order to take the country under the direct control of the Tsar. The parliament in Sofia, however, elected an Austrian cavalry officer, Prince Ferdinand of Saxe-Coburg, as their next king: he was also a relative of Queen Victoria. The Tsar was furious, while the Habsburg Emperor had military credits voted for the army and the fortifications strengthened on the borders of Galicia. Bismarck, however, insisted on keeping the peace in the Balkans. 'What's Hecuba to us?' he asked. 'It is a matter of perfect indifference to us who governs Bulgaria, or what becomes of that country.' He secretly promised Russia that Germany would remain neutral if Austro-Hungary attacked in return for Russian neutrality in case of a French assault. Faced with no allies against the Tsar, the Emperor Franz Josef opted for the quiet continuation of his disparate empire, which his Minister President Count Taafe was just holding together with the soft wax of more concessions to minority peoples.

Following his mother's example, the Crown Prince Rudolf was a supporter of the Hungarian position, which wanted Magyar domination of the Slavs supported by Russia. He wanted no compromise with the Tsar Alexander the Third, who was soon to die, leaving Franz Josef as the senior of the three Emperors in their League. Rudolf called himself a liberal and wrote anonymous articles for the journalist Moritz Szeps and the *Neues Wiener Tagblatt*. Szeps was actually of little importance, yet he was thought to be politically dangerous. He encouraged the Crown Prince to believe that the secret police and reactionary Court circles were hounding them. 'I am constantly being followed and suspected,' Rudolf wrote to his editor, 'and I notice more and more every day how I am dogged by spies and informers, and how my movements are watched.' The Crown Prince was falling into the conspiracy theories of his mother, who avoided the Court at the Hofburg in order to escape any prying into her affairs. 'Unfortunately,' Rudolf continued, 'I know my enemies' tactics only too well.' As Elisabeth had, he too had to endure 'many abominable and shameful examples' of backstabbing and plots against him.

In another way, the Crown Prince was criticised for behaving like Edward, the Prince of Wales, in his relationships with Jewish financiers, who lent the heirs to their thrones large sums of money in return for future support. When Edward came to Vienna, Rudolf gave a supper for three. The only other guest was Moritz von Hirsch, the Brussels financier of the Orient railway scheme. Although both his father-in-law Leopold, King of the Belgians, and the Emperor Franz Josef were wealthy, the Crown Prince received little from the state purse or his wife's dowry. He was, however, more trapped in Austria by convention and rumour than the Prince of Wales, who could move freely from casino to music-hall to spa to shoot to boudoir and bedroom, without attracting too much adverse comment from the press at home. Rudolf's audiences and military duties and manoeuvres constricted him inside a uniform and a regime that left him with little power to exercise the command which he felt was his due, and which was not assigned by his father.

His political views were part of his bitter sense of being wasted as a ruler in limbo. 'Every year I become older, that is, less vital and less able,' he told Szeps. 'The eternal period of preparing oneself, this continuous waiting for the time when construction can begin, saps my creative energy!' His ambitions were hid under a cynical pessimism. While he appeared to back the nationalism that was sweeping Europe, he knew that it would be the downfall of the Habsburg Empire. On his birthday, he wrote: 'Thirty years mean a great period, if not one to rejoice over; much time is gone, spent more or less usefully, but without real deeds or successes. We live in a tottering, decaying age. Who knows how long things can still drag on?'

Curiously, his home and his ideal was the army, in which again his father would allow him no great place. Instead of being put in charge of the Second Army Corps, he was given the indeterminate post of the Inspector-General of the Infantry under the supervision of his uncle, the Archduke Albrecht. He resented such a restriction. His mind turned to a military coup, which was perhaps only wishful thinking. In two letters to Szeps, he had put forward his views on officers leading the nation.

> The army is the only depository of the imperial idea. One must protect and foster it, and secure its sympathies. The army is almost exclusively middle-class, liberal, imperialist, and animated by the idea of the great centralised State . . .
>
> I am persuaded more and more that serious, perhaps bloody, days are ahead, and that, for a short while or long, the army, as the last champion and bulwark of the state idea, of law and order, will have to intervene to save the bourgeoisie and imperial organisation.

Heirs to the throne were bound to become the rivals of their fathers. Greater than Oedipal jealousy over the mother was the wish to replace paternal power. The Empress Elisabeth saw these characteristics too clearly in her son. She once observed that in all ages the old regarded the young as a danger to the state and strove to keep them away from politics. This explained the emphasis in Ancient Greece on gymnastic and musical competitions. Such distractions took youthful minds off serious matters. Their ambitions were in winning games, which exhausted their desires. 'We do the same,' she said. 'We throw a ball to the young to tire them out. Play is the substitute for war. There would possibly be more wars if the old were not so selfish. They are just as eager for war as the young, except that they have other motives, but not better ones. The young allow themselves to be sacrificed, and forgive those who sacrifice them, if only to be rid of the superfluous energy that stifles them . . .'

Yet Rudolf was estranged from the wisdom of his mother, who had never been much of a restraint on him. 'She loved the Crown Prince well enough,' his old tutor Colonel Latour von Thurnberg would tell the Emperor's aide von Margutti. She was, however, 'far too tolerant of everything he did, good and bad alike, and always gave him help and protection so that even when he grew up he always relied on his mother getting him out of his most foolish scrapes. Unfortunately, too, she never had any special influence on his real training – his childhood, when a mother's hand was so essential. It was just about then that she was away for years at a time . . . The Crown Prince's passion for freedom was an inheritance from his mother and it was so strong that Court life and the strict etiquette which the Emperor always exacted seemed to him a horrible relic of the Middle Ages. Like his mother he had as little to do with it as he possibly could.'

Now the time had come for Elisabeth to lose her adored daughter Valérie in marriage. Her father Duke Max had recently died in the palace in Munich, and there on her birthday, Christmas Eve, she announced the engagement of Valérie to the Archduke Franz Salvator of Tuscany. The Baroness Redwitz was standing to welcome Elisabeth and the young couple, carrying bouquets to offset the effect of the mourning that they were wearing for the Duke. The Empress arrived first, walking quickly up the stairs. 'She looked so young and lovely, so alert and fresh in her complexion, in spite of her fifty-one years. The Archduchess Valérie could not speak for happiness. The Archduke Salvator gave the impression of extreme youth.' After telling an old maid that the betrothed pair looked as if they were dancing on ice, the Empress withdrew to her care from her attendants and did not appear for family meals. 'She was busy studying modern Greek, and had a Greek with her. The rest of her suite consisted of a doctor, a Swedish masseur, a sturdy woman to rub her down, and the usual servants' – an entire menagerie, as Valérie called it. Elisabeth, however, did find the time to pay a solitary visit to the burial place of King Ludwig the Second as well as her father's grave. She kept out of sight as far as possible, so that the citizens of Munich could only glimpse in the English Garden the distant figure of a woman shrouded under a black veil, which seemed to show her grief not only for her father and cousin, but also for the looming separation from her daughter.

In spite of their distance from Rudolf, both Franz Josef and Elisabeth and her Countesses warned him against any connection with the Levantine Baltazzi family and the Baroness Hélène von Vetsera, whose daughter Marie at seventeen was an exquisite beauty with dark hair almost as long as the tresses of the Empress. The Emperor warned Katharina Schratt about riding with Hektor Baltazzi, who did not have 'an entirely correct reputation in racing and money matters'. When Rudolf came to Marie Festetics to ask her to receive the Baroness Vetsera, the Countess replied, 'She may make assignations with Your Imperial Highness elsewhere, but not in my sitting-room. I have no desire for her society.' And the Empress told her husband that the way the Baroness Vetsera behaved with Rudolf was unbelievable. 'She is always in close pursuit of him.' Ten years before, Marie Festetics had laughed away the threat, writing that the Baroness Vetsera was in no way attractive, but 'so cunning and knows so well how to use people to get herself to Court and make herself and her family count for something. Meanwhile her daughter is coming up, slowly, to be sure, but one builds from the ground up!' Now Marie Vetsera had come up and the ground was prepared.

The Baroness Vetsera finally caught up with the Crown Prince at the Shrovetide Polish Ball: the bait was her dark and alluring daughter. Once Rudolf had seen her, he was enchanted. Her mother's long courtship of the Empress's niece, the Countess Larisch-Wallersee, made her agree to the use of her sitting-room for secret assignations between the Crown Prince and Marie Vetsera. She had once aspired to Rudolf's hand, but she had been married off to a cavalry officer by the Empress. What jealousy of him or his mother drove her to act the pander was not revealed in her two inaccurate accounts of the fatal affair. She only displayed her malice and her love of intrigue.

The liaison with Marie Vetsera continued for a year, although Rudolf did not renounce his other amours. The chief of them was the dancer Mitzi Caspar, who gave her favours to him and his fellow officers. He had once had gonorrhoea, which had alienated his wife; but medicines from the Court Pharmacy, zinc sulphate and copana balsam as well as mercury, had cured him. Most probably, Marie Vetsera became pregnant, while Rudolf's wife was now sterile in spite of treatment at the fertile waters of Franzensbad in Bohemia. The condition of the Vetsera girl was the prelude and the likely explanation for the approaching tragedy at the hunting lodge of Mayerling.

The exposure of the affair had begun at the Golden Jubilee of Queen Victoria in London, where the Crown Prince had gone. His wife Stéphanie had refused to accompany him because the Vetseras would be there. Moreover, she was already in love with a Polish count. The couple were so far apart that Rudolf was said to have approached Pope Leo the Thirteenth for an annulment of his marriage, possibly in order to legitimise an heir by Marie Vetsera. However that was, a reception was given in the late January of 1889 at the house of the Ambassador of the German Empire, Prince Heinrich of Reuss. This occasion marked the birthday of the Kaiser Wilhelm the Second, and so the whole of the Austrian Court was in attendance. Rudolf was wearing his Prussian Uhlan cavalry uniform, while his father the Emperor was in Austrian full dress. The Crown Princess Stéphanie was there, as were the four Archdukes led by Albrecht. Along with most of the nobility and diplomatic corps in Vienna, somehow the Vetseras had arranged an invitation. And Rudolf's mistress Marie was dazzling, in the opinion of Count Josef Hoyos. 'Her eyes seemed larger than ever that evening, they glittered with a mysterious light, her whole body positively seemed to glow.' She stood face to face with the Crown Princess Stéphanie and refused her a curtsy. This public insult made the wife of Rudolf leave the room.

The Crown Prince was summoned by his father to the Hofburg and was told that his relationship with Marie Vetsera must end. Certainly, his mistress could never again be allowed to insult his wife in front of the Court and the diplomatic corps. If not, Rudolf would have to resign his commission and perhaps his right to the succession, as Maximilian had before the catastrophe of his Mexican adventure. Possibly Rudolf's request for an annulment of his marriage had also reached the Emperor's ears from the Archbishop of Vienna. Whatever occurred, Rudolf spent his last night in Vienna with Mitzi Caspar, before leaving for Mayerling and inviting two hunting companions, Count Hoyos and his brother-in-law Prince Philipp of Coburg, to follow him there. Shadowed by the secret police, Mitzi Caspar told them that Rudolf had previously asked her to join him in a suicide pact at the 'Hussar Temple' near Mayerling as a gesture to the war dead for Emperor and Fatherland, also as a romantic echo of Goethe's novel, *The Sorrows of Young Werther*. He was always playing with revolvers and kept a skull on his table. There was no question that killing himself was not on Rudolf's mind, probably as a revenge on his forbidding father. For in the explanations of psychiatry, then budding in Vienna with Krafft-Ebing and Freud, the destruction of oneself was also a retaliation against a real or imaginary persecutor. Rudolf had been, indeed, treated by Krafft-Ebing for a 'nervous complaint'.

On the following morning in Vienna, Rudolf told the head-keeper of his shooting estate at Mayerling that he was expecting a telegram. When it arrived, it was rushed to his rooms. 'When I took it in,' the keeper reported, 'the Crown Prince was standing by his bedroom window with his watch in his hand and looking down into the Franzensplatz. He opened the telegram hurriedly, read it quickly, folded it, and threw it on the table. As I was going out I heard the Prince say: "Yes, it must be so."'

Rudolf now arranged for Marie Vetsera to join him at Mayerling through the connivance of his confidential coachman, Josef Bratfisch. With the Countess Larisch-Wallersee as a go-between, the pair reached the hunting lodge unseen, except by Rudolf's servants, particularly his valet Loschek. Marie deceived her family by leaving a

suicide note in her bedroom: 'Dear Mother, By the time you read this
I shall be in the Danube.' On behalf of the Baroness Vetsera, her
matchmaker and the niece of the Empress, the Countess Larisch-
Wallersee, now went to the secret police, who would do nothing, sus-
pecting her involvement in an elopement by the Crown Prince. She
fled Vienna, feeling that she was heavily compromised.

At Mayerling, Rudolf hid Marie Vetsera in his apartment. When
his two hunting friends arrived, Count Hoyos and Prince Philipp of
Coburg, he sent them out on their sport for the day. He excused
himself by telegram from having a dinner of reconciliation and
celebration of Valérie's engagement with the Emperor and the
Empress at the Hofburg, although Prince Philipp of Coburg was
able to return to Vienna for the occasion. The inactivity of the secret
police was extraordinary. They refused to meddle in the scandal. On
the night of 29th January 1889, Rudolf went to bed early, telling
Loschek that he should not be disturbed, even if it were the Emperor
himself. He appeared in a dressing-gown early next morning and told
Loschek to wake him again at 7.30 a.m.: then he locked the bedroom
door behind him. Prince Philipp arrived back from Vienna to find
Count Hoyos and Loschek debating whether to break open the door,
for there was no sign of Rudolf well after eight o'clock. The valet
smashed one of the door panels to disclose Rudolf and Marie
Vetsera lying on the bed, soaked in their blood. Loschek undid the
lock, went in and returned to say, 'They are both dead. They are poisoned with strychnine' – a poison which could cause haemorrhages.

The Prince of Coburg had a breakdown at the bloody sight. Count
Hoyos told Bratfisch to drive him at the gallop to Baden station,
where the train from Trieste would stop. He told the stationmaster
that the Crown Prince was dead, and the official telegraphed the
Rothschild bank in Vienna that Rudolf had shot himself. On his
arrival, Hoyos went to the Crown Prince's Master of the Household,
Count Bombelles, to tell him the news. They alerted Baron Nopsca
of the Empress's household and Count Paar, the aide-de-camp of
the Emperor. They decided to inform the Empress first through the
good offices of her trusted Ida Ferenczy. She found Elisabeth
engaged in her Greek studies, learning Homer from her tutor.

Weeping, Ida begged her mistress to receive Baron Nopsca, who told her that Rudolf was dead. He had been poisoned by his mistress.

Elisabeth went into convulsions, crying, 'No, no, no.' But when the Emperor was announced, she recovered herself and asked to be alone with him. After a while, she took him to Katharina Schratt, who was in the Hofburg as well. The two women comforted Franz Josef as best they could, Elisabeth hiding her own grief, allowing her rival the actress to solace her husband in the generosity of her spirit. Later, the Emperor would tell Count Paar, 'If it had not been for my wife, who kept me going with her superhuman strength of mind even though she was struck down with sorrow herself, I should utterly have gone under.'

When Elisabeth told Valérie about the death of her brother, the young woman presumed that he had killed himself. As for his wife, Stéphanie, she tried to explain that she knew Rudolf was already mentally disturbed, but the Empress would not hear of that, turning away as if she were being accused of passing on to her son some of the Wittelsbach strain of insanity. In fact, Stéphanie thought that her mother-in-law believed her to be responsible for part of the guilt of the tragedy. The culmination of these dreadful interviews for the Empress was the incursion of the Baroness Hélène von Vetsera, begging her to help to find Marie. Elisabeth had to inform her that her daughter was dead along with the Crown Prince. What the Baroness always had to assert was that Rudolf had died of a heart attack. This was the version which appeared the following morning in the Viennese press. There was no mention of any other body.

Nothing could be hidden for long. Three of many versions of the tragedy were soon current in Vienna – the poisoning of the Crown Prince by his mistress, his suicide with hers, and his death by natural causes. A medical deputation of five led by the imperial doctor Widerhofer set out for Mayerling to examine the two corpses. Widerhofer's immediate report was that Rudolf had shattered the top of his skull with his army revolver, blasting his brains all over the room. The half-naked body of Marie Vetsera had been killed at short range by a single bullet in her forehead, although her hair had been arranged loosely over her shoulders. A rose had been placed between her folded hands. The right index finger of the Crown Prince had stiffened round the trigger of the murder weapon. The glass on the bedside table contained brandy and not strychnine. Rudolf had apparently shot his mistress some eight hours before himself in a suicide pact. When Widerhofer informed the Emperor of his findings, Franz Josef angrily insisted that his son had died of poison, not a bullet wound. Widerhofer's only crumb of comfort was that the remnants of Rudolf's brain seemed to be abnormal, proving that he was not of sound mind when he had killed himself, so allowing for a Catholic burial. Eventually, the Emperor accepted the medical evidence, sobbing that his son had died like a tailor and a coward.

A new version of the end of the Crown Prince was now put in circulation. He had been shot in a hunting accident; the death of Marie Vetsera was suppressed. This rumour led to another later explanation of the tragedy. Rudolf had been having an affair with the attractive wife of a local gamekeeper, who had crushed his skull with his gun butt in rage and jealousy. Various park keepers later asserted to Count Apponyi, the Grand Chamberlain of Hungary, that they had carried the corpse of the Crown Prince from outside the game-keeper's lodge to his bedroom at Mayerling. This account held the death of Marie Vetsera to be a suicide, when she found that her lover had been killed. According to von Margutti, Count Hoyos himself believed in this murder of passion and informed a Hungarian relative of the case.

The Crown Prince had left farewell letters to his mother and his wife and others, but not to his father. To Elisabeth, he declared that he no longer had any right to live; she later had the letter burned. To Stéphanie, he stated that she was rid of his presence and burden; she should live happily in her own way. He was going calmly to his death which alone could save his good name. And yet to Valérie, he wrote, 'I do not die willingly.' Even so, there was no immediate proof of a conspiracy to assassinate him. In the sudden deaths of royalty, theories of malpractice are like knots of vipers. At each attempt to unravel the mystery, new snakes writhe off in a squirm of possibilities. The eggs of the serpent hatch for ever.

The body of the Crown Prince was carried in a sealed railway wagon to Vienna and the Hofburg, where an autopsy took place and a death mask was impressed. For the lying-in-state, the shattered head was reconstructed with wax and hair and rouge. An official bulletin was issued that the Crown Prince had killed himself while temporarily insane. The story of his apparent slaughter of Marie Vetsera had to be suppressed, although most of Vienna had already heard of the rumour. Whatever the truth of the events at Mayerling, it was wholly important, as the King of the Belgians wrote to his brother, that the fiction of self-destruction was maintained. 'Suicide and madness are the only means of avoiding an unforgettable scandal.' The murdered mistress had to disappear, and yet receive a Catholic burial.

Her intriguing mother, the Baroness Vetsera, was persuaded to flee to Venice by the Minister President Taafe himself. She would never set eyes on the body of her daughter, but she insisted that two of her relatives be present at Marie's burial in the cemetery of the Shrine of Heiligenkreuz. The abbot there had been persuaded to allow her last resting-place to be in consecrated ground, even though an arranged post-mortem examination declared that Marie had died by her own hand, and not from the gun point of the Crown Prince.

The report of the Police Commissioner Habreda was a ghoulish account of her burial. Two of her relatives, her uncle Alexander Baltazzi and her brother-in-law Count Georg Stockau, dealt with her body at Mayerling. To stop the head lolling, a stick was fixed along her spine, held in place by scarves knotted over her forehead and breasts. She was clothed in her shift and her dress, her shoes and her stockings, and then was covered with a hat and coat of otter fur. The two men lifted the corpse into a closed carriage and held up their dead relative between the pair of them. As if she were the Cid, the lifeless victim rode out in a grisly charade on her last journey to Heiligenkreuz, three miles down the slippery road in a howling storm. The report of Commissioner Habreda continued:

> At last, we were able to make out the cortège in the darkness. Count Stockau and Alexander Baltazzi were in the first carriage. They had the body of the young baroness between them and were

holding it up by the arms . . . I motioned the carriage to go straight on to the cemetery, without stopping at the convent. Owing to the hurricane which was raging and roaring and to the rain which was falling in torrents, the carriages had the greatest difficulty in making any progress at all.

Count Stockau's coachman was even forced to screw footnails to the shoes of his horses, which were sliding all over this hilly and icy road. By this means we at length reached the cemetery gates. The bell of the church was then striking midnight.

Count Stockau, Mr Baltazzi, Commissioner Gorup and I dragged the corpse out from the depths of the carriage, and we carried it as best we could into the chapel, where we found the coffin, fashioned very roughly out of four planks, and in it we deposited the body.

But the grave was far from ready; the work having been greatly retarded by the bad weather. In spite of all his efforts, Commissioner Gorup could not persuade the two diggers to work faster. The walls of the grave crumbled in several times and, in their superstitious fright, the two men refused to continue their work, saying it was a bad omen.

We returned then to the Abbey, leaving some police officers guarding the corpse . . . The grave was not ready until seven o'clock in the morning. We then went back to the cemetery, nailed down the coffin, over which Father Grünbock said prayers for the dead, and then bore it to the grave. The howling tempest made it difficult to keep on our feet, as we lurched and stumbled on our way. Count Stockau, Mr Baltazzi, Commissioner Gorup and I could advance no quicker than one step at a time.

The gravediggers, who were crossing themselves all the time, persisted in raising all kinds of objections, although the benediction given by the Prior ought to have reassured them. At last, the first handfuls of earth struck the coffin. It was half-past nine in the morning before we left the cemetery.

There was no death certificate, although months later, an agent from the office of the Court Marshal did sign the parish register of deaths in the name of Marie Vetsera. Eventually a vault would be constructed for her remains within the Shrine. This monument would bear the inscription from the Book of Job: MAN COMETH FORTH LIKE A FLOWER AND IS CUT DOWN.

All copies of Viennese papers which denied the official version of the tragedy were confiscated. But even with censorship, the facts could not be suppressed. German newspapers soon began to report on the likelihood that there had been a double suicide or that the Crown Prince had died at the hands of a jealous gamekeeper. Two other witnesses, the Italian ambassador at Vienna and the father of Princess Louisa of Tuscany, who saw the body of Rudolf, asserted later that his skull had been stove in by a champagne bottle, wielded either by Marie Vetsera or by his drunken companions or by assassins. The ambassador told an Italian journalist from the *Corriere della Sera*, 'The skull appeared to be smashed – shattered as if from a blow of a bottle or a big stick. It was horrible. The hair, the fragments of bone, had been driven into the brain. The wound gaped open beneath and behind the ear in such a fashion that it seemed materially impossible that it could have been self-inflicted. A suicide? Surely not! It was an assassination – I am absolutely positive of that.'

This conspiracy theory started more serpents of rumour. Investigations by the secret police disclosed Rudolf's connections with Count Károlyi, a Magyar patriot who was encouraging Rudolf to be crowned as King of Hungary and perhaps mount a coup there against his father. Certainly, the sick Andrássy paid a private visit to Elisabeth after the death of the Crown Prince to discuss the future of Hungary without him. There would be little backing for Budapest within the imperial family, for Rudolf had been Elisabeth's lone supporter in her campaign for more Magyar independence. As she told Valérie in Vienna, 'All the people who have had nothing but evil to say of me, ever since I came here, now have the satisfaction of knowing that I shall leave this life without a trace of myself remaining in Austria.'

Elaborately dressed and made up, Rudolf was put to lie in state in the Hofburg chapel for two days before being taken to the burial shrine of the Habsburgs, the Capuchin Church. At the funeral service, the Emperor was accompanied by his daughter Gisela; neither Elisabeth nor her daughter Valérie nor Rudolf's wife Stéphanie could bear to go. A veiled Elisabeth visited the crypt the following night to stay with the body of her son for some time before she left. She is said to have cried out his name once. Her calm remained impenetrable. 'We shuddered at the Empress's terrible composure,' one companion of Andrássy recorded of their visit of condolence to Vienna, 'and at the expression in her eyes. No one could bear sorrow more nobly than this splendid woman.'

Doubtless, the assassination of the heir apparent was the quickest way of toppling the regime. Other local witnesses testified to a huge struggle in the bedroom of Mayerling with smashed furniture and many bullet holes in the walls, while the Archduchess Maria Theresa and Duke Miguel of Braganza claimed that Rudolf had been badly hurt in his resistance to the murderers. The German ambassador in Vienna confirmed that the wounds on the Crown Prince's body were not where they were meant to be, and that six shots had been fired from the revolver in his hand, which did not belong to him. Soviet troops would desecrate Rudolf's tomb after the Second World War. Some of his relics would be destroyed, but in a later exhumation, his skull was found to have an oval hole seven centimetres wide at the top with no sign of an exit wound made by any bullet.

Insinuations that Rudolf might have been eliminated by Austrian secret agents for political reasons had two curious corroborations at the time, when political figures shed their ambitions. The ally of the Habsburgs in Serbia, King Milan, decided to abdicate. He declared that Rudolf's suicide had made him fear for his own sanity and life. And Rudolf's cousin and friend, the Archduke Johann Salvator of Tuscany, who had been a radical critic of the Austrian army as well as a supporter of Bulgaria and Hungary against the Emperor, also gave up the fray. In a civil ceremony in London, he married an opera-singer, renouncing his rank and titles, and assuming the name of Orth after one of his castles. He proceeded to buy a ship in Liverpool, named the *Santa Margarita* after his morganatic wife. He had all available records of the vessel destroyed and set off over the oceans, as if he were the Flying Dutchman. After the death of the

Crown Prince of Austro-Hungary, Orth seemed to inherit the persecution mania of Rudolf. He believed that secret agents would follow him to the ends of the earth to do away with him as well. The unreliable Countess Larisch-Wallersee later claimed that there had been a plot by him and Andrássy to seize the throne of Hungary; Rudolf had given her a sealed box for safe-keeping, which she passed on to the Archduke Johann after the débâcle at Mayerling. Although his flight seemed to add weight to her melodrama, only his temperament connected him with the fate of the Wittelsbachs and the Habsburgs. 'Believe me,' he wrote to an old mentor, 'I know that I have failed. Yet I have conducted an inquest on myself of a kind I would not wish on my worst enemy.' For the time being, it had 'broken my spirit and clouded my soul'. He chose exile rather than immolation.

Other theories of the deaths at Mayerling had Rudolf committing suicide because of the failed *coup d'état* in Hungary. The other corpse on the bloody bed there was stolen from a mortuary, while Marie Vetsera was taken on an Austrian battleship to Texas, where she married an American farmer and became the mother of a large family. There were also reports of an 'American duel' over Countess Aglaia Auersperg, who had been Rudolf's mistress. In this version, the Crown Prince drew the black bullet offered to him by her brother, and so was obliged to kill himself within six months. One of the four Baltazzi brothers, Heinrich, was also said to have confronted Rudolf over his niece Marie at Mayerling. Firing at the intruder, the Crown Prince was alleged to have killed his mistress accidentally, before having his skull smashed in by her uncle. Some groups even claimed that Franz Josef had once had an affair with the Baroness Hélène von Vetsera, making Marie the half-sister of Rudolf. Once the young couple had found out that their love was incestuous, they did away with themselves.

The snakes of conspiracy and innuendo slithered in every direction. Although the assassination theories were largely discounted, an amazing assertion would be made by the last reigning Habsburg Empress Zita of Bourbon-Parma in her very old age. She would claim in 1989 that she had heard from both of Elisabeth's daughters, the Archduchesses Gisela and Valérie, that Rudolf and Marie Vetsera had been murdered by French agents, after he had refused to carry out a *coup d'état* in Hungary. Indeed, Lord Salisbury had told Queen Victoria a hundred years before that he was positively convinced that the Crown Prince had been murdered, although the Queen had discounted the theory, writing in her journal, 'It seems poor Rudolf has had suicide on the brain for some time past. Everything points to it.' According to the Empress Zita, who had only come to the throne because of the assassination in 1914 of the Archduke Franz Ferdinand and his morganatic wife Sophie Chotek at Sarajevo, the attempts by Franz Josef to hush up the truth about the end of Rudolf were forced upon him in order to save his throne. 'I could not do otherwise,' he is said to have said to her. 'The existence of the monarchy was at stake.' By her version, Mayerling was the first act of the destabilisation of the Habsburg Empire, while Sarajevo would bring down the curtain.

Of all the motives given for the tragedy, the revenge of Rudolf on his father is the most likely. His killing of himself was a lethal protest of impotence and defiance. The catalyst may well have been a botched abortion on Marie Vetsera. The deluge of blood on their funeral bed was too great to come from their official head wounds. The act appears to have been premeditated, for an onyx ashtray was found in the Hofburg rooms of the Crown Prince, on which Marie had scrawled, 'Better a revolver than poison. A revolver is more certain.' She had also written to a family friend, 'We are curious to see what the next world looks like.' The haemorrhage caused by a failed attempt to terminate her pregnancy was likely to have forced Rudolf into the murder of his mistress and his own suicide, which might be passed off by state propaganda as an assassination because of his dabbling in politics in Hungary.

Yet the imperial efforts to cover up the crime would not hold. This was already the age of mass journalism and the telegraph and the photographer. The German press soon published the truth of Rudolf's suicide, followed by allegations about the tragic end of Marie Vetsera. At the same time, Elisabeth was thought to have become insane with grief. She had banned the Countess Larisch-

Wallersee from the Austrian Court because of her complicity with the Vetsera family. Yet she did not go mad, even if she tortured herself with the possibility that she had transmitted a mental disorder to Rudolf. As she told one of her medical advisers, Dr Kerzl, '"The Emperor should never have married me; I have inherited the taint of madness! My son did too, or else he would never have treated me so!"' As Kerzl went on to say, 'In moments of mental depression she unguardedly used similar words to others, so that many people gradually came to believe it was true and in the end that view was held. Quite wrongly! The Empress certainly had her peculiarities: she was none the less one of the most intelligent and pleasant women I have ever met.'

In her magnanimity, Elisabeth brought in Katharina Schratt to help her husband in his grief. 'Your true friendship and your comforting, quiet sympathy', the Emperor wrote to the actress, 'were a great consolation to us in these recent terrible days. The invitation to call yesterday came from the Empress, who is so glad to have you here.' Although he praised the strength of Elisabeth, he could not disguise her general melancholy. She did not want to recover from the loss of her son. 'We live on quietly in silent grief,' he wrote after some weeks to Katharina. 'In my opinion, there is no improvement in the sad mood. It will prove very hard particularly for the Empress to rid herself of some of the pain.'

Elisabeth's state of mind became worse. Franz Josef found her growing sadder and quieter. She could not decide 'to see anyone at all, so that she stays alone much too much with her gloomy thoughts'. He could still occupy himself for twelve hours a day working on the necessary affairs of state, but with the cold winter weather, the rheumatic pains in the legs of the Empress recurred violently, affecting her nerves and making her sleep badly. Her only distractions were her walks in the gardens and her Greek lessons.

Another disaster also threatened her, the loss of the great love of her life, her daughter Valérie. Her betrothal to the Archduke Franz Salvator provoked a storm of love from her mother, which she recorded in her diary. 'I really love nobody but you,' Elisabeth wrote. 'If you leave me my life is at an end. But one can only love like this once in a lifetime. All one's thoughts are of the beloved, it is entirely one-sided – one requires and expects nothing from the other person.' Indeed, she spoke in another vein to Franz Salvator, as if she had already renounced her passion for her daughter. She declared that she did not want to marry Valérie to him in order to keep her nearby. 'Whenever she marries, it is the same to me whether she goes to China or remains in Austria.'

In fact, the loss of her son to the grave and her youngest daughter to a husband would send Elisabeth on her own restless wanderings until her own death – if not as far as China, then soon to Corfu. Meanwhile, the furthest exile from Mayerling was to sail on the *Santa Margarita* to Montevideo. Loaded with gold bullion, that ship would set off with Johann Orth and his diva and disappear without trace off the coasts of Argentina. There would be no survivors and no wreckage. Searches would be carried out on the orders of the Emperor Franz Josef; but nothing has yet been found of his Habsburg relation and his crew. Orth and his vessel may have foundered in the terrible seas off Cape Horn. His intention was said to have been the purchase of a ranch in Chile. Rumour had him leading a rebellion there and even serving as a general in China. Yet these stories were as wild as many of the fabrications about the end of Rudolf and Marie Vetsera at Mayerling. Imperial tragedies breed fantastical plots without end over the decades. The bones of the royal families are never allowed to rest in peace. The ashes blow always in the wind.

CHAPTER TEN

Greece, with Gifts

❖

The Emperor Franz Josef ordered the destruction of Mayerling and the building of a convent of Carmelite nuns in its place. He wished to hallow the ground of the crime of the Crown Prince, to replace bad memories with constant prayer and penance. When he visited the new cloisters and chapel to celebrate Mass on All Souls' Day, he was moved to write to Katharina Schratt about the comforting and soothing peace in the region and the decision of the nuns to bury themselves within the stern walls. 'In each cell and on the dining table of the nuns, there stands a stone skull. Yet they seem well pleased and will pray a good deal, so that the purpose of my bequest will be fulfilled.' Two days later, he heard on Edison's phonograph for the first time a 'Hurrah' shouted for him in Berlin and the *Radetsky March* and the national anthem played by the band of the Austrian Railroad Regiment. With the burial of the past, the future of mass communications had come with a vengeance. The scandals of the Habsburg family would be transmitted more quickly round the globe.

Franz Josef was providing for his beloved actress as well as for his wife, who had commissioned the building of a dream palace in Corfu. To Katharina Schratt, he gave a house at 9 Gloriettegasse, backing on to the gardens at Schönbrunn and built in the baroque style with a conservatory, which led Katharina to call the place 'her glass palace'. Elisabeth would never visit her there, although the Empress would present her with the key of a new villa at Ischl, named the Villa Felicitas, again across the park from the imperial villa. The triangle of connivance persisted with the Emperor using his wife's need to take a cure, in order to persuade the actress to return from the South of France and be with him. Elisabeth would not go to Wiesbaden for treatment, unless Katharina returned to console Franz Josef. As he wrote, it was 'her obstinate resolution not to leave me so long as you are not back in Vienna'.

In the end, Elisabeth did leave for her brutal massage at the hands of Dr Metzger, while Katharina brought back holy water from Lourdes to bless the melancholy of both the Emperor and the Empress. Soon Elisabeth was back on the Jainzen with her Greek tutor. Franz Josef was amused at the prospect, hoping that the walk on her favourite mountain would cheer up his wife, but he was curious 'as to how the Greek climbs and how often he will fall on the way down'. He himself missed Rudolf less and less except when stag-hunting; then the remembrance of his promising young heir killing game with him made him weep.

Valérie now agreed with her dead brother that Austro-Hungary would fall apart along with the breakdown of the Habsburg family. Only her father held it together by his devotion to duty in a decaying state. She was a witness to the growing gulf between Franz Josef and Elisabeth, so opposite in their characters, so noble in bearing their mutual grief. Her mother made her anxious, as she was great in spirit and incompetent in detail. Her father, however, accepted the monotony of his dedicated existence, alleviated by his breakfasts with Katharina Schratt. Elisabeth was afraid that her increasing melancholy and her belief that God had intended her to become a hermit could lead to a misunderstanding with her husband. Valérie heard her mother asking Jehovah to take her to Him, so that Franz Josef would be free and her daughter undisturbed in her marriage by the thought of the sad life Elisabeth would lead without her.

These attacks of self-pity were aggravated by wild assertions of insanity. After the death of her cousin Ludwig of Bavaria, Elisabeth had paid an unexpected visit to the lunatic asylum at Bründlfeld in

Lower Austria. There a shrieking young woman, driven mad from a fatal love affair, had torn off the hat of Elisabeth. She had stated that she was the true Empress of Austria, while her visitor was only pretending to be – something that Elisabeth often thought herself, when she was play-acting in all her jewels and silks at Court ceremonies. The Empress was hustled away, but she insisted on returning to find the young madwoman in tears and begging her forgiveness. She had been reminded of the slippery line between the imaginary and the real. As the Countess Festetics thought of her imperial mistress, Elisabeth lived on the frontier of two worlds, 'that which our eyes see, and the immaterial world, divine'.

The Empress was more and more haunted about passing on a taint of madness both to her children and to her grandchildren. To be an inbred Wittelsbach was bad enough; but then to marry into the Habsburgs and their incessant consanguinity, with the Coburg streaks of insanity enmeshed in the blood line . . . After Rudolf's death, who would succeed to the throne? The brother of the Emperor, Karl Ludwig, whose mania for quoting the Bible would offend all liberal opinion? His eldest son, Franz Ferdinand, who was very stupid and liked to slaughter unoffending creatures even more than Rudolf? His younger brother Ludwig Victor, so open a predator after young men that the Viennese called him the Archduke of the Public Baths? Even Rudolf in his wild excesses would have been a superior heir to the empire. In fact, Karl Ludwig died soon after contracting typhoid from drinking the holy waters of the River Jordan, while Franz Ferdinand recovered from a long bout of tuberculosis, settling the succession in his favour.

If there was no insanity among the relatives of the Empress, as in the case of Maximilian's Coburg widow Charlotte and King Otto of Bavaria, there were a great many eccentrics among the uncles and brothers of the Archduke Johann Salvator, who had been drowned under the name of Orth. The mania of Karl Salvator was for picking locks and travelling anonymously on trams. The learned Salvator, however, was Ludwig, and the Empress particularly enjoyed meeting him on her travels because of his lack of snobbery and his erudition. He lived on the Balearic Islands, always wore the same baggy coat or single military tunic, and ran his yacht like a floating commune. In the extremes of her wanderlust, he even recommended her to flee to Tasmania or the Americas. Yet she could never quite persuade Franz Josef to slip the leash and let her run so far. In a sense, as for Ulysses, when she found her Ithaca, it should be far enough to go. She would choose Corfu, one of the fabled havens of the *Odyssey* of Homer, as her refuge of dreams.

Her tragedies were hardly over. She had retired from the public eye for a year after Rudolf's death at Mayerling, only to hear that Count Andrássy had passed away in Hungary, her great supporter who had made her Queen of the land. 'Not until now have I felt wholly deserted,' Elisabeth told her daughter Valérie, 'without a single counsellor or friend.' She knelt beside the Hungarian's coffin in prayer and laid on it a wreath of lilies of the valley. On a visit to southern Germany, she met one of her few imperial friends, the sympathetic and widowed German Empress Victoria, who was as broken by the death of her husband Frederick as Elisabeth was by the end of her son Rudolf. Victoria said that her loss was equal to that of Elisabeth, while the ingratitude that both of them met in Court and government circles was more than flesh or blood could bear. When Elisabeth said that all events were fated, Victoria did not agree, saying, 'I believe that God in Heaven in the long run orders all things for our own good. As for the rest, I simply wait. For no one can know what comes after death' – exactly the sentiments of Elisabeth herself and her dead son.

There was no end to the series of tragedies. Elisabeth's elder sister Hélène, the Princess of Thurn and Taxis, died after a long agony. When the pain was over, Elisabeth declared that she understood suicide now as a way of escaping the fear of such a lingering end. She withdrew more and more into herself as the wedding of her last love Valérie approached. Franz Josef had to run the ceremonial functions in Vienna alone, for Katharina Schratt could not aid him because of the demands of propriety. The German ambassador reported that the idea of an imperial Court was disappearing, and the gap between the Emperor and the nobility and society was becoming dangerous to the state.

On Valérie's wedding day, 31st July 1890, the pallor of Elisabeth was whiter than a corpse, and she wept bitterly when she helped her daughter into her going-away dress. She had the poem of hers which Valérie liked the most set to music and sung by a male choir.

> Inquire not of tomorrow,
> This day is set so fair.
> Let us scatter our sorrow,
> Winds blow away our care.

She did not reproach her daughter for leaving her side, but she merely declared her thanks to Valérie for being such a good child. She would leave Austria too, for years on her restless odyssey. No Wandering Jew would appear as condemned as the Empress with her itch for sensation and physical exhaustion. She was embarked on a search that could never discover an end to her guilt and her memories.

Her flight started in a Channel gale, when she was lashed to the mast as Ulysses had been to endure the songs of the Sirens. She survived to continue her voyage under the name of Mrs Nicolson. The bad weather took the English cutter *Chazalie* round into the Mediterranean without docking in Spain. Wherever she landed, at Oporto and Gibraltar and Tangiers, the Empress prowled the streets for the length of the day, unless her companions collapsed. 'The mania for movement of Her Majesty is on the increase,' Baron Nopsca wrote to Ida Ferenczy. 'God knows what it may lead to.' It was clearly leading to her shaking off her guards and leaving herself open to any planned or random assault. The Countess Marie Festetics was plunged into a loving despair. The beautiful soul of the Empress was 'foundering in egosim and paradox'.

Passing through Algiers and Ajaccio in Corsica and Marseilles and the Isles Hyères, the Empress avoided Rome, but she visited Florence and Pompeii and Capri and Naples, where the imperial yacht *Miramare* was waiting to take her to her final destination, Corfu. She had bought Italian statues to adorn the villa she wanted to build there, including two busts of the earliest Greek poets, Homer and Sappho.

Following the example of her dead cousin Ludwig in Bavaria, she had always intended to construct her ideal of a palace. So she bought the ruined Villa Braila near Gasturi to the south of the old Venetian fortress and port of Kerkera or Corfu. In the bay, she built a jetty of white marble to ensure an easy landing from the imperial yacht. The pier is still there, but the bridge over the modern road is as broken as her dreams of finding a paradise of her own, anywhere.

Between cypress and olive and orange trees, mimosa and pomegranate and oleander, a winding road led up the mountain slope, covered with bushes and scrub, black oak and yellow broom. When Elisabeth's plans were realised, great wrought-iron gates led to steps and an ornamental fountain and then to a cupola on columns crowned by an angel with a laurel wreath. But unlike Ludwig's dome on pillars which crowned the hill above Linderhof and was dedicated to Venus, this little temple was consecrated to Heinrich Heine; a statue of the poet sat in an armchair under the marble canopy, looking out to sea and holding a scroll with a verse chiselled upon it:

> What means this tear alone?
> It still dims everything.
> Too many a year is gone
> For this long lingering.
> My dilatory tear,
> Time now to disappear.

Beyond the shrine and the landscaped wilderness park rose the palace of the Achilleion. Influenced by her memories of Munich, which King Ludwig the First had remodelled in the Greek style, Elisabeth tried to reconstruct a classical Doric and Ionic palace with a superb peristyle and atrium facing a garden of the Muses. In a sympathetic description of the original Achilleion, her biographer Karl Tschuppik gave an admirable account of it before its looting in the World Wars and its conversion into a modern casino.

The pillared vestibule led straight into the atrium open to the sky. It recalled the hall of the Vienna Parliament: a lofty, cool apartment with Corinthian pillars. The coldness of the polished marble was tempered by red carpets on the floor and on the walls. Tall mirrors, hitherto unknown in these parts, multiplied the room. On each side of the entrance stood gigantic vases of bronze and porcelain, containing palms whose foliage reached up to the roof. From this hall doors opened into the various apartments of the palace, the dining-room, and the Empress's own rooms. A small room on the right of the entrance to the atrium was fitted up as a Chapel; above the altar was a statute of 'Notre Dame de la Garde', the Virgin of the Marseilles seamen. 'I brought her with me from Marseilles,' said the Empress; 'she is the protectress of all seafaring folk.'

The marble staircase, that led up from the broad approach in the lower garden to the upper garden terrace, was adorned with statues of Venus, Artemis, and handsome youths. The pillars supporting the roof were painted scarlet, the capitals richly gilt, and picked out with blue and red. The further wall of the atrium was adorned with fresco-medallions of Apollo and Daphne, blind Homer, Theseus and Ariadne, Aesop; and the Odyssean landscapes; between them stood Hermes with antique heads.

On a level with the palace, facing north and towards the sea, stood a white marble figure, Peri, the Light-Fairy, gliding over the waves on the wings of a swan. Some of the marble figures, such as the Apollo Musagetes, Elisabeth had bought in Rome from the collection of Prince Borghese. One of them, the 'third Dancer' of Canova, had a history: the model for the gracious naked body had been Pauline Borghese, Napoleon's favourite sister. Elisabeth knew the previous history of the statue. 'I love her,' she said. 'She does not belong to the Muses, but I hope they will make her feel at home.' Antique bronze lamps hung from chains between the pillars. In the garden of the palace were ancient cypresses, magnolias, and olives, and here and there beds of roses and hyacinths. By a fountain stood a black statue of a satyr carrying the boy Dionysus on his shoulders.

At the edge of the garden, where it began to slope down to the sea, Elisabeth had a pavilion erected, hung with brightly coloured stuffs embroidered in antique designs. From here there was a wide view over the sea to the far-off mountains of Albania. Towards the north were two more terraces; at the extreme edge of the first gleamed the 'Dying Achilles', Elisabeth's favourite. 'He was strong and bold; he despised all kings and all traditions; he worshipped nothing but his own will, and he loved nothing but his dreams.' From this point a flight of marble steps led to the second terrace lower down. Here, amid a bower of roses, lay the sleeping Hermes, a copy of the famous Herculaneum bronze. Thence a double half-circular staircase led to the third, the 'Achilles' terrace. Elisabeth called them her hanging gardens. A stalactite grotto below the marble staircase was quite in Elisabeth's style, glittering with green, mysterious light, and with an arrangement of mirrors at the back reflecting to infinity the moving surface of the sea. It was Elisabeth's Calypso Grotto. Shady alleys of foliage bright with blossom led up to each side of the 'Dying Achilles', wood nymphs and a drunken faun shimmered against the green background.

In the building of the Achilleion Elisabeth had a completely free hand: whatever she desired took form. The palace swallowed up gigantic sums of money; and, even so, the Empress sacrificed part of the scheme in order not to have to save on fitting up the interior. As far as possible every piece of furniture was modelled on an original, and made of the finest material. There were chairs like the one Adrastus set before Helen, inlaid with silver and ebony, and covered with a huge sheepskin; elaborate stools and coffers imitated from the antique. The greatest care was taken over the broad Greek bed, which stood only a few inches above the surface of the floor. On the shining bedposts were modelled the bent forms of nymphs supporting that 'dream-haunted pillow'; a silk coverlet was thrown across the bed – indeed, all was just as Helen had bidden the women prepare for Telemachus. Against the walls stood magnificent blue glass vases, like those that are found in ancient graves. On the central storey, which had no direct communication with the garden, were the guest-rooms and living-rooms for the Emperor and the Archduchess Valérie.

Making a palace of dreams is not the same as living in a palace which is made. The Emperor and Valérie would rarely come to the completed Achilleion, where the Empress did not find the peace which she sought. They did not often mount the great staircase with its colossal fresco by Franz Matsch of the triumph of Achilles, dragging the corpse of Hector round the crumbling walls of Troy. Nor did they visit overmuch the monument to Crown Prince Rudolf with an angel over his cameo portrait, supported by a broken pillar. Elisabeth herself was a recluse in her own domain, except for a succession of Greek tutors, who indulged her in her romantic philosophy. She was often seen wandering alone through the olive groves on the mountain or along the beach, as if she were a refugee on her own estate. As Ulysses, she seemed to prefer to be a vagabond rather than live in her new home – a place to approach, yet not to inhabit.

She would explain that she loved the Achilleion because there was a boatman on the shore who resembled Charon. Without a word, he would row her out to an island where a hermit lived, 'as if I were a dead soul bound for the shades'. The hermit also would not speak, but fed her with honey and almonds. 'I remain motionless in this solitude for hours at a time, forgetting the world altogether.' She would also spend a while contemplating the statue of Heine and repeating his queries, for which she had no reply. 'From where does evil come? From where suffering? Is it chance? In that case, is God unjust? . . . These terrible questions haunt us. Yet the day comes when our mouth is closed with a handful of mother earth. Is this an answer?'

While the architecture and statues of Ancient Greece remain the arbiters of the ages, their imitations such as the Achilleion have travelled badly in recent times. Within this century, the revolution of Modernism has condemned the Greek fantasy of Elisabeth as kitsch with luxury, rather than spirit with simplicity. In the statues, Athenian grandeur and line of body were replaced with Austrian languour and puerile curves. The stark beauty of the classical temple was mocked by the badly painted frescos of Homeric myths. So expensive and inferior was the Achilleion that Elisabeth's heirs would sell it to Kaiser Wilhelm the Second, a monarch of little taste himself. He used it as an occasional summer residence; but with the declaration of the First World War, it fell into the hands of the Franco-Serbian forces and was used as a military hospital. Many of the statues and friezes were defaced.

More destruction ensued in the Second World War, when the Achilleion became a military hospital and headquarters for the German and Italian occupying troops. Then the temple of Heine was removed; he was a converted Jew, even if he was also one of the greater German poets. A small statue, however, of Lord Byron did survive the conflict. Lush restoration inflicted more damage on the fantasy palace of the Empress under the reign of a private Greek company, which leased it from the government to run as a rather melancholy casino, more to the taste of Edward, Prince of Wales, than of its creator. Renovated again by the Greek Tourist Board, the Achilleion has regained some of its lost and mistaken elegance, particularly in the view past the giant statue of Achilles down to the salt-marsh of Halkiopoulos and the tourist sea resort of Kanoni with the great mountain of Pantokrator, still suggesting the dominion of the ancient Hellenic gods in the distance.

While the Achilleion was being completed, Elisabeth returned to Vienna and some activities at Court. This made a good impression at last, according to the German ambassador, the Prince of Reuss, 'for the comments about this exalted lady, so tried by fate, have really gone to extremes'. The married Valérie left her husband at his garrison duties and came back to see her mother, who told her that she was as numb as a log. Whatever happened to her must happen. In the middle of January in the New Year, she turned a great festival into a funeral by appearing swathed in black crêpe de Chine. She then went to visit Valérie and her husband in their army home before taking them with her on the imperial yacht *Miramare* to view the progress in building the Achilleion. She would like to be buried there, she said. She did not even look forward to Valérie having a child. The birth of another human being always seemed to her a misfortune.

The voyage continued to Corinth and Athens, where the young couple left the *Miramare* before it sailed on to Sicily. Elisabeth was pursuing her studies in ancient and modern Greek, and she had attached to her entourage two brothers named Christomanos, who spoke German as well. One of them was a romantic hunchback, Constantine; he became the tutor of the Empress's translations of Shakespeare's tragedies into his language. As the astute Count Corti suggested, an affinity developed between Constantine, over-conscious of his deformity, and Elisabeth, obsessed with her fading beauty. In a mutual admiration for the good and the noble in ancient Hellas, a sympathy for the past was discovered, which forgot the present.

Through her studies of classical times, Elisabeth was trying to detach herself from the great changes taking place in the Habsburg Empire. Vienna was becoming modern despite the old-fashioned policies of the ageing Emperor. Technology and industry and limited democracy were putting paid to a benevolent autocracy. The rising tide of nationalism was condemning the authority of a Dual Monarchy or a federal empire. The Minister President Count Taafe promoted slow change within the existing institutions; the conserv-atives were becoming the party of social reform, introducing insur-ance and legal protection for the working man. The Emperor agreed with Count Taafe's general policy, which opposed the liberals and the radicals, encouraged a little autonomy for the various peoples within the Habsburg Empire, and approved the Magyar oppression of the Slavs, who were told to look to Vienna rather than St Petersburg for support for their rights. In fact, however, the Austrian bureaucracy ran the imperial domains, subject only to the will of the Emperor and the brake applied by the Hungarians for their own purposes.

The power of Franz Josef lay in his command of the imperial army, which was now full of conscripts from every one of the groups of subjects in the whole dominion. National service linked the dis-parate tribes and races and faiths in a mutual order. The young Sigmund Freud himself accepted his compulsory service as a surgeon-lieutenant without regret. The hatreds of civil life in politics and economics and between creeds were relaxed by a common loyalty. Class prejudice gave way to brass buttons, bigotry to braid. And the distant Emperor toiling in the Hofburg was set on high as a symbol over all.

The empire could not last by denying the logic of the times. But it was on hold. The tragedy of the military and the bureaucracy, which were ordering the state under the Emperor, was their divorce by caste from the intellectual ferment, heralding modern times in Vienna and Budapest and Prague. Rarely have so many artists and doctors and scientists flourished in the decline of their society. In music, there was Strauss and Brahms and Bruckner, Mahler and Dvořák, Smetana and Janáček, and the popular Lehar. Psychiatry was in its infancy with Sacher-Masoch and Krafft-Ebing, Bruer and Freud, who would collaborate on *Studies in Hysteria*. Poetry and the theatre had von Hofmannsthal and Schnitzler, while Rilke and Kafka would be scribes of imperial confusion and the loss of direction. In the visual arts, Klimt and Schiele in their opulent carnalities would give way to the shocking mercilessness of Kokoschka, who would rend apart Habsburg society more viscerally than even the losses of the First World War.

With genius almost a commonplace in the cafés of the capitals of Austro-Hungary, the Emperor was cut off from the general stimulation by his military education and the Empress by her restlessness and her misery. She did not seek for psychiatric help herself, although her dead son had consulted Krafft-Ebing over his nerves. She had, however, heard of hypnosis. Dr Mesmer's work by this method had been a strong influence on Freud in his early practice. The Empress arranged for Mesmer to treat a distant cousin, who was an alcoholic. The cure was successful, the prince became a teetotaller. Elisabeth then visited the asylum, where hypnosis was used on the disturbed patients. She was particularly interested when an aged amnesiac recalled his life in his youth, and so was restored to memory and his family. Her own neuroses were incurable in her opinion, because they were hereditary. Her mental and physical pains were the result of her experience and over-exercise. Currently, sciatica was giving her more problems than any headache. The sun would be her cure, and she took the *Miramare* off to Corfu, and then on to Egypt, where she stayed at the Shepheard's Hotel in Cairo. Her spirits and her pace returned. She was walking the hind legs not only off a donkey, but also off her fat guardians. 'The secret police said it was intolerable,' the Austrian consul reported, 'to have to follow Her Majesty except in carriages.'

This was the problem of her wandering and her fame until her end. She would die, because she would not be protected. Her choice was to run away from safe convention. She spurned imperial security. She was not scared of assassins or strangers or beggars as the other royal families were. She put herself in the way of the poor and those who loved her. She took an interest in everyone who wished to meet her, if she chose to face the public for her pleasure. A Mrs O'Donoghue always remembered a day from her hunting with the Meath as a girl. She had felt ignored because so many grandees clustered round the Empress, 'who, escorted by Earl Spencer – who, I am sure, must remember it – slackened rein a bit, and, glancing round, addressed a pleasant word just when I was feeling particularly small, and then for one delicious moment I rode by her side and answered her prettily put queries respecting my experiences of Irish sport. She cared nothing to know them – how could she? But she evidently did care that a young rider with a flushed face and eyes of eager longing had been debarred from speaking to her.'

In the contradiction between her grace of contact and her pathological shyness, Elisabeth always lived. Yet with her increasing seclusion, she had given up politics even more than people. On her return to Vienna from Egypt, she had been consulted by her husband the Emperor on Hungarian politics. After the death of Andrássy, he had few counsellors whom he could wholly trust. Yet she would not and could not help him, as she told Christomanos. 'I have too low an opinion of such things. Politicians always think that they are directing events, while really events always take them by surprise.'

'How well the Emperor stands out' Walpurga, Lady Paget wrote in Vienna after the tragedy of Mayerling. 'In the beginning he was overcome, but soon his piety and sense of duty showed him the right way and he not only worked as usual, but he has constantly been seeing people, giving dinners and appearing to be interested and pleased with everything. The Empress on the contrary bore up very well at first, but she has been getting steadily worse. Having led a life

of unalloyed selfishness, worshipping her own health and beauty as
the sole objects in life, she has nothing to fall back on now. At new
year she refused all congratulations. She will, of course, never show
herself again, and she will become a ghost in her own lifetime.'

This verdict was one of envy as well as prophecy. Feeling alone,
the Empress chose to be more alone, except for her entourage,
including her masseuse and her hairdresser. Vanity was, indeed, a part
of her solitude with servants. Yet she had a justification for her
choices. The people, she said, did not know what to make of her. 'I
do not fit their idea of an Empress, and they do not like me to upset
their fancies.' She found it hard to deal with people who did not know
or understand her. It would be madness for her to try and convince
them. All individuals should follow their nature. 'All I ask, too, is that
I should be left in peace to follow my own nature.' She found it very
hard to put up with the company of strangers, and she thanked God
that she was an empress, otherwise things would have gone badly for
her. Especially as the indulgent Emperor continued to pay for her
considerable bills.

She had no thought or knowledge of money, assuaging her melancholy with activity in far places and with thoughts of easeful death.
As a fatalist, she was almost fearless and did not consider her own
safety. She ignored the company of other people, whom she did not
wish to see. On her voyage on the *Chazalie* lashed to the mast, she
had felt in the tempest that she herself had become a breaking wave.
She had found oblivion in the elements, yet wherever she fled, her
incognito was useless. For her picture had travelled before her over
Europe as the most beautiful royal icon of her age. The more she
avoided mass recognition, the more she was given it. Even if her
vagabondage might end in her death, she did not believe she would
achieve eternal peace, as Countess Irma Sztáray told her. 'What do
you know about that?' she asked. 'No voyager on that journey has
ever returned to tell us what was found at the end of it.'

After the death of Rudolf, she had dressed only in black. Her
gowns made her look like a nun, although they were in crêpe de
Chine and lace. Sometimes she wore a large red rose over her heart
to show that she had been struck there. Her veils and pearls were

black as well. Her hats seemed to derive from Rembrandt, while her beads appeared to be a rosary. She kept a lock of Rudolf's hair in a sombre medallion at her waist. Her tutor Christomanos found her exercising in her private gymnasium on the hanging ropes, clad in a black silk gown, because the Archduchesses might see her improperly dressed. She knew 'her duty to such important persons'. On her long gliding walks Christomanos thought that she moved like the neck of a swan, but he had still to scurry behind her, carrying a spare dark costume, so that she could change her clothes half-way and get rid of the sweat and the dirt.

In spite of her commitment to physical exercise, Christomanos saw her as a shadow that had taken on a body. 'I had the feeling that she incarnated something which lived between death and life.' She inhabited an atmosphere that was different to the air he breathed. She had set the fashions of Europe for thirty years, but now she was retiring from her celebrity into the world of Heine and Homer and the Titania of Shakespeare. She would be the empress of the imagination.

At the end of January 1892, the oppressive mother of Elisabeth, the Archduchess Ludovika, died of pneumonia at the age of eighty-four years, while her daughter Valérie gave birth the next day to an infant girl, also named Elisabeth or Ella for short. Instead of showing any devotion to the baby, the Empress fled to Corfu to walk Christomanos off his legs. She regretted now turning the ruined Villa Braila into the palatial Achilleion, for it had lost its solitary charm under its great trees. Dreams, she said, were always finer when they were not made real. People spoiled things, which were better left alone. A hundred years on, no one belonging to her time would still be alive, and probably not a single throne would exist. 'There will be a constant succession of new people, new poppies, new waves. They are like us, we are no more than they are.'

CHAPTER ELEVEN

The End of the Odyssey

❖

W HILE AGE was withering the beauty of Elisabeth, the Empress of Austria and Queen of Hungary, she kept her magnificent *coiffure* and figure. But she was fasting to the point of anorexia and bulimia. Although these nervous diseases were not recognised at the time, the causes of Elisabeth's excessive denial of appetite were the same – an obsession with her personal good looks and a low esteem of herself. At Karlsbad to take the cure, she became giddy on her long marches and fainted when her hair was being done. Marie Festetics told her that eating so little would bring on a stroke. She looked ill and pale. 'She is obsessed with the idea that she is becoming stout.' If Marie Festetics had not persistently been persuading the Empress to take some food, she would long before have died of starvation. She enjoyed, however, mocking Katharina Schratt's efforts to slim at spas by taking a dangerous thyroid treatment. Elisabeth still saw herself as Titania, the Fairy Queen, although the actress had played the role on stage. So in a little aphorism, she wrote:

> Imitation is her way
> In spite of pounds of fat.
> Titania she wants to play,
> Poor Katharina Schratt.

Both of them were trying the hay bath treatment at Gastein, which Franz Josef maintained was the Tyrolese custom of burying oneself naked in a stack. To Frau Schratt, he could only express his wonder at her strong constitution 'that stands up to all these baths, waters, liquid medicines, powders, and cold and warm treatments. God protect you!'

At one of the rare appearances of the Empress at a reception at the Hofburg to celebrate the engagement of her grand-daughter Augusta, she would tell the German ambassador Count Eulenburg that she was preparing herself to become a great-grandmother. People could then, perhaps, allow her to retire from the world for good. Actually, her first great-grandchild, as Franz Josef pointed out, would be a Baron Seefried, for Augusta's sister had run away with a minor Bavarian noble. At the Hofburg reception, however, Lady Paget was alarmed to see how much Elisabeth had aged: 'Nine and a half years ago when I saw her first she was still a beautiful and apparently young woman, in a white dress gleaming with embroidery of gold and silver with jewels in her hair standing in the blaze of hundreds of candles. Now she stood in a waning light, clad in transparent but deepest black, a crown of fluffy black feathers on her auburn hair, a ruche of black gauze disguising as much as possible the thinness of her throat. Her face looked like a mask, the lips and cheeks too red.' Queen Victoria confirmed this impression, writing in her journal that the last time she saw the Empress she was much altered and all her beauty was gone except for her figure. The British Queen herself was flourishing with age; although she had lost her servant, John Brown, she had won the devotion of the Conservative Prime Minister, Benjamin Disraeli, who had also made her an Empress of India.

The handsome Count Eulenburg was making the Emperor jealous in his obvious admiration for Katharina Schratt, whom he described in his memoirs as ravishingly pretty with golden hair and great blue eyes and a lovely complexion. More interesting, though, was his description of the relationship between the actress and the Empress, which he claimed was very close. They often consulted each other about the Emperor's health and exercise. Elisabeth showered Katharina with lucky charms and porcelain and tin pigs. 'In some ways the Empress is more intimate with the actress than with her own daughters, for even her love for Valérie is no longer the same as it was.'

The vagabondage of Elisabeth now became the process of the rest of her life. Leaving what she said in her contradictory way were 'the only three roots binding her to earth', the Emperor and Frau Schratt and her daughter Valérie, she migrated as a wild duck between northern Europe and North Africa. At the end of April 1892, the Empress had added to her travelling household an Alexandrian, Frederick Barker, half-Greek and half-English. He joined her new lady-in-waiting, the Countess Janka Mikes, who found her imperial mistress far too candid about her miseries. No one on earth could feel so unhappy and misunderstood, but nobody else could do anything about it now. Elisabeth took winter cruises for three months in search of the sun with destinations unknown, even to the captain of the *Miramare*, the secret police and her husband. Her birthday on the Christmas Eve of that same year found her exploring the alleys of Valencia before visiting Malaga and the Alhambra palace in Grenada. She pleaded sciatica to avoid visiting the Queen of Spain, causing offence because she was obviously walking everywhere and shopping too much. She wrote to Valérie that she would be in a debtors' prison, if Marie Festetics were not there to bargain in the souks and the markets. After sailing on to Gibraltar and Seville and Cadiz, Elisabeth returned to Majorca and Barcelona, the Riviera and Turin, where she heard that Valérie had given birth to a son and heir, a godsend that made the Emperor think of the lost Crown Prince Rudolf. 'It is a poor substitute,' he wrote to his wife, 'but still a kind of substitute.'

The Empress crossed the Alps to Geneva and the resort of Territet on the Swiss lake, where she walked her companions through their shoe-leather. She even persuaded the Emperor to visit her there, although his guards and spies believed he would be assassinated in such a hotbed of anarchists and nihilists and socialists. Irresponsible press stories claimed that Franz Josef had only left Vienna for Switzerland because Elisabeth had gone insane and had tried to drown herself like King Ludwig of Bavaria in the water. His visit did not allay her restlessness, and she moved on to Lake Como, then to Milan and Genoa and Naples. She would not return to the Achilleion on Corfu, because its completion had disenchanted her. What was having a dream palace and living in it compared with building it? She had once confessed that wherever she might happen to be, if she were told she would have to stay there for ever, 'even Paradise would become a hell for me'. Perhaps she could find a rich buyer and give the money to Valérie, so that her grandson could have everything. Franz Josef was sad at this prospect. He had hoped that the Achilleion would settle his wife and stop her 'travelling and roaming about the world'.

As the Empress knew, her endless movement did not imply progress in coping with her inner demons. Brief visits back to Vienna only led to further journeys. This time her boat was the wallowing *Greif*, which made everyone seasick except herself. Her destination was first Algiers and then a return trip to Madeira, where she had fled thirty-two years before from the rough embraces of her husband. Again she spent her Christmas Eve only with her chosen Argonauts, leaving Franz Josef to wish her by letter a little peace, a good understanding between them and fewer misfortunes. On her voyage home, she touched at Alicante to renew her friendship with the Habsburg relative she liked the most, the free-and-easy intellectual Archduke Ludwig Salvator in his old clothes. He was the only one in the family as eccentric as she was – that is, out of an asylum, where King Otto of Bavaria was now confined. For him, too, a house was on the waves. As he wrote of his yacht, it was the only place he felt at home. 'In all my palaces and places of residence in Austria and Hungary, and even on my beloved Island of Majorca, I feel just as if I were in a hotel, and almost as if I were in a prison. There is no sense of home in such places – no sense of home whatsoever.'

When Elisabeth reached Cap Martin in the South of France, Franz Josef came to visit her once more. The Empress Eugénie had left England to make her final retirement there. Elisabeth could not avoid her all the time, yet she was bored by the troubles of the widow of Louis Napoleon. Her presence led to the Habsburg Emperor visiting his wife in some secrecy in her hotel, for he wished to revive no fears in Germany of inclining to a French alliance. Katharina Schratt could not be invited to stay there. For, as Franz Josef wrote to her, there was no question of being incognito, they were continually observed. The place swarmed with the curious and the nobility and the press. The actress and the imperial couple would be compromised. As for Elisabeth, he discovered that his wife had become skin and bones and lived on a diet of milk and sorbet flavoured with violets and oranges, which gave her indigestion. She even had herself packed in seaweed to reduce her weight. 'These incessant cures', Franz Josef observed gloomily, 'are really terrible.'

He had now kept the peace in the Habsburg Empire for nearly thirty years, except in the ever troublesome Balkans. Although Andrássy was dead and Count Taafe had been forced from office to be followed by a succession of unsatisfactory ministers, the Dual Monarchy continued to function well by allowing the Hungarians in Budapest to rule over the many other peoples in the east, while Vienna controlled the west. Her persuasion of her husband to accept the Magyar partnership had been Elisabeth's great political triumph. Sharing power had been the secret of maintaining power, along with the defensive triple alliance of Austro-Hungary and Germany and Russia. As the elder statesman of Europe, Franz Josef deserved the thanks of the many nationalities within the patchwork of his domains. He had given them prosperity and industry without the need to fight any more major wars.

During the summers, Elisabeth visited spas near the Rhine and the Bavarian and the Carpathian mountains. President Carnot was assassinated by an anarchist in France, but she continued to take little care of her personal safety. She revisited both Gödöllö and Corfu, yet these old refuges brought her no peace of mind. Again two winter cruises on the *Miramare* took her around the Mediterranean. On board, her dieting became even stricter and her gymnastics more taxing. Her weight was forty-eight kilos or seven and a half stone, too thin for a woman who was five foot six inches tall. The Emperor could not understand why she punished her growing hunger by more fasting. Other people ate, while she starved. 'The case is beyond all remedy,' he observed, 'so we will pass over it in silence.' She tried all the fashionable medical treatments of the time, even Dr Kuhne's sand cure with Katharina Schratt. Not much harm, the Emperor wrote, was done to either of his women, thank God.

The seal of the marriage and the diplomacy of the Emperor and the Empress was signified in the late spring of 1896 at the celebration of the millennium of the constitution of Hungary, a country still devoted to Elisabeth. Although she hid her face behind her fan as she drove in the imperial carriage to the ceremonies, she was moved to tears by the words of the Cardinal Prince Primate in the Coronation Church, as he spoke of the grateful love which the nation had for her. An article in a contemporary Hungarian newspaper, quoted by Count Corti, gave a most complete impression of the Empress at the state reception of the Hungarian parliament:

There she sat in the throne-room of the royal palace in her Hungarian costume of black, adorned with lace. Everything about her was sombre. From her dark hair fell a veil of black. Black were the ornaments in her hair, black her pearls, everything black, only her face was marble-white and ineffably sad . . . It was the same face as of old, well known from her bewitching portraits; the free, noble features with the hair cut short in front and waving round her brow like a silken fringe, and above this her luxuriant braids, the loveliest of all crowns. She was still herself, but sorrow had left its mark upon her face. The picture was still the same, but as though shrouded in mist. The lashes drooped over her sweet eyes, so full of life. Still and impassive she sat, as though seeing and hearing nothing. Only her soul seemed to range far and wide. Not a movement, not a glance to betray her interest. She sat like a statue of marble pallor . . .

The magnates of the realm waved their hats. Still the cheering would not abate. The orator was forced to pause and the Queen inclined her head. Her snow-white cheek showed a faint flush. Its milky whiteness was tinged with pale rose, then a crimson wave surged up, flooding it with a living red. As though by magic, a Queen appeared in all the hues of life seated at the side of the

King. Her eyes dilated and flashed with their former splendour. Those eyes, whose captivating smile had once had power to console a sorrowing land, now filled with tears. Once more the current of sympathy flowed back and forth. The land, now happy, had succeeded in consoling its Queen, but only for a moment. Majestically she raised her lace handkerchief to her eyes to dry her tears. The orator resumed his speech. Slowly the flush of life faded from the Queen's countenance, and soon by the King's side, there sat once more the woman shrouded in mourning, the Mater Dolorosa.

After the celebrations, the Hungarian admirers of the Empress would never see her again. A few months later, Elisabeth developed a red skin complaint, a rampant rash that was probably the effect of her starvation of herself. She now wore a veil much of the time, as well as hiding her face behind her fan or her sunshade. When the Emperor again stayed with her at Cap Martin the following year in the early spring, he wrote to Katharina Schratt that Elisabeth's poor appearance had exhausted and depressed her, as well as leaving her in agony from her disease, which she dosed with sulphur and iron pills. A contemporary description by the royal observer de Burgh commented on the increasing mania of the Empress in rushing from place to place:

> She was a familiar figure in nearly every one of those Baths in the centre of Europe in which women especially seek relief and deliverance from the miseries of diseased bodies and diseased minds. Kreuznach, a beautiful little town in a valley only half a hour's railway journey from Bingen-on-the-Rhine, is a favourite place for women, and is supposed to alleviate their manifold troubles. This resort was visited by the Empress, and her habits there were as peculiar as elsewhere. She would get up about four o'clock in the morning, and by six had completed that two hours' walk before breakfast which is part of the cure. Early as the people of Kreuznach were, there was nobody about at that hour in the morning. The next walk was between nine and eleven – again a

time when few were about, as most of the patients were then either at their breakfasts or in their baths. The Empress did not care to be seen by anybody; she shrank from the vulgar and embarrassing stare to which royalty is generally subjected.

At Territet in Switzerland, which was also a favourite resort, she followed similar habits; there she used to take her bath punctually at five o'clock every morning; then she sat on the terrace until eight o'clock, when she was served with a breakfast of iced milk and biscuits; and during the rest of the day she would roam about, dressed in black, with short sleeves, a short skirt, and tan boots. She hardly ever wore gloves, and when passing anyone she invariably covered her face with a fan. On returning to her apartments, which were extremely simple, she would respond to the respectful salutes of her suite with a gentle wave of her hand. She always retired to rest very early.

The grand and sentimental occasion in Hungary had been too much for Elisabeth, who withdrew after a visit from the Tsar to isolation at Ischl, where she had spent an idyll in her youth with her husband. She would try at steam baths, as they were called before saunas, and cold plunges. She went for the winter to Biarritz instead of to the sun. She now enjoyed the gales and the roaring of the sea. Franz Josef rightly thought that this delight in stormy weather reflected her sad state of mind. She should listen to her Dr Kerzl and exercise less and eat more. She should not be obsessed about her weight. As her doctor often exclaimed to her, 'If it were not for those damned scales!'

Elisabeth did reach the French Riviera in the January of 1896, where she was more cheerful, but still thin and tired. The iron and sulphur pills she was taking to bolster and purify her system did not help her. She told her husband on his visit that she would perform no more public duties. Her joints were swollen, probably because she took so little food. She was told that she would have dropsy, if she did not eat more. She added two glasses of ewe's milk to her orange diet.

She recovered enough at Territet on Lake Geneva, however, to return to Austria. Before her end, she would visit the one member of the imperial families of Europe whom she appreciated. Unannounced and wearing her stained walking dress, she dropped in to see the Empress Frederick of Germany. When she told the guard that she was the Empress of Austria, he merely laughed; but a chamberlain recognised her. She was admitted to pay a last visit to the daughter of Queen Victoria, who could hardly recognise this strange visitor in her odd costume. In her will, Elisabeth would only remember, of all her royal contacts, the Empress Frederick, leaving her a silver horseshoe with a golden effigy of St George in the middle of the piece.

When Elisabeth returned in May to the Villa Hermes at Lainz, another tragedy destroyed any composure she still possessed. 'In all its circumstances,' Queen Victoria was told by her Prime Minister, the fire in Paris was 'more terrible than anything that has happened in this century.' At a charity bazaar, attended by most of the nobles in the French capital who were interested in seeing each other doing good, an early cinema stood next to the embroidery booth, supervised by Elisabeth's sister, the Duchess of Alençon. A magic lantern powered by electricity showed moving pictures, which would be the chief publicity machine of the celebrities of the next century. There was a short circuit in the wiring, the celluloid film caught on fire, the metal housing exploded. The sparks and shrapnel set fire to the tissue paper and baskets of confetti and flimsy drapes within the marquee to make an instant inferno. Panic and cowardice gripped the people choking in the smoke. The counts and marquesses of Paris trampled their way to the inadequate exits. Women and children came last. One hundred and thirteen victims were discovered after the débâcle. The bodies were of the most prominent ladies of fashion in Parisian society, the kind who still run charity events to this day. Most of them were crushed by the charge of their escorts or burned beyond recognition. They had died in pursuit of social fame in the largest slaughter of the aristocracy since the French Revolution, the days of the tumbrils and guillotine.

Sophie, the Duchess of Alençon, had behaved heroically, pushing her young assistants out of the burning embroidery booth before herself. Her last words were said to be: 'Duty before all – *le devoir avant tout.*' All that remained of her was her charred skull and bones. She would be identified by the fillings in her teeth and her wedding ring. Although badly burned himself, her husband had survived the conflagration along with most of the other gentlemen there. Accompanied by his wife's two sisters, the Queen of Naples and the Countess of Trani, he spent the night searching the hospitals to find if Sophie had survived. She had been left behind in the rush to get outside.

The effect on Elisabeth was devastating. Only two of her sisters were now living. She felt that the Wittelsbachs could not escape their tragic destiny. Sophie had been engaged to King Ludwig of Bavaria. She now had met her fate as well, as if she were one of Wagner's Valkyries at the fiery Twilight of the Gods. 'The end is not yet,' the Empress said, 'but the end will come.' Mentally and physically, she was in great pain. A grape cure at the Karersee and Meran failed to ease her. She spent the winter again in Biarritz, but even for her, the cold and the rain were too much. Racked by nerves and insomnia, she decided to leave for Paris for another cure by Dr Metzger and for a visit to Sophie's grave.

The three surviving sisters met at the Hôtel Dominici. As Elisabeth did, so Mathilde, the Countess of Trani, travelled under a pseudonym, plain Fräulein Nelly Schmidt. This was to avoid the attentions of any potential anarchist or assassin in that radical capital. Elisabeth laid wreaths on the graves of Heine and the Duchess of Alençon. And she continued to exercise. She was the despair of the French secret police, who were meant to protect her. She would rise before five in the morning and leave for the Bois de Boulogne on foot or on horseback. The detectives scurried after her as best they might. She was unpleasant to them, if they crossed her path. She hated being under supervision.

She was, perhaps, the first royal woman to be stalked. Known from portraits and photographs all over the world as the most beautiful empress of an age when the nobles were the film stars, she insisted that she remained anonymous although she was so celebrated. Her official alias was an advertisement of her arrival.

However discreet her bodyguards, they stood out like buffalos on her errands through the streets and the forests. According to Xavier Paoli of the Sûreté, who was responsible for keeping foreign royalty from being assassinated, the Empress Elisabeth drove him to distraction with her habits. She often walked twenty miles a day with her Greek reader, and once she went to see Notre-Dame by moonlight, ending with an onion soup in the meat and vegetable market. At Biarritz and Cap Martin, which she visited for three years in succession, she would never let Paoli or his agents know what she was doing or where she was going. Warned of the danger of assassins, she replied, 'What! More of your fears. I repeat, I am not afraid. And mind you, I make no promises.'

Her husband Franz Josef was more aware of both general and personal security. As he wrote to her, he found himself in a very difficult situation in Vienna, where there were scandals in the Reichsrath, the Chamber of Deputies. Mass demonstrations of students and workers were bringing back memories of the 1848 revolutions. Yet the secret police and the Hussars counter-attacked and pacified the streets of Vienna. Franz Josef was forced to deal with Karl Lueger, a handsome demagogue and politician, whose rise to power would serve as a model for Adolf Hitler. He was anti-Semitic and anti-Hungarian, a supporter of extreme Austrian nationalism allied with a sort of Christian Socialism. As mayor of Vienna for thirteen years, he would change his tactics in office and become a catalyst between the imperial regime and the modernising forces and the working classes. He would put in electricity and gas all over the city, build new schools and hospitals, and even aid the cause dear to the Empress, the construction of the new Steinhof insane asylum.

The Empress left Paris for Marseilles and San Remo. She returned to her walking, usually with her Greek tutor, Frederick Barker, who despised the rest of her ageing household, bitter old maids and gentlemen. He excused her new and decisive Controller, Major-General Berzeviczy, whose bluff wit suited the irony of Elisabeth and reminded her of Captain Middleton. Barker read to her a lot of poetry and the romances of Marie Corelli and the Mafia novel *Corleone* by Marion Crawford. He wrote, 'There were days when I talked, sang, and read to her for twelve hours together. I read as we walked, or I recited. Sometimes we sat down and I sang Greek shepherd songs, or poems, to a guitar.' Too fat to keep up with her mistress and jealous of this young pretender, Marie Festetics was becoming more possessive and malicious, losing her role to Ida Ferenczy as the most trusted adviser of Elisabeth. In the Empress herself, Barker even noticed a manipulative streak. She enjoyed setting the members of the household at odds by asking them, 'Who do you love most of all?' The answer had to be her, of course. Like the stepmother of Snow White talking into her mirror, she had to be the fairest of them all.

In the March of 1898, the Empress returned to Territet for long mountain walks with her tutor. She was persuaded to go for yet another cure to Kissingen, where the Emperor would meet her for a week, followed by her daughter Valérie. She was happier, but still melancholy, saying that the words 'hope' and 'rejoicing' had been struck from her life for ever. She progressed to Bad Brückenau and then to Ischl, where she told Franz Josef that she certainly was still too ill to come to his approaching Jubilee celebrations. This was the last time that the Emperor would see his wife alive. A bulletin was issued to excuse her absence. She was said to be suffering from anaemia, inflammation of the nerves, insomnia and a heart condition. These maladies called for treatment at Bad Nauheim, where she refused to have X-rays taken of her chest. 'I greatly dislike being photographed,' she said. 'For every time I have had a photograph taken, it has brought me bad luck.' Her luck was to run out in Switzerland without the need for the pursuing lens of a camera.

CHAPTER TWELVE

Death of an Empress

❖

Now celebrated for its neutrality in two World Wars and its security – even outside its banking system – Switzerland attracted the radicals and the refugees at the end of the last century. Geneva and Zurich rivalled London as the sanctuary of the socialists and the communists to come, the nihilists and the anarchists, those who believed that monarchy had to be destroyed before the people might rule. When the Emperor Franz Josef pointed out that the Austrian secret service counselled his wife against any Swiss residence, she replied that she was now a poor woman with little concern in politics. She had nothing to fear. 'If I tremble when I hear talk about anarchists, it is only because of the Emperor that I tremble.'

She had met hostility on her long marches. In England, she had helped a poor country woman, bringing her charity which proved intolerable to her husband, who had stopped the Empress with a gun on his shoulder to denounce the whole imperial system. She was in her old walking clothes. He had no idea who she was and shouted that he wished he had a crowned head at the end of his gun. 'Your wish is granted,' she said. 'I am the Empress of Austria.' She walked away, and he did not shoot her.

Entries in the diaries of Frederick Barker may show the Empress meeting her murderer before he knifed her. On one of her long walks with her tutor, she was accosted by a young Italian beggar, who was referred to her Controller, the Major-General tagging behind her. Berzeviczy was unkind to the young man, who was sent packing. His mistake was to identify the thin woman in the sweaty black dress as the Empress of Austria. Whoever the vagrant was, he boasted that he was an anarchist, who cared nothing for majesty. If he were her eventual killer Lucheni, a personal motive can be seen in this random encounter, which was to prove the point of the mother of the Empress, the dead Duchess Ludovika of Bavaria. Her daughters found it easier to be heroines and martyrs than to be good wives and mothers.

Luigi Lucheni was abandoned as a baby in Paris by his mother, a labourer from Albareto in the Apennines in Liguria. She could not bear the shame of having an illegitimate child, and she emigrated to America, where she disappeared. He was brought up in orphanages in Paris and Parma and then fostered and put to work on the railways. The navvies of the time took jobs where the iron lines were being built, and Lucheni went to Switzerland at Ticino and Geneva, before reaching Austria and Trieste. Penniless and starving, he was deported into Italy, where he was drafted to serve in the disastrous campaign to conquer Abyssinia.

While serving in the cavalry, Lucheni distinguished himself by his daring and was promoted to lance-corporal by his squadron commander, Prince Raneiro de Vera d'Aragona, who engaged him as a valet on his discharge. He acted as a servant for a few months, asked for more wages, and was discharged again. He left for Lausanne in Switzerland, where he came across anarchism in the cafés, particularly inflamed by the evidence of aristocratic corruption in the Dreyfus case. One of the doctrines of the movement was the need to destroy the feudal order by the act of assassination. A single blow might cut the rotten veins of the blood royal, which would bleed to death and oblivion.

The potential murderer needed a weapon and a victim. In the market, Lucheni spent a few pennies on a long rusty file with three edges, which he sharpened, adding a wooden handle carved with his pocket-knife. He hoped that this clumsy dagger would serve its purpose. The question was who would be the victim. Prince Henri of Orleans often stayed in Geneva and was a witness for the prosecution in the Dreyfus trial; yet he was still in Paris. The visit of the Empress of Austria to Caux near Montreux was being announced in the Swiss press. She would be a greater and easier mark. At his interrogation, Lucheni would say, 'I struck at the first crowned head that crossed my way. I don't care. I wanted to make an example and I succeeded.' Prince or empress, king or president, they were all the same to him. 'How I should like to kill somebody,' he also said to a friend. 'But it must be a person of great importance, so that it gets into the newspapers.'

The Swiss newspapers had already enabled the Empress to get within the reach of his blade by publicising her arrival at Caux, although she was travelling under her usual incognito of the Countess of Hohenembs. Although smaller than usual, her household made her very recognisable. With General Berzeviczy and the Countesses Festetics and Sztáray, there travelled her Chamberlain, the Prince of Auersperg, and her private secretary, Dr Kromar, and the Count Bellegarde and the Countess Harrach and two maids. Also in attendance were the Count of Kuefstein, the Austrian minister at Berne, and the controller of the imperial train. Elisabeth had always believed that her endless movements would elude any plot against her life. Yet this was hardly so, given the publicity that surrounded her, as well her retinue. In the end, she felt fated to do what her caprice made her do, saying, 'I am always on the march to meet my fate. Nothing can prevent me from meeting it on the day on which it is written that I must do so. Fate often closes its eyes; but, sooner or later, it always opens them again, and sees us.'

So predestined was her end in her mind that Elisabeth asked the chief of the police department in Geneva to remove the detectives whom he had placed round the Grand Hôtel in Caux as a precaution. She was taking a steamer across Lake Geneva to visit the famous park and hothouses of the Baroness Rothschild at Pregny before moving on with her household to the Hôtel Beau Rivage at Geneva, within walking distance through gardens and squares of the Quai du Mont Blanc, the landing-place. The Habsburg standard was waving from the flagpole of the Villa Rothschild when the Empress arrived, but it was hauled down because she wanted to maintain her pretence of being a countess. She drank champagne and wrote to her husband that the ice-cream had never tasted better, nor the chamber music sounded sweeter. The orchids and the aviary of exotic birds and beasts were superb, including miniature porcupines from Java. On the trip back to Geneva, the Empress told the Countess Sztáray that she did fear death although she often longed for it. 'It is the moment of passing and the uncertainty that make me tremble.'

At the Hôtel Beau Rivage, Elisabeth spent a bad night. She had a large corner room on the second floor, the street was noisy, an Italian tenor sang ballads, the blinds were not drawn, the moon shone on to her face. She lay awake until two in the morning and rose late at ten, ordering her household to take everything before her on to the boat for Caux. She wished to shop in the city with Irma Sztáray, and she would meet the rest of her entourage on the landing-stage. At Bäcker's music shop, the Empress heard the latest mechanical music played on an Orchestrion, which simulated a brass band when it was wound up. Elisabeth bought a smaller version of it, the Ariston, for Valérie and her grandchildren. She would not be introduced to an intruder, who claimed to be a Belgian countess, and she hurried back to her hotel, where she drank a glass of milk before setting out for the lake steamer and her fate.

The *Journal de Genève* and the *Tribune* and the *Genevois* had all announced that the Empress of Austria was staying at the Hôtel Beau Rivage under the pseudonym of the Countess of Hohenembs. Her appearance was well known from the photographs and drawings of her that appeared regularly in the picture papers. Lucheni sat on a bench outside the front of the hotel, observing the departure of the imperial household with the luggage. When the Empress and Countess Sztáray came out of the Beau Rivage to cross the park towards the Quai du Mont Blanc, where they would catch the boat, he followed them. The two women had no protection at all.

By the balustrade on the lake, Lucheni confronted the pair of ladies, who stopped to let him by. He stumbled in front of the Countess Sztáray, then sprang at the Empress, who was hiding under her sunshade. He struck her with his sharp file a huge blow on her breast. She fell backwards on the pavement, knocking herself out briefly, although her mass of hair cushioned the shock. The Countess Sztáray screamed, a cab-driver rushed to help the Empress rise along with an English tourist, while Lucheni ran off. When Elisabeth was asked if she was hurt, she said she was not. 'It is nothing.' At his interrogation, Lucheni would insist that he had acted alone. There was no conspiracy. He was the dedicated stalker with the knife. He would say of the crime, 'I ran toward her and barred her way. I bent down and looked under the parasol. I didn't want to catch the wrong one. They were both dressed in black. She wasn't very beautiful. Quite old already. Anybody who says different doesn't know what he is talking about. Or he lies.'

The two women walked along the quay towards the steamer. On the gangway, the Empress staggered and said in a weak voice, 'What has happened?' On deck, the Countess and a manservant tried to hold her up, but she slipped down unconscious on to the planking. 'A member of the Chamber of Commerce of Geneva', an official witness testified, 'carried Her Majesty in his arms to her cabin after she had fainted on deck. The captain was reluctant to order his vessel to proceed, but upon the request of the suite of Her Majesty he gave the signal to leave the jetty. However, very shortly afterwards it was noticed, to the terror of all, that the Empress seemed unable to recover her consciousness. The ladies about her, who had done everything possible to assist the Empress, observed a small spot of blood upon her bodice. Her condition seeming to be serious, the steamer turned back, and a stretcher was improvised of oars and sail-cloth, and upon this she was reverently and carefully carried back to the hotel by officers and sailors of the boat.'

According to the evidence at the inquiry given by the Countess Sztáray, she was first sure that the Empress had suffered a heart attack when she had reached the steamer. On a bench on the upper deck, the Countess opened the blouse of her mistress and the silk corset to let her breathe more easily. She then saw on the chemise of the victim a drop of dried blood. There had been an assassination attempt. Only then was the captain summoned by the Countess: 'Sir,' I said to him, 'on your ship lies Empress Elisabeth of Austria, Queen of Hungary, mortally wounded. One cannot allow her to die without medical and priestly assistance. Kindly give orders to return at once.' The captain hurried away without saying a word, and immediately the ship changed its course back to Geneva.

The Empress was brought back to the Beau Rivage. One witness heard a rattling sound in her throat, but this was not the evidence of Frau Fanny Louise Mayer, the wife of the proprietor of the establishment:

> It was two o'clock when the Empress was brought to the hotel, and carried into her bedroom. I was called to give such assistance as was in my power. We took off her clothes, which had already been partly loosened, when we noticed two small drops of blood, and one a little larger of very light red colour: on the body itself there was only a small wound, but no blood was visible. Countess Sztáray exclaimed in consternation, 'The Empress has been stabbed!' The Empress was lying with a pale face and closed eyes upon her bed. Soon after she arrived in her room she sighed twice deeply: these were the last signs of life. She lay on the stretcher as if asleep, and with no outward show of pain. When we removed her from the litter to the bed she was evidently dead: she must have died when still on the stretcher. Two physicians, Dr Golay and Dr Mayer, arrived at this moment, and also a priest; but all remedies proved vain.

The autopsy by Dr Golay showed why the Empress had been able to walk to the steamer after her fatal stabbing. The pointed file broke the fourth rib in her chest, pierced the lungs and the pericardium, then passed through the heart to come out in the left ventricle. So sharp was the file that it caused slow bleeding. If it had been left in the wound, the Empress might have survived. Even so, she managed with her usual courage to walk along the quayside while her pericardium was slowly filling up with blood. The abandoned murder weapon was later found by the police, while Lucheni himself was followed by two cab-drivers and a sailor in his flight, caught and handed over to the authorities. 'It was not a woman I struck, but an empress,' he boasted. 'It was a crown that I had in view.' He felt sure that he must have killed her. 'I hope I did not botch it. I hope she is really dead.'

The body of the Empress was robed in white and laid in a triple coffin of polished oak with silver fittings, lined with white satin and later given a glass top. This was placed in a carriage, in which it would be taken to Vienna, but converted into a chapel for the time being. As de Burgh observed: 'Now the bier was a prie-dieu, on which lay a rosary and a cross; the floor was covered with a black carpet with flecks of silver, and the walls were draped with black cloth relieved by silver stars. Nuns, sent by the Bishop of Fribourg, knelt beside the coffin. The adjoining rooms were filled with wreaths of flowers, of which a great number had come from Geneva itself. Most of them were tied with red and yellow or yellow and black ribbons. Among those who sent floral tributes were the foreign officers attending the military manoeuvres in the neighbourhood.'

The blessing of Elisabeth's remains and her procession to the station were carried out with full military honours in front of huge crowds, carrying bouquets and in tears. The hearse and the two carriages behind were decked with wreaths and flowers and drawn behind black horses. The great bell, known as La Clémence, of the cathedral in Geneva tolled on and on. Absolute silence reigned as the Empress moved on her final journey. The funeral train rolled through Innsbruck and Salzburg, where all the houses were draped in mourning. Vienna itself was transformed. Crêpe and black banners hung from the flagpoles in the Ringstrasse and on every balcony, as the coffin was carried from the train to the Habsburg chapel, also draped in black. There the last rites were recited in front of the Emperor and the imperial family and the Court. At last, Elisabeth had returned for ever.

Two days later, the body was taken towards the Habsburg chapel of the Capuchin Church, where there was space in the crypt for only one more imperial burial, that of the Emperor Franz Josef himself, if the remains of the Emperor Maximilian were to be removed. The vast and silent crowds carried forget-me-nots and lilies and white roses, swathed in dark muslin. They watched the glitter and the clatter of the Austrian and Hungarian and Polish cavalry, as the hearse was escorted through the streets. Eighty bishops crowded into the small whitewashed church along with the mourners, who included the Emperor Wilhelm the Second of Germany. At the end of the ceremony, after the choir had chanted the *Dies irae, dies illae,* the Emperor fell on his knees and sobbed for several minutes. Then he rose to continue with his official duties.

Elisabeth had finally left Franz Josef, and by the method that was feared most by all the crowned heads of Europe. Yet she could do the least of them, she had given up politics long ago. Her murder caused amazement as well as terror. 'Who could have hated her so much?' her friend the Empress Frederick mused. 'She would not hurt a fly, poor soul.' Although Elisabeth was so melancholy and unhappy, so sick and tired of life, 'the horrible way of being hurried to one's grave – struck down by the dagger of an assassin – a helpless harmless woman – is too dreadful for words.' Elisabeth had never recovered from the death of Rudolf and never would have. She was shy and strange and hated society, and yet she did not deserve to be the victim of anarchist influences. 'It is *too* shocking to *think* of destruction and cruelty being preached and taught to foolish young people – whose *heated* imagination takes up these wicked inhuman principles – and is ready to carry out these hideous deeds of violence and attack the most innocent people.' The Empress Frederick would hardly outlive the Austrian Empress; but she would die naturally as would her mother, Queen Victoria, who also heard of the heartrending and revolting details of 'the assassination of the poor dear Empress. Thank God she did not suffer, or realise what had happened. It was a painless end and she never recovered consciousness.'

The Emperor Franz Josef was also struck to the heart. When he had first heard of the death of his wife from Count Paar, he was silent before saying, 'I am spared nothing in this world.' Due to start army manoeuvres, he declared that they should go on, although they were later cancelled. As always, he tried and failed to put his duty before his feelings. He would hardly admit to himself that Elisabeth had gone from him. She had so often been far away in her life.

Hunting at Gödöllö, he wrote back to Katharina Schratt that he had visited the rooms of the Empress twice. Nothing was changed: they were decorated with her favourite flowers. 'She could walk in at any moment. It was quite sad and yet rather comforting . . .'

CHAPTER THIRTEEN

The Legacy

❖

W HEN THE EMPEROR FRANZ JOSEF had the Count Károlyi
executed after the Hungarian rebellion, the Countess was said to
have pronounced a curse against him and the Habsburg family: 'May
heaven and hell blast his happiness! May his family be exterminated!
May he be smitten in the persons of those he loves! May his life be
wrecked, and may his children be brought to ruin.'

When Elisabeth was assassinated, a newspaper in Vienna made a
summary of the effects of the curse, which were naturally coin-
cidental:

On January 30, 1889, Crown Prince Rudolf took his own life in his
hunting-box at Mayerling. In May, 1897, Sophie, the Duchess of
Alençon, at one time betrothed to King Ludwig the Second of
Bavaria, was burnt to death in Paris. On June 16, 1867, the
Emperor Maximilian of Mexico, the Empress's brother-in-law,
was shot by a firing-party at Queretaro. His consort, the Belgian
Princess Charlotte, lost her reason, and has been, for the last thirty
years, under restraint at the Château of Bouchout. Archduke
Wilhelm Franz died, in the summer of 1894, at Baden near
Vienna, from injuries sustained through a fall from his horse.
Archduke Johann of Tuscany, who had resigned his rank and
taken the name of Johann Orth, disappeared on the high seas off

the coast of South America. King Ludwig of Bavaria, the Empress's cousin, committed suicide on June 13, 1886, drowning himself in the Lake of Starnberg in a fit of insanity. The Count of Trani, the husband of Duchess Mathilde of Bavaria, the sister of the Empress, committed suicide at Zurich. Archduchess Mathilde, the daughter of Field-Marshal Archduke Albrecht, was burnt to death in her father's palace as the result of a blazing log from the fire [actually a cigarette] having set alight to her ball dress. Archduke Ladislas, the son of the Archduke Josef, came to grief while hunting by an accidental discharge of his gun. And now we learn that the Empress Elisabeth has been murdered.

These ten deaths of relatives of the Austrian Emperor were the result not of an anathema, but of accident and a heredity which had a touch of insanity. Although the Habsburgs and the Wittelsbachs were not always responsible for their actions, they thought that they were because of their duty to the state. Elisabeth believed that fate was her guide, when in fact she chose the risks of her wandering life and her flight from her obligations as Empress. As one sympathetic Magyar, Count Cziráky, burst out to von Margutti: 'There is no doubt that the dead Empress did a great deal of lasting good for us Hungarians. I am a Hungarian myself body and soul. Yet I cannot be enthusiastic about her . . . She never had the least idea how to play the part of her husband's partner on the throne, or to make his very difficult duty any easier for him. But as the wife of so sorely tried a sovereign, that is exactly what she was there to do!'

Another historian with Magyar sympathies, Emil Niederhauser, summed up the life of the Empress Elisabeth as a story of missed opportunities.

Her tragedy was that for forty-four years she was a ruler of a great European power, but also a partisan of republicanism. She made a love match, but she was unhappy all her life because of it. She was expected to fill the role of Mother of her Peoples, but she could not even be a mother to her own children. She wanted to be emancipated as far as the times would allow, but her position made this impossible. She was attracted to many of the ways of a new world, but everybody saw in her the representative and incarnation of the old ways. When she married, she was the adorable Sisi; when she died, the lovely wanderer. Her many good qualities were senselessly wasted. And then her tragic end! Perhaps this is why, in spite of all criticism, this modern woman on a very ancient and dilapidated throne is somehow a winning personality.

Even the Emperor was once known to complain about his dead wife, when he said to an unmarried aide-de-camp, Baron von Höhnel, that he was to be envied. He ought to be very glad. Only those who had been married knew how terribly trying life could be. The Emperor himself was speaking from bitter experience. He had, indeed, indulged Elisabeth in her every caprice, and to him, her eccentricity must have often appeared to be egocentricity. As his Empress, she mostly did what she wanted to do, while he, as she often declared, was a slave to his duties. And this obedience to his imperial role led to his neglect of her.

Although Krafft-Ebing and Freud were then establishing modern psychiatry in Vienna, the causes of Elisabeth's estrangement from her husband and of her obsession with her beauty were insoluble at the time. Now the motives for her incessant wanderings and exercise are more apparent. As a child in Bavaria she had loved her father Duke Max, who had wandered away from her all the time to the Near East. When they had ridden together to the Bavarian inns and fairs, she had performed with him and earned the only honest pennies in her life, glorying in the independence and freedom from convention which he had given her along with his wayward love. Married at sixteen in a romantic dream, she had been crippled by the tortuous conventions of the Habsburg Court, which she could not tolerate.

Once she had children, her mother-in-law had effectively removed their education from her. The ladies of the Court would never accept her; to them, she was a naïve provincial. Feeling inadequate, her revenge was her own person. With her exercises and her beauty treatments, she made herself into the icon of all Europe, the most beautiful royal woman of her age. And yet, when her husband contaminated her purity and gave her an excuse to avoid the Habsburg Court as well as her role as Empress, she took it with restless feet. Her flight all over Europe and the Mediterranean was a denial of her adolescent marriage. Her celebrated and flashing beauty was her revenge against the tedious splendour of the ceremonial in Vienna. She asserted her own role as the first independent empress in history, who renounced a dominion to fulfil herself. Both in Hungary and in Ireland, her display of personal freedom and resistance to tradition inspired their movements towards independence. Her example became their cause.

If the conservative people of Vienna had disapproved of their Empress during her life because she had run away from her imperial role, she became a cult after her murder. Statues of her were set up all over the city: these were always covered with garlands. She became the symbol of the sorrowing mother, almost a Madonna, who had also lost her son most tragically. As for her assassin, sixteen thousand working women signed a petition of hate: 'Murderer, beast, monster, the women and girls of Vienna sigh to avenge the fearful crime which you have committed against our beloved Empress . . . Accursed be the whole of the rest of your life, miserable, cruel monster. May what you eat do you no good. May your body be a source of nothing but pain to you, and may your eyes go blind. And you shall live in eternal darkness.' In fact, Lucheni was sentenced to life imprisonment and, like Judas Iscariot, hanged himself with his own belt before his descent into eternal darkness.

Elisabeth had been so distant from her husband and Vienna for so long that his life hardly changed with her death. He resumed his daily duties and his regular life with Katharina Schratt, although the death of the Empress caused a rift between them. Elisabeth had told her daughters to continue to nurture the relationship between the Emperor and the actress, but Valérie with her many children was an extreme Catholic and disapproved of the liaison. Her Jesuit chaplain and the Christian Socialists around the charismatic mayor of Vienna, Karl Lueger, encouraged her to strike against Schratt and her imperial lover. This was done through the conscience of Franz Josef, as Schratt complained to her tattle-tale friend and admirer Count

Eulenburg, the German ambassador: 'They never stop worrying the poor old gentleman. All this talk of prayer and repentance gets on his nerves, but he lets himself be influenced and keeps going to confession when he has nothing to confess. When I tell His Majesty, "What would a dear kind person like yourself have to confess?" he replies, "Don't you want me to become better in my old age?" and I say, "That is so. But there is no point in Your Majesty going to confess when you have no sins on your conscience to confess."'

A sense of public propriety as well as guilt drove Franz Josef to deny the honour and recognition which the Viennese actress wanted above all things in front of her home audience. For the Jubilee celebrations, a special medal for women had been created, the Elisabeth Order. Before her death, the complaisant Empress had assured Katharina Schratt that she would be one of the first to be awarded the prize. Yet her assassination made impossible this for-giving complicity. The Emperor would seem to be acknowledging and rewarding his mistress after the death of his wife. Katharina was not given the Elisabeth Order. She lost her temper with Franz Josef, accused his daughter Valérie and the Clerical Party of blocking her acceptance in her role as the mainstay of the Emperor, and soon took herself away from him to the Riviera, where Elisabeth had often fled. And when she visited the Pavilion of Sport at the Paris Exhibition, she let the Emperor know that he had a life-size photo-graph there, which was a testimony to his killing 48,345 head of wild game to date.

There was talk of the remarriage of Franz Josef, who was young enough at the age of seventy still to father a son and save the empire from the succession of Franz Ferdinand, who took his recovery from tuberculosis as a sign that he should succeed Rudolf as the heir to the Habsburg Empire. He was a man of strong loathing. He hated the Jews and the Serbs, he distrusted the Hungarians and the Italians, he wanted to end the Dual Monarchy, which Elisabeth had encour-aged and which had preserved his inheritance. On only one matter did he break protocol and custom, his infatuation with the Countess Sophie Chotek, said to be the only woman who could cure his rumoured impotence. Franz Josef would not tolerate a dynastic wedding to a minor noble. Yet when his minister Count Goluchowsky told him that if he did not give way he would face another Mayerling, the Emperor decided to accept a morganatic marriage by his heir.

The price was high. An Act of Renunciation was drawn up, by which Franz Ferdinand gave up all royal rights for the children of his union with Sophie Chotek in front of the fifteen Archdukes of the Empire. He was made to take an oath on the Bible facing the fearsome assembly: 'We bind Ourselves with Our word never to attempt to nullify Our present declaration . . .' The brother of Franz Josef, the late Emperor Maximilian, had been made to swear a similar form of renunciation before he departed on his Mexican catastrophe. Franz Josef seemed determined that the blood line to his succession remained free of all taints except those contained within the Habsburg and Wittelsbach genetic inheritance.

Even so, the death of the merciful Elisabeth seemed to soften the Emperor in his harshness over unsuitable unions within the family. He accepted the marriage of his granddaughter, Princess Elisabeth of Bavaria, to the Protestant cavalry officer, the Baron von Seefried, perhaps because she was named by Gisela after his dead wife. More difficult was the request by Rudolf's widow, the Coburg Princess Stéphanie, to marry a Chamberlain in her own household, Count Lonyay, a minor Hungarian nobleman. Even her father, the King of the Belgians, objected to such a demeaning marriage. Yet in memory of Rudolf and Elisabeth and their love for Hungary, Franz Josef permitted the alliance and allowed Stéphanie to keep the titles of Her Imperial and Royal Highness from her marriage to the dead Crown Prince. He would not meet Count Lonyay officially, yet he allowed Stéphanie to retain her pride and her position. And when her daughter by Rudolf, also named Elisabeth, insisted on marrying Prince Otto von Windischgrätz and not an arranged European royal sire, Franz Josef also acceded. He seemed to have lost the taste for a direct descendant.

Certainly, he would not marry again. He seemed to prefer his isolation in his devotion to duty, and his attachment to Katharina Schratt. His rift with her had widened, when he refused to support her against the managers of the Burgtheater, who desired to end her contract. Most probably, the Emperor wished his mistress to leave the limelight and devote herself to him alone. In the end, she resigned and gave up her career. According to another actor, Hugo Thimig, Katharina Schratt now suffered from the dead Elisabeth's affliction, 'a morbid (or should I say healthy?) thirst for liberty. The slavery of being the favourite, bound by golden chains, seems to have ruined her nerves.' Katharina did recover from her chagrin and her efforts to escape. She returned to Vienna to see the Emperor through the long decline of his empire.

The Boer War was also the herald of the waning of the British Empire. The commitment of an imperial army to defeat the best mounted guerrillas outside the Apaches isolated Britain in Europe, especially when the atrocity of the first concentration camps came to be known. Queen Victoria died before a pyrrhic victory and a forgiving peace. Her dominions were overlarge and could not be maintained, although two World Wars would be necessary to prove the case. Franz Josef would live on almost as long as she had into his late eighties, but his hotchpotch of nine potential nations would only just survive his death by a couple of years. The new King Edward the Seventh, indeed, would form an alliance with France and Russia, which would encircle the German-speaking powers. They would always have to plan to fight on two or three fronts at the same time.

Although dismissed by the Kaiser Wilhelm the Second, the great Bismarck left his memoirs behind him, when he expired in the same year as Elisabeth. These writings warned against the Austrian alliance, which he himself had sustained. Nationalism would rend the fraying fabric of the dying Habsburg Empire, although the old Emperor seemed able to control the Reichsrath, the Chamber of Deputies of his peoples. Russia would intervene to pick up territory in the Balkans. Its ally would be the aggressive new Serbia, looking for a Pan-Slav state, instituted by a bloodbath in 1903 in Belgrade, when military conspirators would murder the compromising rulers of their country. Franz Josef's riposte would be to break his treaty obligations and annex Bosnia and Herzegovina. Russia would be mollified by a secret agreement that Austria would support the right

of the Black Sea fleet to pass through the Dardanelles. This stirring
of the brew of Balkan nationalism would culminate in the disastrous
assassination of Franz Ferdinand and Sophie Chotek in 1914 at
Sarajevo, when their open car had stalled. Another poor anarchist,
Gavrilo Princip, would shoot them both, one in the chest, the other
in the stomach. The dying words of Franz Ferdinand would be those
of the stabbed Elisabeth, 'It's nothing.' Yet his death and Austrian
mobilisation against Serbia would lead to the twenty million victims
of the outbreak of the First World War.

Royal assassination still had fearful consequences for the world at
the turn of the century. Although she was only a child when the
Empress Elisabeth was murdered, the English author Rebecca West
later recorded that her life had been punctuated by the slaughter of
royalty. Newsboys were always running down the street to shout that
somebody had used a lethal weapon to turn over a new leaf in the
book of history. When she was five years old, she heard of the death
of the Empress from her mother, become a stone in reading a newspaper. She remembered the scene much later, when she talked to her
nurse and told her that Elisabeth was one of the most beautiful
women who had ever lived. 'But wasn't she mad?' the nurse asked.
Thinking of the 'lovely triangle of Elisabeth's face', Rebecca West
answered, 'Perhaps, but only a little, and at the end. She was certainly
brilliantly clever. Before she was thirty, she had given proof of greatness.'

So Elisabeth became a beacon for the feminists of the twentieth
century. Yet her death also shocked American men such as Mark
Twain because of its significance. As he wrote in 1898:

> That good and unoffending lady the Empress is killed by a
> madman, and I am living in the midst of world history again. The
> Queen's jubilee last year, the invasion of the Reichsrath by the
> police, and now this murder, which will be talked of and described
> and painted a thousand years from now. To have a personal friend
> of the wearer of the crown burst in at the gate in the deep dusk
> of the evening and say in a voice broken with tears, 'My God, the
> Empress is murdered.' . . . It is as if your neighbor Anthony should

come flying and say, 'Caesar is butchered – the head of the world is fallen!

The feeling that a part of ordinary life and chat has been taken away – as if a friend or cousin were lost – links the death of the Empress Elisabeth to those famous people who were to follow. By the quality of her beauty and her sympathy, she had turned celebrity into family. Her going coincided with the coming of mass communications. Gossip columns had begun with her birth, photography in the middle of the nineteenth century. Her death and that of her sister Sophie, the Duchess of Alençon, heralded the birth of cinema: to date, some thirty films and series have been screened of the life of the Empress and the tragedy of Mayerling. Most dangerous of all, the yellow press and tabloid journalism, then called the Illustrated News, had begun to stalk the movements of the renowned. And Elisabeth was the reigning star of her age.

Her very elusiveness, indeed, made her more attractive to the newsman and the photographer. Unlike those celebrities who would succeed her, she had no idea of how to use the press. Public relations had not been invented, nor the handlers of the black art of playing with opinion. Truly, she tried to avoid the fame which she had created for herself by her beauty and long odyssey. Her contemporary observer, de Burgh, wrote a whole chapter of a book on Elisabeth as 'The Recluse', who hated to be the celebrity she was:

She began to shun people; and when travelling every contrivance had to be resorted to in order to guard her from the stares of the many who found pleasure in looking upon her . . . When sailing in her yacht, she could be observed promenading the deck alone for hours and hours; not a soul was allowed to approach and disturb her. But more than anywhere else was she able to indulge in her passion for solitude when residing at her palace in Corfu . . . Her apartments there were completely isolated from any other part of the building; she had her private entrance, and could leave or enter the palace entirely unobserved at any moment during the day or night. Her meals she took by herself, waited upon only by a lady-in-waiting and one footman. She would spend a few hours during the day in the society of some of her suite, or with her teachers and readers; but the nights were her own – then she would wander alone through the dark groves and along the gloomy walks. When every one had retired and night covered the landscape, in the subdued glimmer of the moon or the stars, the Empress was often seen entering the gardens, clad in dark, closely fitting garments, a black veil thrown over her head, as she glided along the terraces and the paths of the park, and found her way to the beautiful monument she had erected to her son Rudolf in one of the most enchanting spots of her domain. So far as it was practicable she had in reality become a recluse, and her desire to still more thoroughly bury herself in some place far from all she knew and had once loved was expressed to her intimates over and over again.

The fear of the fame which would bring about the death of the Empress was even more pronounced in the year before her murder.

In the Tyrol she took up her abode principally in Meran, where she was joined by other members of the imperial family, and where also her brother the Duke Karl Theodor with his family owns a villa, which they occupy during the winter months. There the guide Buchensteiner won the special confidence of the Empress, not so much on account of his thorough acquaintance with the mountains, as because he understood her so well, and knew how to keep back the curious crowds who were anxious to see her . . .

The Empress Elisabeth had expressed a wish to arrive at Meran entirely incognito. However, her arrival, in spite of precautions, had become known on the same day. To the many enquirers at the hotel as to what time she would arrive it was answered, 'At seven o'clock in the evening.' An enormous mass of people crowded the approaches to the railway station and the Hotel Kaiserhof at that time, when a lady, in simple black dress, with a stick in her hand, walked unobserved along the street, and entered the hotel from a side door; it was the Empress, who had arrived many hours before, and had just returned from a mountain excursion of which not a soul knew anything. However, the wish of Her Majesty to be left alone was fully respected by the natives, and it was only the foreigners who, without any consideration, almost mobbed her when she went out in the daytime.

Elisabeth was too well known not to be recognised, even by those who wished her no good. Although only an adolescent, she had consented to her union with the Austrian Emperor. Finding herself trapped within marriage and child-bearing and the Viennese Court, she had taken her opportunity to rebel and escape because of her husband's contamination of her. For that reason, she had even won the temporary sympathy of Queen Victoria. Her later revenge was to turn herself into a fashion plate for other women, who were also trying to escape stifling conventions. Her lifestyle was her banner of revolt. Her gymnasium was her drill square, her saddle was her cavalry charge over the hazards to a victory by leadership. She could be no feminist, given her birth and circumstances. Yet she could set an example by her daring and her ways.

In the last decade of her life, female emancipation and even suffrage was making great strides in the United States and the United Kingdom. In Lord Bryce's opinion, American women talked less about politics than English women – but then, he was used to conversation in aristocratic circles in England, where politics was a normal subject. Indeed, it had been the aristocratic Lady Amberley's public demand for the vote which had sparked off Queen Victoria's famous diatribe against the early feminists. 'The Queen is most anxious to enlist everyone who can speak or write or join in checking this mad, wicked folly of 'Woman's Rights' with all its attendant horrors, on which her poor feeble sex is bent, forgetting every sense of womanly feeling and propriety. Lady Amberley ought to get a *good whipping.*' Jealousy of feminine rivalry for her position of pre-eminence may have made the Queen choose this masculine remedy for stopping women's rights by flogging. Yet there is no doubt that the majority of her subjects of both sexes agreed with her dislike of the feminists. Victorian England remained more traditional than Victorian America, outside the South. Supporters of women's rights in parliament were ahead of those they represented and of their Queen, who was royal before she was a woman.

That was also true of Elisabeth, a Bavarian princess before she became the Empress of Austria and the Queen of Hungary. Her personal struggle for independence and free expression did not lead her to wish the same liberties to be given to all of her sex. Indeed, her privileges were supported by a great deal of privilege. When she dashed over the fences and banks of Gödöllö and Meath to be in at the death of the fox and the stag, her supporting staff of ninety people would rival that of a modern travelling group of singers. Her cartwheels from hunt to resort to spa did not come cheap. Her luck was never to break her husband's exchequer nor his patience.

Yet she tried him sorely. For she never counted the costs of her caprice. Money was as unreal to her as madness was real. She took for granted the subsidy of everything she wanted to do, even though it flouted the traditions of her paymaster. His forbearance was her good fortune and the condition of her rebellion. In her genuine concern for the insane and working women and the poor, she did not question her birthright and her finances. Her option was not self-sacrifice and living like a pauper to show her contempt for worldliness. Her God-given role was her charity and her understanding. She could show other ladies what they might become.

Short of saintliness and beatitude, Elisabeth's generosity and care for the unfortunate was exceptional in her unquestioning role as an empress. She was known for her sudden acts of private charity. She was a spontaneous visitor to the sick in the hospitals of Austria and Hungary. She met the troop trains carrying back the wounded from the imperial wars. She saved an old woman from the edge of a precipice, and she paid a pension to the family of a railway worker who was drowned at Cromer in Norfolk. Her giving was instinctive and no substitute for state welfare. Her example was the good she did in her personal life.

Elisabeth did not deserve her death, which was the result of her fame. Yet the greatest of the imperial tragedies was to coincide with the final collapse of the three dynasties of Europe, the Habsburgs and the Hohenzollerns and the Romanovs, at the end of the First

World War. The Bolshevik Revolution had deposed the Tsar and sent him and his family into exile in Siberia. There they were murdered by bullet and bayonet on the orders of Lenin. The jewels which the Tsaritsa Alexandra and her daughters had stitched into their corsets deflected the points of the murder weapons and made their ends even more grisly. The corpses were burned by acid and buried. From this time on, the lives and deaths of royalty would not be reported so much. Other celebrities would rise to stand on the pinnacles of glory. Majesty would no longer make the news.

CHAPTER FOURTEEN

Death by Fame

❖

THE EIGHTEENTH CENTURY was that of the Agricultural Revolution, when the Europeans learned to produce enough food for the growing masses in the city slums, the labour force for the Industrial Revolution of the nineteenth century. The next hundred years, heralded by the deaths of the Empress Elisabeth and Queen Victoria, would become the modern decades of the Communications Revolution. Indeed, conflicts would be no longer continental, but global. There would be two World Wars, followed by creeping connections between the economies of all countries, so that conglomerates and multinational companies would dictate the fortunes of humankind more than the governments of minor powers. The coming of computers would also enable words to put a girdle round the earth instantly, not in Puck's forty minutes. Even swifter than an arrow from the Tartar's bow, news travelled everywhere in a flash, particularly if it was bad.

These communications were expensive, and commerce had to pay for them. This affected the nature of what they carried. Court circulars were out of fashion. Disaster stories and celebrity gossip came to rule the radio waves and the print columns, while the explosion of the cinema created new dynasties of film gods and goddesses. Their reigns would often be as short and tragic as those of the Habsburgs and the Wittelsbachs, but they were far more accessible to all countries on earth, their giant presences filling the hoardings and the screens. They hardly shrank from having their pictures taken as the Empress Elisabeth had. Their images were their power.

The First World War had ended so many of the great dynasties, the Hohenzollerns in Germany, the Habsburgs in Austro-Hungary and the Romanovs in Russia. Only the House of Windsor hung on with the enfeebled British Empire. Even in London, there were fears of another Russian Revolution with a General Strike and the rise to power of the Labour Party. Yet the public was less concerned with the deaths of kings and queens than with the early end of a Valentino. Only the abdication of King Edward the Eighth of England in order to marry the American divorcée Wallis Simpson caught the popular imagination, as imperial scandals had in previous times. That mixture of renunciation and romance was almost as potent as the film of *Gone With The Wind*.

Royalty, indeed, was no longer presented as a blood line, but as a studio concoction. In the eyes of the world, Katharine Hepburn came to represent Mary, Queen of Scots, and her sad execution. And films about the Empress Elisabeth and her husband and King Ludwig of Bavaria began to proliferate. In 1920, Carla Nelsen played the Empress, to be followed by Leni Riefenstahl, Lil Dagover, Danielle Darrieux, Edwige Feuillère, Romy Schneider and Ava Gardner with Catherine Deneuve and Omar Sharif in the 1968 tragedy of *Mayerling*, made in another year of urban revolutions. The screen transmitted past images into present imaginations. The stars lent their faces to the dead and gone, as if the Empress Elisabeth had looked in her mirror and seen not herself, but Romy Schneider, who had replaced Katharina Schratt as the toast of Vienna.

Before and after the Second World War, more thrones tumbled, in Spain and Italy and Greece. The Russian control of eastern Europe wiped out the aristocracy in all the old Austrian dominions except the western heartland itself; the Habsburg capital was divided between four occupying powers. The death of the Duke of Kent in an air crash seemed to matter less than the similar fates of Carole Lombard and Leslie Howard and the bandleader Glenn Miller. Waning interest in royalty was offset against mass fascination with celebrity. The stars of screen and song were presented as the future, while crowns and tiaras almost appeared obscene in the rigours of war.

One extraordinary American woman would become the catalyst between blue blood and box office. Uniquely, Grace Kelly would achieve a Hollywood fantasy off the sound stage. She was the film star who became a real princess, even if the whole of Monaco was no bigger than the studio back lot. In one sense, her marriage was arranged, as that of Elisabeth of Austria had been. In another way, she also achieved her practical and romantic desire. She adored her father, Jack Kelly, a handsome and dashing Irish-American politician in Philadelphia, as her predecessor had Duke Max of Bavaria.

As a child, Grace had a streak of natural melancholy. In the words of a friend, she did what sad little girls do, she became an actress. Her strategy for success was immaculate – to work with Alfred Hitchcock, who always counterpointed her ladylike reserve and hidden sexuality against physical danger and outburst. A world star after making *Rear Window*, Grace was the choice of the single Prince Rainier of Monaco, who could only save his failing principality on the Côte d'Azur by a marriage to a celebrity who would attract new tourism to its antique casino and produce male and female heirs. For the publicity departments of Hollywood and Monaco, this marriage between a screen princess and an ancestral domain was a dream team.

The comments on Grace's wedding in Monte Carlo could have been made about the Disneyland of the Bavarian castles of King Ludwig the Second. The new princess by marriage looked like Snow White in her wedding dress. She was the most terrific Cinderella available, who created a royal bubble as she walked. She had the true grace of her name; she played the role of her imagination as she had in one of her films, *The Swan*, where she had put public duty above personal feeling. As was the fate of Elisabeth of Austria, she was resented by what passed for the aristocracy and Court of the principality. But as the Empress had, Grace ignored her enemies or won them to her side with her good works, particularly with the Russian ballet school and orphanages and old people's homes. She insisted on a private family life in a villa up the rock face above the sea. The press, which had made her a celebrity in Hollywood, were now excluded from the lives of her son and two daughters, the wilful Caroline and Stephanie. She shunned the fame which had given her the opportunity to become a princess.

Yet her withdrawn presence brought the crowds to Monte Carlo and enabled her husband to wrest back control of the casino from Aristotle Onassis, who would have his own celebrated marriage with Jacqueline Kennedy, the widow of another Irish-American politician who became a murdered president. Onassis had wanted to preserve Monaco as the fading oasis of the retired rich. Princess Grace helped her husband to modernise the ageing structure of the city on the sea and ensure the future, as Elisabeth had done in Vienna by her glory and example.

As if Elisabeth had come again, Grace fled more and more from the press. In the words of a bridesmaid at her wedding, she felt like a hunted animal with the hounds after her. When her car spun out of control on the Corniche and killed her, although not her daughter who was with her, she died too young as Elisabeth had, trying to drive her own way from the fame she had chosen. She spurned the safety net of her secure position. She was at the wheel of the tragic accident, which ended the fairy-tale she had worked to make come true.

Grace had observed all the royal conventions, although she had frequently lived apart from Prince Rainier during the last decade of their marriage. Her excuse was to educate her daughters in Paris, where she set up an alternative court for poetry reading, as the Empress Elisabeth had for Heine and Homer. On one occasion, she had met the young Diana, the Princess of Wales, who had complained to her about the harassment of journalists and photographers. Grace told her not to worry, saying, 'It can only get worse,' as it did. Press intrusion was to become even more destructive after the death of Princess Grace, who could manage to disguise her separation from her husband. Future famous people would not be able to paper the cracks.

The Kelly confusion between the royal blood and the silver screen was stirred even deeper by early and celebrated deaths. Marilyn

Monroe had played with Laurence Olivier in *The Prince and the Showgirl*, as if it were another true romance between an actress and an aristocrat. She then became linked to the American President John F. Kennedy, before he was assassinated in Texas. She herself committed suicide, leaving as many clouds of conspiracy swirling about the double deaths as followed the tragedy at Mayerling. The Hollywood actress Sharon Tate was butchered by the anarchist Charles Manson, while another lone assassin murdered the Beatle John Lennon. His aim was that of Lucheni, to achieve his own fame by killing a great person.

The targets were now shifting. The mark at the end of the knife or the gun was not always an empress; it could be an actress. Not always a president; it could be a pop star. The victims merely had to be celebrated, whoever they were. Then their murder would lift the assassin from nothing and obscurity into an infamous name and celebrity. 'Herostratus lives that burnt the temple of Diana,' Sir Thomas Browne had noted, 'he is almost lost who built it.' As with Judith and Holofernes, to the killer might belong the glory. He or she would be, as Alexander Pope had suggested, 'damn'd to everlasting fame'.

Of course, fame was always a double-edged sword. The Roman Seneca called it the shadow of virtue. To Sir Walter Raleigh, it was a hollow echo. And to Ralph Waldo Emerson, it was proof that people were gullible. They were, and the use and misuse of self-publicity has always distinguished wily greatness from mere vanity. There are those from the Empress Elisabeth through Grace Kelly to Diana, the Princess of Wales, who have been condemned by the fame which they may have sought at first, but then rejected. All three of them were the victims of the image which they had set in their mirrors. So, in a sense, the Count Frankenstein of Mary Shelley was destroyed by his monstrous search for personal perfection in a made self.

The irony of the tragedies of these famous women would lie in the envy and the jealousy which they aroused along with the mass adoration. If ever a person created a career from self-promotion and mediocrity, it was the American artist Andy Warhol. So he knew well what he was saying in the age of instant global communications which he exploited so brilliantly, that anyone could be famous for quarter of an hour. Due to television and news programmes and voracious gossip magazines, each shocking parade or attack could catapult the performer from nonentity to notoriety. The worth of the deed did not matter. The act was all, for it ensured the exposure. The medium was the message – and the murderer.

In 1959, a prolific writer of chaste and aristocratic bodice-rippers, Barbara Cartland, had shelved her many historical romances to write a short biography, *The Private Life of Elizabeth, Empress of Austria.* Based on the dramatic facts of that tragic story, the tale was still redolent of the Cartland style of bleeding hearts and roses. Earl Spencer was hardly mentioned, except as the host of the Empress when he was Master of the Pytchley Hunt. Later, Barbara's daughter Raine was to marry another Earl Spencer. Her stepdaughter would be Diana, brought up with her brother Charles in Norfolk and at Althorp Park before she was to marry the Prince of Wales. The sad parallels of the lives of these two royal people, killed by their fame, were hardly foreseen in this Cartland book. Yet there were descriptions of Elisabeth complaining to the Countess Festetics about being the target of malignant gossip, as she had always been. There were also scenes of the Empress hurrying away from the chattering at Court, so that she could not hear what was said of her. 'I can feel who likes me,' she whispered, 'and who does not.'

Unique in royal archives and only possible after tape recorders were invented, Diana, the Princess of Wales, left her views on her life indelibly. Her feelings about those who liked her and those who did not were often as misplaced as those of the Empress Elisabeth. The recordings which she made of her opinions on her childhood and marriage into the House of Windsor were entrusted to a medical friend, who was not worthy of her belief in him any more than the Countess Marie Larisch-Wallersee had been. He enlisted the services of an obscure journalist, Andrew Morton, who would publish some of her opinions in a meretricious account of her life. She was later to regret this misuse of her confidence. After her accidental death, Morton would republish his trivial work, including nearly twenty thousand words from her own mouth. Unwittingly, in his Warhol ambition to leap to instant fame and fortune, he made available what his glib prose could not, the revelations of a princess about herself and her troubles and how she overcame them by her many acts of nervous recreation.

Rather like the child Elisabeth, Diana Spencer liked being brought up in the country, where she was close to her young brother Charles, just as Sisi had been to Karl Theodor in various trials against governesses and nannies and discipline. Both young girls had adored their fathers, who had chosen them as their favourite. Earl Spencer was divorced from his wife, while Duke Max had merely whistled for forgiveness from the Duchess Ludovika in the long corridors of the Munich palace, when he came home from his adventures. And both Elisabeth and Diana as children had a sense of some sort of destiny, of being different and set apart for a special marriage. Diana, indeed, felt that she had to keep herself very tidy for whatever might come her way.

What came her way was what had come to Elisabeth, an arranged marriage to the heir to the throne. Diana's grandmother Ruth Lady Fermoy had already brought together the eldest Spencer daughter Jane with Robert Fellowes, who became private secretary to the British Queen, herself a godmother to Jane's younger brother Charles. Very friendly with the Queen Mother, Ruth, Lady Fermoy agreed with her that Diana would be a perfect match for the Prince of Wales, who showed few signs of settling down and having children to confirm the succession. His courtship with Diana was brief and formal. Later, she would claim that she went into the marriage as a call to duty, so that she could work with the people.

Lady Fermoy had warned her grandchild that the lifestyles of the Spencers and the House of Windsor were far removed. That had been the case for Elisabeth, caught between her Wittelsbach upbringing and the infinite proprieties of the Habsburg Court. And the press harassment began with the royal betrothal. When Diana got into her car, she was chased everywhere by more than thirty photographers. Yet she remained polite, weeping only in private. She had always had a natural gift for getting on well with everybody from gardeners to policemen, following her father's advice to treat each person as a special individual. This gave her a rapport with the newspaper men, however much she suffered early at their hands, particularly when she was not yet protected by any palace security.

Although Diana felt persecuted, she found within herself an inner determination to survive. She was told about Camilla Parker-Bowles and her place in the life of the Prince of Wales; but she did not accept the relationship as Elisabeth had done that between Franz Josef and Katharina Schratt. Feeling tubby and fearful and loathing herself, Diana began her eating disorders, gorging and vomiting to give herself a perfect figure. She lost six inches round the waist before her fairy-tale wedding, and her bulimia was acute even during her honeymoon on the royal yacht *Britannia*. Although on board she conceived an heir to the throne, she became thinner and also suffered from morning sickness. She felt so unhappy and inadequate in royal circles that she took to self-mutilation and attempts at suicide, which were cries for the help and love she was not able to find. But with the birth of two sons and princes, she fulfilled her duty and now could look for her own self and role.

She could never overcome her sense of failure, even when she made herself into the royal icon of all the world, as the Empress Elisabeth had been. At first, she concentrated on her fitness and her beauty and her wardrobe, using the gym and the hairdresser and fashion to create the image of an independent and caring woman, who happened to be the Princess of Wales. Then she chose as her good causes and charities the people who had the most need. Once English kings had touched those who were afflicted by the King's Evil, a skin disease. Now Diana touched those who were untouchables to many, those with leprosy or AIDS or who were limbless from land mines. The hurt within herself was transmuted into easing the hurts of others, far worse off than she ever was. In helping to heal the ill, she healed her own ills. She liked glamorous occasions less and less. She preferred the mutual cure of visiting the sick one to one.

Someone who knew her, the previous Director of the Victoria and Albert Museum, Sir Roy Strong, described in *The Times* the kaleidoscope of the images which she created for her role, 'fairy princess, field-worker, fashion model, loving mother, international playgirl and hospital visitor'. These pictures were not taken from official portraits, but from the snapshots of paparazzi and television appearances. 'Mass photography and filming may have killed her, but it also made her, and she was unashamed in responding to its possibilities in a way no other member of the royal family has ever done before. And as a result she has insured her own immortality on the grand scale.'

If Diana again allied the monarchy with the press, she used the press to promote her alternative version of what the monarchy might be. After her separation and divorce from the Prince of Wales, she was largely refused a public role by the royal family. And so, she decided to create her own myth. She would be the independent princess of the people, not of the palace. Her first vehicle would be the world of fashion, then where fashion met charity, then charity alone, however far it led her on her wanderings abroad. For she, too, was another Empress Elisabeth in her estrangement from Court practice and policies, pursuing her own fate rather than what was prescribed for her. She would follow the Empress, indeed, to the very end, preferring foreign places and admirers to her own homeland.

Her going into the world of fashion and its designers gave Princess Diana all the attention of the media at the danger of compromising her position. She might well become friends with Catherine Walker and Giovanni Versace, but she moved toward the perilous world of the catwalk and the catcalls for doing so. At the parties were all the celebrities of wealth and screen and song, pursuing the damnation of temporary fame. Diana could not preserve her privacy and her mystique against this disparate and competitive group of stars. Some of them would prove black holes, dragging into their churning waste the glorious constellation of their age.

All the good books have said that charity is an act which should be private. Now that it is confused with celebrity, those who display their giving may expect uncharitable comments. To give to the poor and the sick is best done backstage, only known to the donor and the divine. Mercy and generosity thrive in secret. In the case of the Empress Elisabeth, she hid her good works. She shunned charity events and raised no funds, but she dipped deep into her own purse

and begged her husband for more. Her compassion was only fully
known after her death, through the fame which she tried so hard to
avoid. Although she cultivated her beauty, she did not put it on show.
Her mirror was to her a reason for her personal pleasure and worry.
Her fan and her veil and her parasol were her shields from the photographer and the voyeur. Rarely has so lovely and celebrated a
woman courted publicity less and kept her feelings and her good
deeds so closely to herself.

After the murder of the Empress, the tragic Diana, Princess of
Wales, would be the victim of her fame nearly a century later. She
would die in a car crash as Grace Kelly had, the film star who finally
confused celebrity with royalty and publicity with being a princess.
Diana had found it hard not to be used by various charity organisa-
tions for her glamour and ability to attract millions of pounds to the
good causes which she chose to support. Although she paid private
visits as Elisabeth had to the terminally ill, she was the modern Helen
whose public face launched a thousand glitz events, where the rich
and famous were to be seen and pictured in their contributions. The
stars of screen and song mingled with the wealthy and the notorious
and the blood royal in orgies of self-awareness at these scenes in the
global theatre of mercy. By their glittering presence, they were very
well known.

This strange confusion between merit and occasion, between
tragedy and popularity, would reach its apogee at the state funeral of
the Princess of Wales. This had been preceded by the murder of a
gay fashion designer. Versace was gunned down by a serial killer, who
may have been his lover. At his memorial service, Princess Diana reconciled herself with a rock pianist and singer, Elton John, who had
met her at previous AIDS charity events. Her treading on the shifting sands of fashion and pop stardom had put her in the company
of celebrities whose sexuality and standards were not her own. Her
reaching out to the minorities and the despised had always had the
whiff of the flash bulb about it, until she made use of her cultivated
fame to campaign against land mines, the scourge of the poor people
of Africa in their endless genocide. Politically attacked for treading
literally through a minefield, Diana by her accidental death would go

a long way towards helping to ban a nasty and indiscriminate means of war. The publicity of her example for the best of her causes would make a martyrdom of her ill-considered end.

She had emulated the Empress Elisabeth in becoming far too close to a cavalry officer. James Hewitt, who taught her to ride well, was the 'Bay' Middleton of her married life. Yet her choice of Dodi Fayed as her last amour and unknowing architect of her doom was even more extreme than the Empress with her selected Greek tutors and Hungarian admirers. The rich playboy was a Muslim, although his father gave him access through his ownership of Harrods and the Ritz in Paris to the helicopters and yachts and fast cars of international celebrity. The public fling of the Princess of Wales with him before their death together with a drunken driver at the wheel, fleeing the newshounds of hell in Paris, was a defiance of all convention. This flaunting of her independence as a famous woman might have distorted all the other images of her as the merciful sister of the maimed and the forgotten. As after Mayerling, there were even conspiracy theories that the couple had been killed by British and French intelligence to stop them having a Muslim baby. The fact was that Diana's sudden death, far too young, unleashed a tidal wave of emotion that struck the foundations of Buckingham Palace, almost submerging it under the piling breakers of flowers.

At Diana's state funeral, which was controlled by the palace and by her brother Charles, now Earl Spencer after the death of their father, the reformed drug-addict Elton John was permitted to sing a rewritten lyric. This had mourned the death of Marilyn Monroe, and now that of Diana Spencer. For blonde bombshell, read England's rose. The two women had little in common except their fame and their early deaths, although the camera and the people had loved them both. To equate the significance of their different lives was to trivialise what they had done so well, yet so apart. To perform such a song in Westminster Abbey was a slap at majesty and ceremony. This was the product of the witches' brew of the revolution in communications, which had spent a century confusing the popular with the important, and the headline with anything of worth. And so Elton John became the funeral bard of his people, and the wind started by the media blew out the luminous candles on the bier of the Princess. Sir Elton was knighted for his pains, an honour not even achieved by William Shakespeare.

Another wind of public emotion was raised by the passing of Diana. The blast would rock the very throne of the House of Windsor, which would be asked to modernise or give way. In his coded funeral speech, Earl Spencer had told the monarchy to adapt or die, particularly with the education of his sister's two sons, the elder of whom would inherit the throne. The monarchy had wasted so much public sympathy by its cool treatment of Diana after her divorce from the Prince of Wales. With the tragedy of her death, the resentment of the people in their love for her became an ocean of blooms. The millions of bouquets banked against Buckingham and Kensington Palaces and thrown on to the hearse travelling to Althorp Park along the motorway outshone even the floral tributes that had decked the last journey of the Empress Elisabeth through Geneva and Innsbruck and Salzburg to Vienna.

Republican sympathisers in Britain would try to use the estrangement of the Princess from the royal family to make a case for a lessening or abolition of the powers of the Crown, but the wise new Labour Prime Minister Blair saw that he would need the support of the palace to reform the constitution in the way that he desired, just as the Christian Socialist Karl Lueger had to have the acquiescence of the Emperor Franz Josef to bring Vienna up to date. The Empress Elisabeth, indeed, had preserved the Habsburg dynasty by including Hungarian nationalism within a Dual Monarchy. Her distance from her husband had actually increased his popularity in Vienna, where she was thought to neglect her imperial duties. And even the republicans in Budapest, where she was always revered, never succeeded in using her personal show of independence as a signal for their own revolt. There is equally no question that Diana was a monarchist, and no republican. Even if she could not be Queen, she wanted her son to succeed to the kingdom.

What the Empress Elisabeth would never have done was to supply confidential information to the press about the breakdown of her marriage to Franz Josef, and the reasons for her long wanderings. She knew nothing about manipulating news stories in her favour 'to set the record straight'. That was not done in her time, and she did not do it. Her indiscretions and fears were only revealed after her death by those she trusted and should not have believed, such as the Countess Marie Larisch-Wallersee – a role played by the cavalryman James Hewitt in his indiscretions to a woman journalist. Elisabeth fled from the early paparazzi and publicity even in Ireland, where her incognito became her fame. Accidents were caused by her efforts to avoid the crowds and the curious, notably to 'Bay' Middleton, her version of Queen Victoria's John Brown, and the forerunner of Prince Diana's horse and news-whisperer. In the end, her murder by Lucheni resulted because of the reports of her coming to Geneva and the pictures of her, so he knew where to seek her out. She had also outrun her bodyguards and escorts, hating their supervision. She was too quick for most of her pursuers, yet she could not avoid the final stalker with the knife.

Although both Elisabeth and Diana fell victim to the frenzy of their celebrity, Diana had more insidious assassins, the thousand thousand pricks and soundbytes of modern networks. Although she had milked the media for her own purposes, she hated their intrusion on her intimacy with the very few she loved. The spies of the camera and the print-out broadcast the least detail of her doings to every green screen and tabloid paper in the globe. At her death, the Internet made it possible for anyone with access and a computer to share in mourning for this royal stranger. Although the million million viewers never knew her, they felt that they did because of all the reports of her life. 'She was more than a royal,' one message on a Website read, 'she was real.' Of course, she was not. She was the unreal creation of the media, which had invaded her managed privacy to project the image of the caring friend of all the world. For that is what Diana wished to appear.

The death of the Princess of Wales in Paris coincided with the passing away of Mother Teresa in Calcutta, where she had worked for fifty years in the streets for the poor and the lepers of society. In Westminster Abbey, Earl Spencer said in his moving tribute to his sister that it was not right to make a saint of her. Mother Teresa will probably be beatified; but Diana eclipsed her in their dying. Communication had won its final victory. Celebrity was more important than sanctity. A princess was worth more coverage than a poor nun. And ironically, all that publicity certainly stimulated the giving of hundreds of millions of pounds to Diana's memorial fund. This fortune would buy more good services for more disadvantaged people than could ever be achieved in filling the poor boxes of Catholic charity.

The great gift of the Empress Elisabeth had been to create an image of concern for all, which would unite the nine nations, Christian and Muslim, ruled by her husband, the Emperor of Austro-Hungary. That was also the gift of Diana, Princess of Wales. By stretching out her hand to those in need in Africa and Asia, America and the British Isles, without fear and without discrimination, she put a royal seal on a country and commonwealth of many cultures. Both of these lonely ladies, who courted fame and were killed by it, had the human touch. However much they were devotees of their own beauty and fashion, they were leaders in their independent show of concern for everybody. Diana once said that she wished to be the princess of all the world. Her celebrity made her appear so. Fame is a double-edged sword, and its sharp cut sent both Elisabeth and Diana to everlasting glory. The Empress and the Princess joined Lord Byron's *Childe Harold*:

> Mortals, who sought and found, by dangerous roads,
> A path to perpetuity of fame.

Acknowledgements

I am most grateful to Her Royal Highness Princess Michael of Kent, who helped me with her Habsburg family connections on the research and the pictures in the early stages of this book. All its opinions and comparisons, however, are the responsibility of this author alone. I am also obliged to the staffs of the archives and libraries which I have consulted, but most particularly to the Curator of Althorp Park, Joyce H. Coles, who thinks with me that the lifestyle of Princess Diana was like that of the Empress Elisabeth. I must also thank Elizabeth Spicer for her meticulous work on this and other manuscripts of mine. And I owe all to my wife Sonia, without whom, indeed, nothing would ever now be written.

The sources of the longer quotations are cited in the text, and there is a select bibliography of the books which I have used. I am grateful to all the authors who have led the way, particularly to Count Corti, whose work on the Empress remains the best, although Brigitte Hamann has done superlatively well in her most recent biography of Elisabeth. The illustrations are taken from contemporary photographs and lithographs and etchings and illustrated magazines in the public domain, except for some photographs taken by this author and the colour picture on the cover, which is courtesy and copyright of Earl Spencer at Althorp Park. Where permissions are necessary, efforts have been made to trace copyright holders. Any omissions brought to the attention of the author will be remedied in future editions.

Select Bibliography

ARCHIVES

Althorp Park
Public Record Office, London
Royal Archives, Windsor
State Archives, Vienna
Swiss Federal Archives
Wootton Hall Park, Northampton

OTHER WORKS

ADALBERT OF BAVARIA, PRINCE *Through Four Revolutions*, London, 1933.
ADLER, H.G. *The Jews in Germany*, Notre Dame, Ind., 1969.
ANDRÁSSY, JULIUS *Ungarns Ausgleich mit Österreich vom Jahre 1867*, Leipzig, 1897.
Anonymous *Kaiserin Elisabeth von Österreich*, Vienna, 1898.
— *Private Lives of Two Emperors*, London, 1904.
BAGGER, EUGENE *Francis Joseph*, New York, 1927.
BARKELEY, RICHARD *The Road to Mayerling*, New York, 1958.
BATTENBERG, PRINCE ALEXANDER VON *Kampf unter drei Zaren*, Vienna, 1920.

BEUST, COUNT *Memoirs*, 2 vols., London, 1887.

BLUNT, WILFRID *The Dream King: Ludwig II of Bavaria*, London, 1971.

BOURGOING, JEAN DE, ed. *Briefe Kaiser Franz Josephs an Frau Katharina Schratt*, Vienna, 1964.

BÜLOW, PRINCE BERNHARD VON *Memoirs*, 2 vols., London, 1931.

BURG, KATERINA VON *Elisabeth of Austria: A Life Misunderstood*, London, 1995.

BURGH, A. DE *Elizabeth, Empress of Austria*, London, 1899.

CARS, JEAN DE *Elisabeth d'Autriche: ou la fatalité*, Paris, 1983.

CARTLAND, BARBARA *The Private Life of Elizabeth, Empress of Austria*, London, 1959.

CHANNON, HENRY *The Ludwigs of Bavaria*, Leipzig, 1934.

CHRISTOMANOS, CONSTANTINE *Die graue Frau*, Vienna, 1898.

—*Tagebuchblätter*, Vienna, 1899.

—*Die Wachspuppe*, Hamburg, 1929.

COBURG, LUISE VON *Autour des trônes que j'ai vu tomber*, Paris, 1920.

CORTI, COUNT EGON *The House of Rothschild*, London, 1928.

—*Elisabeth, Empress of Austria*, London, 1936.

—*Franz Joseph*, 3 vols. *Vom Kind zum Kaiser*, Graz, 1950. *Mensch und Herrscher*, 1952. *Der Alte Kaiser*, 1955.

—*Die Tragödie eines Kaisers*, Vienna, 1952.

—and HANS SOKOL *Kaiser Franz Joseph*, Graz, 1960.

CRANKSHAW, EDWARD *The Fall of the House of Habsburg*, New York, 1963.

—*The Habsburgs: Portrait of a Dynasty*, New York, 1971.

—*Maria Theresa*, New York, 1969.

CUNLIFFE OWEN, MARGARET *The Martyrdom of an Empress*, London, 1900.

DORFMEISTER, F.N. *Kaiserin Elisabeth von Österreich*, Vienna, 1898.

Elisabeth von Österreich: Einsamkeit, Macht und Freiheit, Vienna, 1987.

ERNST, OTTO *Franz Josef in seinen Briefen*, Vienna, 1924.

FAYE, JACQUES DE LA *Elisabeth von Bayern*, Halle, 1914.

FRIEDMANN, E. and J. PAVES *Kaiserin Elisabeth*, Berlin, 1898.

FUGGER, PRINCESS *The Glory of the Habsburgs*, London, 1932.

GAILLARD, HENRI *L'impératrice idéale*, Paris, 1899.

GILBERT, MARION *Elizabeth de Wittelsbach*, Paris, 1932.

GRIBBLE, FRANCIS *Life of the Emperor Francis Joseph*, London, 1914.

HACKER, RUPERT *Ludwig II von Bayern*, Munich, 1980.

HAMANN, BRIGITTE *Elisabeth: Kaiserin wider Willen*, Vienna, 1982.

HARDING, BERTITA *Golden Fleece*, New York, 1937.

HASLIP, JOAN *The Lonely Empress*, London, 1965.

—*The Crown of Mexico*, New York, 1972.

—*The Emperor and the Actress*, London, 1982.

JOHNSTON, WILLIAM M. *The Austrian Mind: An Intellectual and Social History 1848–1938*, Los Angeles, 1972.

JUDTMANN, FRITZ *Mayerling, The Facts Behind the Legend*, London, 1971.

KETTERL, EUGEN *Emperor Franz Josef I*, London, 1929.

KIELMANSEGG, COUNT ERICH *Kaiserhaus, Staatsmänner und Politiker*, Vienna, 1966.

KÜRENBERG, JOACHIM VON *A Woman of Vienna*, London, 1955.

LARISCH-WALLERSEE, COUNTESS MARIE *My Past*, London, 1913.

—*Secrets of a Royal House*, London, 1935.

—*My Royal Relatives*, London, 1936.

LONGAY, COUNT CARL *Rudolph – The Tragedy of Mayerling*, London, 1950.

MACARTNEY, C.A. *The Habsburg Empire*, London, 1968.

MAREK, GEORGE R. *The Eagles Die: Franz Joseph, Elisabeth, and Their Austria*, London, 1975.

MARGUTTI, BARON VON *The Emperor Franz Joseph and his Times*, London, 1921.

MATRAY, MARIA and A. KRÜGER *Der Tod der Kaiserin Elisabeth von Österreich*, Munich, 1970.

MCGUIGAN, DOROTHY G. *The Habsburgs*, New York, 1969.

MAY, ARTHUR J. *The Hapsburg Monarchy 1867–1914*, Cambridge, Mass., 1951.

Mayerling Original, Das, Vienna, 1955.

METTERNICH-WINNEBURG, PRINCESS PAULINE *The Days That Are No More*, London, 1933.

MITIS, OSKAR *Das Leben des Kronprinzen Rudolf*, Vienna, 1971.

MORTON, ANDREW *Diana: Her True Story – In Her Own Words*, London, 1997.

NETHERCOTE, H.O. *The Pytchley Hunt Past and Present*, London, 1888.

NIEDERHAUSER, EMIL *Merénylet Erzsébet Királyné Ellén*, Budapest, 1985.

NOSTIZ-RIENECK, GEORG, ed. *Briefe Kaiser Franz Josephs an Kaiserin Elisabeth*, 2 vols., Vienna, 1966.

O'DONOGHUE, MRS POWER *Ladies on Horseback*, London, 1896.

PAGET, WALPURGA, LADY *Embassies of Other Days*, 2 vols., London, 1923.

—*The Linings of Life*, 2 vols., London, 1928.

PALÉOLOGUE, MAURICE *Elisabeth, Impératrice d'Autriche*, Paris, 1939.

PONSONBY, SIR FREDERICK *Letters of the Empress Frederick*, London, 1928.

—*Recollections of Three Reigns*, London, 1951.

PUTNOKY, MIKLÓS *Carmen Sylva, élete és müvei*, Lugos, 1910.

RADZIWILL, PRINCESS CATHERINE *The Austrian Court from Within*, London, 1916.

—*More I Remember*, London, 1924.

REDLICH, JOSEPH *Emperor Franz Josef of Austria*, London, 1929.

RUMBOLD, SIR HORACE *The Austrian Court in the Nineteenth Century*, London, 1909.

SAINT-AULAIRE, COMTE DE *François Joseph*, Paris, 1948.

SCHLOSS GRAFENEGG *Die Zeitalter Kaiser Franz Josephs*, 2 vols., Vienna, 1984.

SCHIEL, IRMGARD *Stephanie*, Stuttgart, 1979.

SCHNÜRER, FRANZ *Franz Josephs Briefe an seiner Mutter 1838–1872*, Munich, 1930.

STÉPHANIE, PRINCESS OF BELGIUM *I Was to be an Empress*, London, 1937.

STRONG, SIR ROY *The Times Magazine*, 6 September 1997.

SZTÁRAY, COUNTESS IRMA *Aus den letzten Jaren der Kaiserin Elisabeth*, Vienna, 1909.

TAYLOR, A.J.P. *The Hapsburg Monarchy 1815–1918*, London, 1941.

TOSCANA, LOUISA DI *La Mia Storia*, Milan, 1911.

TSCHUDI, CLARA *Elizabeth, Empress of Austria and Queen of Hungary*, London, 1906.

TSCHUPPIK, KARL *The Empress Elizabeth of Austria*, London, 1930.

—*The Reign of the Emperor Francis Joseph 1848–1916*, London, 1930.

TUSCANY, LEOPOLD OF *My Life Story*, London, 1939.

VALIANI, LEO *The End of Austria-Hungary*, London, 1972.

VALLOTON, HENRI *L'Impératrice Tragique*, Paris, 1947.

VETSERA, BARONESS HÉLÈNE VON *Denkschrift* (privately printed, 1889).

WELCOME, JOHN *The Sporting Empress*, London, 1975.

WERTHEIMER, EDUARD VON *Gräf Julius Andrássy*, Stuttgart, 1913.

WOLFSON, VICTOR *The Mayerling Murder*, Englewood Cliffs, N.J., 1969.

WYNDHAM, COL. H. *The Pytchley Mastership of the Fifth Earl Spencer*, Kettering, 1970.

Index